I0582368

The 90s Club & the Clue in the Old Album

by

Eileen Haavik McIntire

Amanita Books
Imprint of Summit Crossroads Press
Columbia, MD, USA

Copyright 2022 by Eileen Haavik McIntire

All rights reserved. No part of this book may be reproduced or transmitted in any form or by any means without written permission of the author. This book is a work of fiction. Any references to real places, events, or people are used fictitiously. Other characters, names, incidents, and places are a product of the author's imagination.

Library of Congress Control Number: 2022916500
Print ISBN 978-1-7368214-3-5
Cover design by SelfPubBookCovers/DianeConsanzastudios

Published by Amanita Books, an imprint of Summit Crossroads Press, Columbia, MD USA.

The author welcomes your comments. E-mail her at eileenmcintire2017@gmail.com. Also visit her website and subscribe to her newsletter at www.secretpanels.net

**If you enjoy this book,
we would greatly appreciate your
writing a review on Amazon.com.**

Books by Eileen Haavik McIntire

The Shadow Series of Historical Mysteries
Shadow of the Rock
In Rembrandt's Shadow

The 90s Club Series of Cozy Mysteries
The 90s Club & the Hidden Staircase
The 90s Club & the Whispering Statue
The 90s Club & the Secret of the Old Clock
The 90s Club & the Mystery at Lilac Inn
The 90s Club & the Clue in the Old Album

Psychological Suspense
The Two-Sided Set-up

Historical Suspense
The House on Hatemonger Hill

Table of Contents

Note to the Reader

When I first began writing the 90s Club series, people in my critique group wondered why my 90-year-old characters weren't deaf, feeble, using walkers or wheelchairs, eccentric, or displaying any of the other supposed traits of the elderly. That's the way the elderly are usually portrayed in the media, especially now that baby boomers have reached their seventies and are a huge marketing segment that can be tapped for chair lifts, Medicare programs, alert buttons, incontinence underwear, and all manner of other products emphasizing decrepitude heavily advertised in the media.

Fighting the stereotypes, my characters Nancy, George, Louise, and Fitz are able, alert, and active as many 90-year-olds are nowadays. I have a collection of articles about people in their 90s—and 100s—who are running marathons, winning canoe races, working, and participating in a full life. One of my own 90-year-old friends jumps out of a plane on her birthday. Another delights in snorkeling whenever she gets a chance.

In the fifties, an African-American was often portrayed in the media as a maid or gardener. In one TV show, the Black character turned white when he saw a ghost. We no longer see that kind of racial or ethnic stereotype in the media, but the elderly are still fair game for ridicule and stereotypes, often portrayed as decrepit, eccentric, childish, bedridden, deaf, etc. etc. Many older people believe these stereotypes and play their roles accordingly.

In my books, I look at what is possible with a healthy lifestyle and positive attitude and so do my characters. Sometimes they employ the stereotypes as a useful tool in detective work, but none of them will ever say, "I'm too old."

Eileen Haavik McIntire

Chapter 1

Nancy Dickinson casually observed a middle-aged couple as she pushed her cart behind them in the grocery store. She recognized the man as Mike Johnson, a county commissioner who was an overbearing blowhard at commission meetings. In the store, he was treating his wife like an incompetent child. Nancy longed to trip him, acting as if it were a little old lady mistake. Then she'd roll her cart over him. Instead, she dawdled behind the couple as she shopped, always curious. How much worse did he treat the poor woman at home where no one watched?

On this trip to the store, she had brought along her neighbor, a tall, elderly man carrying a six-pack of beer. He followed behind her. "Let me kick him," he whispered to Nancy. "I'm rarin' for a good fight."

"Hush," said Nancy. Bill Myers was a cantankerous old buzzard and a retired newspaper man. Nancy didn't doubt he'd do something to start a fight if she didn't watch him. He'd probably fall and hit his head before he got close to Mike Johnson, but she didn't relish the idea of calling for an ambulance to put

Bill's battered remains together again.

The subject of their disdain wore a light summer suit with a white polo shirt stretched over a beer belly. He hurried his wife down the aisle as he questioned her selections, implying to the world at large that she was a dolt. The woman responded in a low stutter, her hands fluttering. Everything from her plain striped dress like old-fashioned prison garb on a gaunt body, lifeless hairstyle, and nervous gestures to her tense little face said defeat. The bully beside her regarded his wife with a sneer, but then he noticed Nancy staring at him. He changed the sneer to a grin and a wink at Nancy.

Nancy turned away in disgust. At ninety years old, she had seen a lot of good and bad relationships. Twice-married and widowed herself, she was sympathetic toward the women but impatient when they persisted in a bad relationship. In her own long lifetime, she had experienced the battles women face in the home and the work world. She savored the fact that nowadays women did have choices and opportunities.

As Nancy watched, the woman dropped a jar of mayonnaise from nervous fingers. It splattered on the floor.

"You clumsy idiot!" her husband spit out. "Can't you do anything right?" He roughly grabbed her arm and pulled her down the aisle away from the mess.

He would have hit her if I hadn't been watching. Nancy pitied the wife following the fat nincompoop through the grocery store. That would have been the end of it if the sad woman hadn't looked at Nancy, eye to eye, with a bleakness that spoke of a life devoid of hope. It was a cry for help.

Nancy followed the couple through the checkout lane, waiting patiently as the woman's stuttering replies to the cashier held up the line. Out in the parking lot, Nancy and Bill joined their friend Louise, who had made her purchases in the produce section. They stowed their groceries into the car trunk as Nancy wondered what she could do to help that poor woman.

On impulse, knowing it was foolish, she decided not to return immediately to her apartment at Whisperwood Retirement Village. Instead, she followed the couple out of the parking lot and down the road.

"Where are we going?" asked Louise, tossing the long, gray braid that hung down her back.

"I'm curious about a couple I saw in the store." Nancy glanced at Louise. "This won't take long."

"Good," muttered Bill from the back seat. "I'd like to see more of that story. We ought to rescue that poor woman."

"One of these days," said Louise, shaking her head at Nancy, "curiosity is going to be your undoing."

"Probably, but you didn't see that poor woman," Nancy said. "The way she looked at me. She needs help."

"And you want to help her." Louise threw up her hands in resignation.

Nancy nodded. "If I can."

The car ahead drove into a subdivision on the edge of town. Pleasant neighborhood, well-kept houses. Nancy chuckled at herself for imagining a grim scenario from a casual observation, but then that's exactly the kind of thing she would do.

The man pulled into a driveway at a two-story white frame home like the others on that street. Nancy stopped at the next house and watched him slam the car door, glance at the houses around him, and stride through his front door without a backward glance, ignoring his wife as she struggled with the grocery bags.

Two tall, teenage boys threw a baseball back and forth on the front lawn. Neither of them greeted or helped the woman. *She must be their mother.* She was living with three louts, thought Nancy. How demoralizing that must be.

She glanced at Bill in the back seat, who was staring grimly at the house. "Looks good on the outside," he said. "Wonder what it's like on the inside."

Louise watched the scene and said in disbelief. "This is what we were following? That terrible man with his domestic slave?"

"I'd use stronger words for him," said Bill. "I recognize him. Do you know who he is?"

"Sure," said Nancy. "That's why I followed him. County Commissioner Mike Johnson."

"That's who it was?" Louise nodded toward the house. "I didn't get a good look at him. He voted against increasing funds for the Domestic Violence Center at the recent budget hearing." She folded her arms and frowned in disapproval.

"You're right, Louise. I've got a file on him," said Bill. "I don't trust him, so I'm keeping track of his voting and activities on the commission. It's our county, too, you know, even if we live in an isolated outpost."

"Outpost?" snickered Louise. "Are you trying to glamorize Whisperwood?"

"That man is not someone I'd care to know," added Nancy. "Did you see how he checked out the neighbors?"

Bill laughed. "Making sure no one saw him leaving his wife

with the bags."

"I didn't like the way he treated her," said Nancy. "Or the way she knuckled under to his abuse."

"You're talking a domestic problem here," Louise said. "Even the police are scared of those. She can get help if she ever finds the gumption, but she's got to do that herself."

Nancy still stared at the house, hands on the wheel. "That poor woman cowered from his words and behavior. She'd get rid of that stutter in a hurry once she got away from him."

"I've seen that happen," Louise said.

"Let it alone, Nancy," Bill said as he positioned the six-pack securely between his feet on the floor. "I've got enough on him to get rid of him with the next election."

Nancy slowly drove past the house and out of the neighborhood. "Sometimes the victim needs a little nudge."

She mulled over the problem and brought it up that evening during dinner at Whisperwood with her three friends, Louise, Fitz, the love of Nancy's life, and George, known for his colorful sartorial taste. As he had told Nancy and Louise, when he retired, he gave away all of his somber, dark suits to indulge in his love of color. Tonight he wore a yellow checkered shirt with a pink, flowered bow tie.

They were all ninety or more and called their group the 90s Club. It was racking up a solid reputation in crime prevention and detection at Whisperwood Retirement Village. In their first case, they had discovered the secret behind Whisperwood's higher than normal death rate. Their last case, just a few months earlier, involved helping the local sheriff nail a murderer and a serial killer.

The dining room hostess led them to their usual table, number fifty-six, placed behind a pillar that gave it a sense of privacy. The dining room was a sea of white tablecloths and teal napkins with residents sitting around most of the tables and the low buzz of conversation filling the room.

A server arrived with a basket of rolls, water glasses, and menus. "Tonight's entrees are London broil, coconut-fried shrimp, and vegetarian lasagna," she said.

The club regularly ordered drinks, which were delivered by the dining room manager because servers, recruited from the local high school, were too young to serve alcohol. While Nancy ordered a merlot and Fitz, a martini, Louise asked for pinot grigio, quickly downed it when it arrived and asked for another.

George abstained. "Can't drink with the meds I'm taking." The short, pudgy man sat back and patted his stomach.

Nancy told George and Fitz about the couple she'd followed from the grocery store.

Louise sniffed and flicked her braid. "Nancy's got a mission to split them up."

"She'll be glad I did," said Nancy, "eventually."

"Give it a rest," was George's assessment. "You have no idea who those people are." He punctuated that statement with a sip of water.

"Yes I do," Nancy said. "Their names are Mike and Emily Johnson. She's a homemaker. He's a county commissioner and owns a garage in town."

"Still not our business," said George. "Interfering could be dangerous."

Louise shook her head. "Nancy's on a roll. How do you

know about the garage?"

"Easy on the Internet," Nancy said. "I feel sorry for his wife. Once you get trapped into a nest of people who put you down," she added, "you get dragged into a downward spiral. Most people caught that way don't even recognize it. Some think they deserve it."

"She's right," Louise said. "Victims get paralyzed and depressed and don't see a way out. Leaving takes courage and support. If we can find a way to help, I suppose we should." She raised her hand to Nancy for a high five.

'Buttinskys are us," George muttered. He looked up to see the others frowning at him. "Well, that's what we are, isn't it?" he said. "Butting in where we don't belong?"

Louise eyed George with a cocked eyebrow. "I think it's a tough job. We have to try to help that poor woman, but I don't have much hope."

"She'll resist you," said George. "Probably hate you for interfering."

"We'd only be a catalyst," Nancy said. "She'll have to want to make a change and the guts to make it happen."

Fitz placed his hand over Nancy's. "And how do you propose to help, Luv?"

"I don't know yet," Nancy retorted, "but I hate it when people stay in the same bad situation year after year without making some effort to develop a better one. Life is fleeting! Move on!" She lifted her glass once more. "Cheers!"

***

Later that night, after nine p.m. when the hall lights were dimmed, Nancy felt the need for exercise. She kissed Fitz on the forehead and left him engrossed in a new book. She and Fitz had known each other since college days but had lost touch until Fitz moved to Whisperwood. They had recently discovered their love for one another, and Fitz now made Nancy's apartment his home, a situation satisfactory to both.

She savored the gothic atmosphere in the spookily quiet and dimly lit corridors of Whisperwood at night. Too many closed doors with secrets behind each one, but this time as she passed an apartment on the fourth floor, she heard giggling and the clinking of glasses. She smiled. A couple was enjoying themselves. She felt a pleasant glow of good will towards them until she idly noticed the apartment number. It belonged to her friend Bill Myers. He lived alone and didn't like it, which is why Nancy had invited him along on the grocery store outing earlier that day.

Now there's a buttinsky, Nancy thought. Bill was a large, gangly man with big feet and hands and an insatiable curiosity. His sometimes intrusive questions made people nervous, if not irritated. A couple of residents had threatened him and some kept their distance, but Nancy found him interesting and enjoyed trading observations with him.

She heard them laugh again behind the closed door and was glad he'd found a companion to laugh with. Several days before after he'd drunk a few beers, Bill had confessed to Nancy how depressed and lonely he felt. She was touched.

The thought sent her down the path leading to her own relationships. She was content having good friends like George, Louise and Fitz. She wished the same joy for Bill. She reached the stairs and paused as she heard a door open behind her down the hall. She glanced back. That was Bill's door. Curious as to whom his friend might be, she hovered, pretending to enter the stairway exit.

Out stepped one of the young home health aides. Nancy couldn't remember her name, but she certainly shouldn't be here this time of night. And she didn't seem to be on the job. Nancy had a bad feeling about this. She entered the stairway as the young woman passed, probably on her way to the elevators and then out of the building. No one would question her.

Only Nancy knew the aide had been enjoying Bill's company. She certainly wasn't paid to stay after hours. The question was why? What did she hope to gain?

***

Ask the Answer Man

Got a question about Whisperwood or the world? Meet Bill Myers, Whisperwood's Answer Man. Whatever your question, this former newspaper reporter will either know the answer or find it for you. Catch him in the Pub cocktail hour from five to six p.m. on weekdays.

The Whisperwood Breeze,
Whisperwood Retirement Village Newsletter

Chapter 2

The next morning, Fitz left early for a bird-watching hike. Nancy slept late. When she finally got up, she dressed in gray slacks and a white, scoop-necked T-shirt. After breakfast, she played with her kitty Malone, wearing heavy gloves because Malone's play tended toward "nature red in tooth and claw." Most people treated the fawn-colored tomcat with respect and kept their distance. Speculation around the building was that he might not be a domestic cat at all.

Malone soon tired of the game and jumped onto the window sill. He stared with twitching tail at the birds outside as Nancy left for the lobby to set up her laptop on one of the tables. The lobby was a reception area designed to feel comfortable and welcoming with plush easy chairs, card tables and chairs, and pots of coffee and tea available. It was her usual post on Tuesday and Thursday mornings.

She waited with her laptop to help residents who were worried about disturbing phone calls and emails that demanded payments or scared residents into buying unwanted gift cards for the extorted payment. Like everyone else at Whisperwood, she was a senior citizen and a target for con artists.

Since she had no takers this morning, she set the laptop aside and shuffled a deck of cards to begin a game of Solitaire. She turned to greet Louise, who walked down the hall towards her, wearing her white beekeeping coveralls and carrying heavy gloves and netted hat. "I didn't see you come in," Nancy said.

Louise tossed the long braid that hung down her back and nodded toward the hall behind her. "I used the back way."

"Back way?" asked Nancy. She was always learning new things about Whisperwood. "You had your key with you? They keep those doors locked."

Louise shrugged. "I know, but the staff likes to duck out for a smoke now and then, so they prop open the back door by the dumpster. That door is probably accessible twenty-four-seven. Anyway, this place is too remote to have lurkers prowling around. It's got security guards and a guard in the gatehouse, too." She smiled at George, who had just seated himself comfortably in one of the easy chairs in the lobby. "I'll join you as soon as I get this gear off and put away."

He winked at her. "I'm looking forward to it."

Nancy returned to playing Solitaire and hoping someone with a question would show up. A few minutes later, Louise returned with a book and pulled an easy chair over to sit next to George. She had shed the white beekeeping outfit and was dressed in rumpled khaki slacks and a plaid shirt. Today she wore a "Reuse—Recycle" button on her shirt.

Nancy smiled as she glanced at them and realized they were holding hands. Despite their contrary natures, Louise and George were close friends. How close? Nancy didn't know, but she and Fitz speculated.

After losing another game, she turned to her two companions. "Did you know the staff here isn't supposed to fraternize with the residents?" she said as she shuffled the cards.

"Why not?" asked Louise in a soft drawl, her legs stuck out straight. "They think we're going to warp their young minds?"

"No," said George. "They don't want our next of kin finding out they've been cheated out of their inheritance by some upstart home health aide." He ran a hand over his balding head and sat back in his chair. With his pink complexion, light blue suit, and red bow tie, he resembled the white rabbit in Alice in Wonderland.

Nancy laid the cards out for another game. "I know one family that ought to be worried."

"Who?" asked Louise. "Those aides are nice enough, but they're all business."

"They're all business to you," put in George. "Some of us have more charm."

Louise playfully slapped his arm. "I've got as much charm as anyone."

"Be serious for a moment," said Nancy. "I'm worried about this situation."

"What are you worried about?" asked Louise. "Or who?"

"Bill Myers." Nancy paused in shuffling. "You know how lonely he is."

"Yeah," said Louise. "I'm surprised some widow here hasn't snapped him up. Easy as duck soup, if you ask me."

"You think a home health aide is after his money?" George leaned forward, his bulbous nose turning in Nancy's direction.

Nancy placed a red queen on top of a black king. "She was

visiting him in his apartment last night after dinner. I was walking down the hall and heard giggling, and then I saw her come out."

George whistled. "If it was after dinner, she had no legitimate reason to be there."

"You're not going to tell on her, are you?" asked Louise. "Let the old boy have some fun."

"Of course not." Nancy shrugged. "I don't agree with the rule they set up. After all, we're adults, aren't we? Life is short, but I do worry about Bill. He's vulnerable right now, and who knows what goes on behind closed doors?"

"I can imagine." George leered.

Nancy picked up the cards and returned them to the box as a frail little man inched his walker forward toward her table.

"You talking about Bill Myers?" he said. "I stay away from him. Talk to him for a minute and the next thing you know, he's set up a file with your name on it, ready to check out your background and your relatives and who knows what."

Nancy smiled at him. "Hello, Axel, I'm open for business. Are you being accosted by an African prince with millions to send you?"

Louise and George nodded greetings. Axel was well-known to the residents for his frequent violin recitals at Whisperwood.

He smiled. "Not today, Nancy. I've got something better. Not quite up your alley, but you're the best person to figure this out for me."

George heaved himself out of his armchair and brought a straight-backed chair over to the table. Axel nodded his thanks and eased himself into it.

"This morning I was sitting at breakfast, and I thought to myself, there's Nancy in the lobby, hoping somebody will come by with a problem." He winked at her. "And here I am with a problem that needs solving." He glanced at Louise and George and looked back at Nancy with a nod to her two friends. "Can they keep a secret?"

"Of course," she said. "We work together. One for all and all for one." You couldn't hurry Axel. You had to wait for him to spill whatever was on his mind. That was okay with Nancy. No one waited in line, and she liked sitting in the lobby—and she loved hearing secrets.

George gave Nancy a thumb's up.

"What's this problem you're worried about?" she asked.

"You'd think I'd ask Bill Myers since he likes this kind of thing, and…" Axel paused and shook his head, "I did give it to him for a couple of days, but changed my mind and got it back. He kind of scares me. I don't think he'd be kind, you know?" He glanced at Nancy. "I think he'd look for dirt, and I don't want that."

"What did you give him?" asked Louise.

Axel pulled a satchel off his walker, reached into it, and drew out what looked like an ancient album. His hands shook, and his grip was tenuous as he laid the album on the table and slid it over to Nancy.

"In there is all I know about my family," he said.

Nancy touched it gingerly. This must contain precious family history. Her grandmother had had one like it, and it was tucked into an old trunk filled with other family memorabilia in storage at Whisperwood. She banished the memories and examined Axel's album. Someone had once decorated the cover with painted flowers, but now only traces remained. "This is very old," she said.

"I'm old as Methuselah, you know," said Axel. "My parents sent it with my sister and me when they shipped us out of Belgium." He squinted at Nancy. "That was in 1939, just months before Hitler invaded the country." He shook his head. "I was too young to know what was going on, but my parents must have been desperate to get us out of there. I remember so little of that time, I think I may have been traumatized, too. They put us aboard a fishing boat in the care of an uncle. Leastways, I think he was an uncle…or maybe somebody they paid to take us to England."

"How terrible," said Nancy. "Just you and your sister?"

"That's right. A lot of tears that day, I can tell you. The man who shepherded us to England knew of a family that would take us. We never saw our mother and father or any of our other relatives again. Nobody could or would tell us anything about what happened to them. The English family adopted us, and our names were changed to Wright. After that, anybody who was looking for us under our birth name of Kuiper would have had a hard time."

"So you were born with the name Kuiper that was changed to Wright when you were adopted."

"That's right. I think 'Kuiper' referred to people who made or repaired wooden containers like barrels. In England, they spell it 'Cooper.'

"You were lucky to have found a good home. Those were dangerous times."

Axel nodded. "My sister and I barely knew there was a war on. We eventually landed here. I don't know…" His gaze turned inward for a moment, but he roused himself and nodded at the album. "That's all I've got left of my family. My sister died three months ago, and her children sent it to me. They're hoping I might remember more about our family from it." He sighed. "Oh boy, if my sister couldn't do it, why do they think I could?"

He seemed lost for a moment, but then he looked at Nancy and winked. "My sister didn't have you on her side," he said, "but I do." He cackled and coughed. "Success is assured!"

"Not so fast," said Nancy. "Did you ever connect with anyone else in your family since then? What happened to your parents? You're talking eighty years ago. How old were you in 1939?"

"I was five, my sister seven. I only have a few vague memories of my parents. I remember we traveled a lot. We didn't stay long in one place." Axel shrugged and pointed to the photos. "My mother was the camera addict. She was always taking pictures."

Nancy opened the album and carefully turned a page. The pages were heavy black paper and fragile. The photos were sepia-toned with age and secured on the page with small, adhesive-backed, black photo corners. On the margins of some of them were faded notes. A large photo of two toddlers standing in front of a clock tower took up one entire page. "Any idea where this was taken?" she asked.

Axel shrugged. "Somewhere in Belgium. Bruges, maybe."

Nancy continued through the rest of the album. "If you

were sent to England in 1939, your parents must have been terrified of the coming Nazi invasion. Was your family Jewish?"

"I don't know, but my name, Axel, is from the Hebrew for Absalom. After the war, we stayed with the British family. When we grew up, we eventually moved to the U.S. This album is the only thing I have left from my birth parents."

"Did your adoptive parents have other children?" asked Nancy.

Axel shook his head. "We filled a need, I guess. They couldn't or wouldn't tell us much about our family. My sister held onto this album all her life, and now it belongs to me. It's our only clue as to who we are, where we come from. His voice trailed off. "Now I'm close to ninety. I'd say it's about time I learned about my family. I want my sister's kids to know who we were. As far as I've been able to learn, they're all that's left of the family after me. I'm hoping the photos in the album will help."

Nancy could see how important the album was to him. How sad that it represented all that was left of his family. Or did it? This kind of search fascinated Nancy.

Axel watched her intently as if to measure her. Was he worried she'd laugh at him? Scoff at the idea? Eighty-plus years were a long time to haul the album along.

"So you were born in Belgium?" asked Nancy.

Axel opened his hands to her. "I would think so, but I have checked with the authorities there, and they have no records. With all the destruction and bombing during the war, I suppose such documents were lost."

"What about passports?" Nancy asked. "Wouldn't you and

your sister need passports?"

Axel shrugged. "I once wrote to my adoptive parents and asked them if they were given any such thing when we arrived, but they said no." Axel shook his head. "I don't remember much except a feeling of chaos and fear because Hitler's armies were invading us. I was shoved aboard the boat, told to be quiet, and shipped off. It wasn't organized like the Kindertransport. I think it was secret, and we were smuggled to England. I guess my parents did the best they could. The war destroyed so much, and we were adopted. It took time, but we got the passports to come here."

"Your family might have been Jewish," Nancy said. "Did you ever find out what happened to them?"

"No. Nothing remains that would tell us. I have read the horror stories of the concentration camps and looked for the victims' names, but I didn't find anything. And yet..." Axel paused and stared down at his hands. "I don't think we were Jewish. I go to synagogue here, I light the menorah at Hanukkah, but it does not feel comfortable like I should know the rituals. I even played the dreidel game, which if we were Jewish, I would surely have remembered, but I had to ask someone else in this country to teach me. I remembered nothing about it."

"I suppose the religious rituals of the family that adopted you would have supplanted anything you might have remembered. You were only a little boy when you left Belgium," said Nancy.

Axel looked at her glumly and nodded.

George had sat quietly, listening to Axel's story, but he glanced at his watch and started. "Got a class," he said, but with a reassuring nod at Axel, he added, "If anybody can find a clue in that album, Nancy can."

"Wait a minute." Axel laid a hand on George's arm. "Don't go telling anyone about this, especially Bill Myers. He has already seen it, and I took it back because I don't trust him, and I didn't like the questions he was asking."

"What kind of questions?" said Nancy.

"He wasn't interested in my family, you know. Unless they were spies or resistance fighters. He was looking for intrigue, maybe, I don't know, but he scared me. Don't tell him I gave Nancy the album."

"Don't worry. Lips are sealed." George stepped away from Axel and headed down the hall.

Louise stood also. "And I've got errands to run. Good luck, Axel." She grinned. "Mum's the word." She walked toward the elevators.

Nancy looked up to see Axel staring at the album. His gaze spoke of a lifetime of longing. Nancy knew the lost family history would haunt her if it had been her family.

"Okay," she said. "It's a challenge."

Axel nodded. "I know."

"But I like challenges," Nancy added.

***

Photo Restoration Services Available

Whisperwood resident Jan Adams is offering a new service—photo restoration. Get those precious albums out of the closet. Now is the time to make sure your irreplaceable family photos are restored and protected for the next generation. Jan can also digitize them for you, uploading them onto the latest digital technology with captions. They'll not only be protected but also provide meaningful identification on each one. If you're interested, place a note in her message box, No. 616.

The Whisperwood Breeze,
Whisperwood Retirement Village Newsletter

Chapter 3

Nancy couldn't erase from her mind the bleak look on that woman's face in the grocery store. Did she have any friends? Did anyone else see she was in trouble and needed help? Nancy remembered the miserable times she'd suffered in life, and a friendly word made a difference. One of those times was less than two years ago after her second husband died, and she was living in Morgantown. Louise pushed her to move to Whisperwood. The change opened up a vibrant new life. *I've got to help that woman like Louise helped me.*

The next day, Nancy donned a dowdy flowered housedress for a comfy, homebody look. She glanced at her white curly hair in the hall mirror as she left her apartment. More like grandmotherly, she thought. All good. People liked grandmothers.

She drove down the mountain into town and parked in front of a small store on Main Street. "Alice's Pet City" was painted in red on the display window. A bell jingled as Nancy walked in.

Alice raised an eyebrow at Nancy's outfit. "Cute get-up," she said. "You're up to something, I'll bet."

Nancy waved a greeting but didn't respond. She knew exactly what she wanted, quickly found a dog collar and leash, and greeted her friend Alice as she pulled out her wallet.

"Did you get a puppy?" asked Alice with a smile. "He'll help you live longer. I can attest to that." She grinned down at the short-legged corgi leaning against her boots. Alice wore a flannel shirt and jeans and owned a farm out of town where she kept rescued farm animals.

"I'm buying these for a friend," Nancy said. "One cat is enough, thank you."

"Especially your cat."Alice shuddered. "We all know about Malone, Whisperwood's notorious feline." She winked. "And I know people who've suggested he ought to be put down, but you'd never do that unless he became terminally ill."

"Sometimes he's hard to appreciate," said Nancy, "but he's a terrific watch cat. He just has a, uh, difficult personality."

"That he does." Alice rang up the sale, bagged the items, and handed the bag to Nancy. "Don't worry," Alice added. "A lot more people praise Malone to the heavens for his role in saving Whisperwood last year when you solved the case of the hidden staircase. Live and let live, my opinion." She walked Nancy to the door.

Nancy felt Alice watch her as she drove away. She probably wondered why Nancy would buy a leash and collar for someone else's pet.

Nancy drove out to the Johnsons' house, just a mile from town, and parked up the street at the end of the block. She grabbed the leash and collar and proceeded down the street, stopping at every other house. At each house, she inquired if they had seen a small dog running around off a leash.

he told them. Her response to Bill was noncommittal.

As long as Bill had lived at Whisperwood, he had tried to pump her for details on the people she met there, the scams she'd unearthed, and the gossip she'd heard. Bill found the stories fascinating and knew he'd only scratched the surface. Whisperwood was full of secrets. The trouble was that he was like a five-year-old at a tea party and apt to blurt out sensitive information that humiliated other people. He didn't deliberately intend to hurt them, Nancy thought, but he didn't recognize social cues. Most people had learned to be cautious about what they said around him.

"Come on. I know you're involved in another adventure." Bill leaned forward and extended his arms as if he could pull new stories out of her.

Nancy shook her head. "I'll keep you posted. What about you? How's everything?"

"I told you. I'm barely keeping the rags on and spirits up."

"Sorry about that." She eyed him closely and finally asked the question. "Don't you have a home health aide coming in to help?"

"Sure I do." His eyes narrowed with suspicion. "She helps out around here, keeps things tidy. A lot of people here use them," he added defensively.

"You think she does a good job?"

"As best she can for an old codger like me," Bill said, sounding defiant.

She didn't respond, hoping he'd fill the silence by saying something more about his home health aide. She studied Bill as she finished her beer. He had health issues, and his daughter had taken away access to his money. It was quite sad. Most people living at Whisperwood were active, even with health issues, and they hadn't relinquished control of their bank accounts. How had his daughter managed to do that?

Bill sat silently, lower lip out, staring at the floor and occasionally sipping the beer. Nancy finally stood to leave. "Let me know if you need anything," she said as she walked out and closed the door behind her.

***

The next morning was Thursday. After breakfast, Nancy glanced at her watch. Too early to set up her laptop on the help table in the lobby, but her apartment felt lonely. Fitz had left for a class and Malone was curled up in a nap. Despite the early hour, she took her laptop and a book and walked to the lobby to staff the help table. The receptionist, Ashley Davis, a petite blonde who had recently graduated from high school, was talking on the phone and smiled at Nancy as she set her laptop on the counter.

Ashley paused in her phone conversation. "Want me to keep that laptop here? You're way early."

Nancy nodded. "I'm going outside for a while."

"Sure, go ahead. I'll watch it." Ashley returned to the phone conversation as she waved Nancy toward the front door.

She ambled outside into bright sunshine. A balmy breeze wafted her hair. A mockingbird sang from the top of the portico, and there wasn't a cloud in the sky. One of the home health aides, wearing the usual uniform of flowered top and blue slacks, sat on a bench by the path that ran around the building. She lifted her face to the sun and ran her hands through her

long, blonde hair. It was a fetching pose, worthy of a glamour shot. She had dreams, Nancy thought, and then recognized
the woman as the home health aide she'd heard in Bill Myers'
room. The scene shifted and took on a darker cast. What exactly were her dreams?

Nancy sat on a bench nearby for a while, enjoying the warm
breeze, then she walked back into the lobby, picked up her laptop, and opened it on her usual table.

As she read her email, she heard a car door slam at the
front entrance, then a man stalked in, his face red with anger.
As he came closer, Nancy recognized Emily Johnson's abusive husband Mike, the county commissioner. Had Emily told
him about her visit? Was he planning to confront her? On the
alert, she lifted her chin and waited for him to approach her.
Instead, Mike veered right and banged his fist on the receptionist's counter.

"Where is that clown Bill Myers? I want to see him right
now."

The flustered receptionist tried to hold her ground. She
would normally provide the apartment number, but her eyes
sparked. "I'll call him for you, sir," she said, pushing the guest
log towards him. "Please sign in."

Nancy silently applauded. Good for her.

"I want to see him right now," insisted Mike, ignoring the
guest log. "I'm not taking his nonsense."

"Yes sir." Ashley picked up the phone and tapped out a
number. After a moment, she said, "I'm sorry, sir. There's no
response. He's not in."

Mike stood at the counter, fuming. "He's not gonna get

away with this." He turned back to Ashley. "You tell him I'll be back, y'hear?"

Ashley nodded, her face deadpan. "Yes, sir. I'll tell him."

Nancy watched him stalk out of the building, get into his car, which he'd arrogantly left parked under the portico at the front door, and roar away. She walked over to Ashley and leaned an elbow on the counter. "You handled him well."

Ashley shuddered. "I hardly ever have to cope with that kind of problem. Most people are polite. Maybe I should have called Security."

"He's gone now and nothing happened." But Nancy was consumed with curiosity. Why did Mike Johnson want to see Bill Myers? Some political business? Bill said he was keeping a file on Mike. What was in that file? Maybe Bill had unearthed skullduggery on the commissioner's part. She wouldn't put anything past that man now that she'd seen how he treated Emily.

Bill was a garrulous old gossip. If she could talk to him today, she might find out why Mike was so upset. She stayed in the lobby past noon, hoping Bill would show up, but she didn't see him. Then she decided to have lunch in the Pub in hopes she'd see him there. No luck.

Later, Nancy arrived for Happy Hour at the Pub to hang around with the eager early diners. This time she was in luck. She spotted Bill as he walked out of the elevator and caught him before he entered the Pub.

They walked in together to the cheers of a group of residents already feeling their early drinks. He joined her at one of the small tables and a server immediately brought a beer for

Bill and took Nancy's order for pinot grigio.

"I hear you've got a problem with a county commissioner," she said. No use beating around the bush.

Bill stopped in mid-sip and squinted at her. "How'd you hear that?"

Nancy told him. "He was ready to punch you," she added. "He scared poor Ashley at the front desk. She didn't give him your room number, though."

"Good thing. Smart gal." Bill nodded. "That was Mike Johnson, I take it? The commissioner and me, we got problems."

"Seems like it," Nancy agreed. "What's it about?"

"I've been going through the commission's finances and the county budget," Bill said, "and he's an operator. He buys things for his own business but charges them to the commission office, paying exorbitant prices for standard office equipment and funneling the excess to himself. He's got a bunch of shady deals going on there." Bill jutted out his jaw. "I'm working on exposing his shenanigans."

"Doesn't the county have controls against that kind of embezzlement?" asked Nancy.

"Sure they do." Bill narrowed his eyes. "He's clever, I give him that, but I see through his little song and dance. I'm onto him."

"Good for you," said Nancy. "What are you going to do with the information?"

"Writing it up for the *Charleston Gazette-Mail*," said Bill. "When I'm done with that, I'm tracking down a fishy land deal he's involved in that smells dirty to me."

"That man's ready to draw blood to stop you."

"He's a pissant. Small potatoes. Not going to worry about him," Bill retorted. "I've been up against the mafia, drug runners, you name it, and I'm still here."

"Stay out of dark alleys," Nancy said. It was a joke. Bill didn't seem worried about repercussions from Johnson, but he hadn't seen Mike storm in that morning.

"Anyway, Whisperwood has good security here." Bill glanced at his watch. "I've got to go. Meeting a few friends for dinner." He nodded a good-bye, waved at the other Pub patrons, and strode into the dining room.

Nancy joined her friends, the 90s Club, as they waited for their regular table. "Bill's been making trouble," she said, as she greeted them. Fitz reached over to take her hand.

"What's he done now?" asked George, resplendent in a blue star-spangled shirt. No tie this time.

Louise looked him up and down. "Where's your white belt and pants with red stripes?" she joked.

He ignored her, and the four followed the hostess to their table. As they seated themselves, Nancy said, "He dug up dirt about the county commissioner, Mike Johnson."

"Gossip here wasn't good enough for him?" said George as he looked around for the server. "He's gotta go annoy a county commissioner, too?"

"More than annoy," Nancy said. "He thinks Johnson's been mishandling government funds."

"I'm all in favor of investigative journalism," put in Louise. "Otherwise, the rats would take the cheese. I'm not calling all political officials rats, mind, but some of them certainly are vermin. They don't give a hoot for the public interest."

The dining room manager suddenly appeared with their glasses of wine and quickly distributed them. The server took their orders and disappeared.

Fitz brought the conversation back to the subject. "I hope Bill has his back covered. He's collecting a sizeable group of dubious characters who aren't happy with him."

Louise laughed. "Let's make a list. His daughter and her husband are watching his money. That's Megan and Don Thompson. Maybe saving it for themselves for when Bill kicks off."

"His home health aide is weaseling into his domestic circle," said George.

Nancy smiled. "Axel and other people here don't like him snooping into their lives."

"And now a county commissioner could lose his position if Bill got the word out about his embezzlement," added Fitz.

Nancy nodded. "Not to mention the people we don't know about yet. He's quite a charmer, our friend Bill."

George lifted an eyebrow. "It seems like a county commissioner is the only one who has any clout."

Louise nodded and laughed. "Bill better keep his back to the wall," She looked at Nancy. "Which commissioner are we talking about? There are three."

"Remember Mike Johnson, the fat nincompoop berating his wife in the grocery store?" Nancy sipped her wine, raising an eyebrow at Louise.

"Bill thinks Johnson has his hand in the till?" Louise shook her head. "I've heard Mike has an explosive temper. Hope Bill locks his door at night. Maybe he should leave town."

"Good idea. He certainly knows how to make enemies," added Fitz. "And I happen to know he's quite wealthy from an inheritance. His family has money."

"How do you know that?" asked Nancy in astonishment.

Fitz held up his hand. "Sorry, Luv. Not revealing my source."

Louise arched an eyebrow. "My, my. Bill has money and enemies," she said. "Sounds like he needs a bodyguard."

***

Voter Registration Here This Monday

Now that you've moved to Whisperwood, you probably live in a new county and maybe in a new state. You need to register to vote here. Important issues are coming up in the county and the state that affect you. Two of the three county commissioners are up for election as well. To make it easy, Whisperwood will have a voter registration drive on Monday. You can also pick up information about getting a West Virginia driver's license and motor vehicle tag. Just drop by the lobby between ten a.m. and four p.m. on Monday. No need to make an appointment. Keep your right to vote! It gives you power.

The Whisperwood Breeze,
Whisperwood Retirement Village Newsletter

Chapter 5

Nancy stayed up later than usual on Saturday night, attending a concert in the auditorium and then chatting with friends. She woke late on Sunday morning and spent several hours poring over Axel's album. She didn't know what she was looking for exactly, and Axel hadn't offered any suggestions. The faded photographs were typical family groups and occasional portraits of lone family members, often dressed for special occasions although their clothes were simple, poor, and worn.

Almost all the men and older boys wore ragged trousers with suspenders over shirts. The women mostly wore simple ankle-length dresses. Some of the women's clothes included scarves and sashes that would have been colorful if the photos hadn't been black and white. In several photos, people were posed in or around a large covered wagon that resembled a Conestoga wagon or prairie schooner, but it was in Europe, not America.

Horses pulled the wagons, but the photos didn't show enough detail to indicate any particular breed. They looked tired and emaciated and didn't appear to be Clydesdales, Arabians, or thoroughbreds.

A few people were identified along the photo margins in faded but elegant handwriting that was difficult to read. She could work on deciphering the writing first. Before she started on that, she called Axel and caught him as he was leaving for a swim.

"You gave me your name and birth date and that of your sister's," Nancy said, "but are you sure you don't have any documentation like a birth certificate or any government-issued papers from Belgium or England. They would help immensely in the search."

"Oh boy," said Axel. "Like I said, all that paperwork was lost in the war. I will drop by later with a list of my relatives that I know about, but that list will be short. I'll look through my papers again. Perhaps I will find something else, I don't know…"

His voice faded away as if he were thinking. Nancy wondered how painful dredging up the memories might be for Axel.

"The more information I have," Nancy said, "the easier it will be to find answers."

"I know that," said Axel, "but all I have is the album. That's why I asked for your help."

"Okay. We'll see what we can do with your list of relatives." Nancy hung up the phone and returned to the album.

This time, she leafed through the album page by page and tried to decipher the phrases sprinkled throughout. She wrote her best guess on a separate sheet. Nancy typed them into her computer and went to Google's translation site. The words weren't Flemish, French, Dutch, German, Hebrew, or Yiddish.

They certainly weren't English. Could they be some obscure Flemish dialect or a Slavic tongue? If Axel was originally from Belgium, as he said, then this family album should also be from Belgium. The names might give her a clue. What kind of name was Axel? What was his sister's name?

A quick search on the Internet took her to a site that identified Axel as the Hebrew name for Absalom. If his family were Jewish, then getting the children out of the country when the Nazis invaded Belgium made sense. The rest of the family might have been deported to concentration camps and murdered, which is why Axel and his sister never reunited with them. If they hadn't found a home with the English family, they would have been murdered as well or left orphans at the end of the war. Or would they? Nancy could imagine the chaos of displaced persons. How would families find each other again? There must be registries. Did Axel or his sister search those?

She continued poring through the album. Several photos showed a man peering out the back of a covered wagon pulled by two horses. Were Axel's family itinerant workers? She found another photo of the same man with a fiddle or violin. Another carried an accordion. Axel had inherited the family's musical aptitude.

The most surprising photo was of a bear wearing a bandana around his neck and looking quite comfortable sitting next to a large, swarthy man with a handlebar mustache. The photo was printed on heavy stock. He must be an entertainer, Nancy decided, and the photo was for promoting his act, but it wasn't signed.

She laid the album aside for the time being. Several elements puzzled her, but she could make a good guess about what happened to Axel's family during World War II.

***

International Family Day: Mark Your Calendar

Whisperwood sponsors an International Family Day every fall. Most of us have interesting family stories to share. What country did your ancestors come from? If you have it, wear the ethnic costume of your heritage and bring items from that country to display. The chef will also provide an international dinner menu that evening. The date is September 10th from 1 p.m. through dinner. Tables will be set up in the lobby for you to display the handicrafts and other items from your country.

The Whisperwood Breeze,
Whisperwood Retirement Village Newsletter

Chapter 6

After lunch, Nancy took a random walk for exercise through the halls of the building, starting at the top floor. As she eventually strolled down the fourth-floor hall, she glanced through the open door of Bill Myers' apartment and stopped. Her jaw dropped, and she gripped the handrail. A security guard came to the door and closed it in her face, but not before she saw a soberly dressed man standing at a gurney. Nancy found herself shaking. She tottered down the hall and knocked on Louise's door.

When Louise opened the door, Nancy stumbled into the apartment, muttering, "I think Bill Myers is dead."

"What? Bill Myers?" Louise looked shocked. "I don't believe it. He was fine yesterday. What happened?"

"I don't know. A security guard and a doctor, I think, are in Bill's apartment. Bill may have seemed okay yesterday, but we all know he was in poor health."

"Most of us still teeter on year after year even though the staff figures we're all about to die."

Nancy stared at her own white curly hair and wrinkled face in a mirror on the wall. She was in good shape and had kept her weight down, thanks to tennis, swimming, and long walks. Bill never exercised, but he kept busy. He was tall and thin but frail. Easy to think he had died of a heart attack but had he? His passing left her immensely saddened. She had enjoyed Bill as a friend.

Louise interrupted her thoughts. "I hear something happening in the hall." She opened the door and looked. Nancy peered out at her side. The sheriff and one of his deputies had arrived. The sheriff clomped into Bill's apartment, closing the door behind him. The deputy stood in the hall and guarded the door, holding a pen and notebook.

Louise turned to Nancy. "This looks bad. Usually, they're very discreet if someone dies here. They wheel the person out when no one's around. We don't know a person has died until an official announcement is made."

Nancy nodded. "That's true. I've only seen the sheriff here when we had that other trouble."

Her mind sifted the rumors and facts about Bill the 90s Club had discussed only the night before.

Louise continued to look down the hall at Bill's place. "Here comes our friend Detective Yost," she said. The 90s Club had helped Detective Yost solve a murder case at nearby Lilac Inn just a few months earlier.

"They must think Bill's death is suspicious," whispered Nancy. She watched as the deputy stepped aside to let Yost enter the apartment.

Nancy edged past Louise and walked down the hall to the guard. "I'm here to visit Bill Myers, who lives here," she said innocently. "Is anything wrong?"

The deputy folded his arms and blocked the doorway. "Sorry, ma'am. No one's allowed in."

"All right." She returned to Louise's apartment. "No use wheedling," Nancy said. "He's good at stonewalling. How about you staying here and keeping an eye on things. I'll go down and see if I can get any information out of Harry Doyle." Doyle was Whisperwood's administrator. With the assistance of the Residents' Board of Directors, he had recently hired a middle-aged woman named Suzanne Craddock as his assistant.

The door to the executive suite was locked. The office windows looking out on the lobby were dark. No one was there. Nancy suddenly remembered the day was Sunday. The executive staff had the weekend off. Sunday was usually a quiet day. Many residents left to visit their families elsewhere, or their families joined them for the early brunch. Nancy returned to her apartment and called Louise.

Then Fitz walked in with an armful of books from the Whisperwood library.

"I'm sorry, Luv," he said. "What happened?"

Nancy shook her head sadly. "I don't know. Bill was fine yesterday. I can't find out anything because it's Sunday and nobody is in the office." Nancy ached to learn more. "Security is handling things, and they've called the Sheriff's Office. I'll have to wait until tomorrow morning."

Accordingly, the next morning, Nancy woke early, dressed, ate breakfast, fed Malone, and then paced back and forth until nine a.m. when the executive offices opened. She arrived as the secretary, Betsy Clark, unlocked the door.

"Is Harry here?" Nancy asked, following Betsy to her desk.

Betsy took her seat and sipped her coffee before responding. "Harry is away on a much-needed vacation with his family," she said. "Suzanne is in charge." She glanced at her watch and looked past Nancy. "There's Suzanne now."

Suzanne bustled in, waved at Betsy, nodded at Nancy, and passed them to enter her office, closing the door behind her.

Nancy breezed past Betsy and rapped on Suzanne's door.

At Suzanne's "Come in," Nancy poked her head around the door. "Got a minute?"

Everyone knew Nancy was curious—nosy is what most people said, but Suzanne Craddock had heard enough about Nancy to pay attention.

"I haven't even had my coffee yet," Suzanne complained. "But for you, okay. What's up?"

"Have you received a report about Bill Myers from Security?"

"I was away all weekend," said Suzanne. "Just got in."

"The sheriff is here with his detective. Didn't Security notify you?"

"What?" Suzanne looked shocked. "The one time I try to get away for the weekend…" Then the phone rang. "Just a minute." Suzanne answered the phone. She glanced at Nancy as she listened. "All right," she said and hung up. "That was Security. Bill Myers died yesterday under suspicious circumstances. His apartment is now considered a crime scene. They're sending a report over." There was a light tap on the door, then Betsy walked in with a folder. "From Security," she said.

Suzanne took the folder and pulled out a form. She scanned it and then looked at Nancy. "You're right. He died during the night, that is, Saturday night or Sunday morning early. A doctor checked him and…" Suzanne read the rest of the report silently. She looked upset.

"What's wrong?" asked Nancy.

Suzanne shook her head. "The sheriff's detective is on the scene, and Mr. Myers is scheduled for an autopsy. Unattended death. Suspicious circumstances." She looked up at Nancy. "That's all I've got right now."

"What suspicious circumstances?" Nancy asked.

Suzanne frowned. Her hands trembled. "I don't know. There's nothing more here." She placed the form in front of her. "I'll check on it right away."

Nancy mulled this over a moment. "Okay," she said. "I'd appreciate your letting me know what you learn and what the autopsy report says. I'm here to do whatever I can to help. Bill was a friend." Since she had helped Suzanne with difficult matters before, Nancy felt she'd be kept in the loop for information now. She liked Suzanne, who occasionally called on Nancy for advice on handling residents' complaints.

Suzanne rose. "I appreciate your offer of help, Nancy, but I have to discuss this with the sheriff and the Board. Now I've got to go check out this report."

"Thank you," said Nancy. "I understand how delicate this situation is." She closed the door quietly behind her, leaving a worried-looking Suzanne staring at the paper in her hand.

Louise had given up on learning anything more about Bill's death and had gone out to the garden to tend to her beehive. George had passed by on his way to the swimming pool. Nancy returned to her apartment to give Malone a little attention.

She was flicking a catnip mouse in front of the cat when she heard a knock on the door. She left a displeased Malone and opened the door. Axel walked in, leaning on his walker and wearing an old-fashioned straw boater, gray slacks, and a white polo shirt.

"I'm heading out for a little walk," he said as he pulled a folded paper out of his shirt pocket. He laid it in front of Nancy. "Here's that info you wanted. Hope it helps. It's all I know." He touched his hat in a salute and whistled on his way out the door.

Nancy unfolded the paper. It contained a short genealogy. The top line listed two names: Nitaka Kuiper and Danior Kuiper with no middle names and no dates. Nancy skimmed the list. They must be Axel's parents. No grandparents listed. The two names on the line below the parents were Axel Bassett Cooper Wright, 1934 - ?, and Rose Cooper Wright Gillray, 1932 – 2020, his sister. Below that were two names under Rose Cooper Gillray's name. Danior Gillray and Lavinia Gillray. They must be Axel's niece and nephew, Rose's children. Axel had no children. She added a note that Cooper could have been spelled Kuiper in Belgium or with some of the family.

Rose was no longer a resource, but she must have told her children something about the family and where it came from. Nancy laid the paper aside and tapped her fingers on the chair arm. She needed to arrange a visit with Rose's children. Nancy opened the album again and began listing questions for them. Then she went to her laptop and ordered a DNA kit for Axel.

Tiring of her apartment, Nancy walked to the lobby on her way to the garden outside and was in time to watch a sheriff's car pull up under the portico at the front door. Nancy immediately thought of Bill Myers. She watched the sheriff lumber in trailed by Detective Yost. They stopped at the reception counter. Yost wore a gray suit and tie, but the sheriff was dressed in the gray slacks and shirt standard for sheriffs in West Virginia. He rapped his knuckles on the counter and asked for the "person in charge." Ashley ushered the two men into Suzanne's office.

Nancy waited at the reception counter for Ashley's return. "What's going on?" she asked. How much did Ashley know?

The young woman glanced around and whispered, "Bill Myers." She tossed her head toward Suzanne's office. "The sheriff is here to investigate."

"Really. Any idea what happened?"

Ashley shook her head, and they both watched as Suzanne shepherded the officers to the elevators.

"Everything okay?" asked Nancy as Suzanne walked past.

"I believe so," was Suzanne's noncommittal reply.

***

About the Whisperwood Foundation

The Whisperwood Foundation provides funds for residents who find themselves in financial need or unable to pay their monthly fees. Donations are tax-deductible. Consider adding a donation to this worthy foundation in your will to help others who enjoy the benefits of Whisperwood. Susanne Craddock, assistant administrator, will be happy to answer your questions and help you find ways to contribute.

The Whisperwood Breeze,
Whisperwood Retirement Village Newsletter

Chapter 7

Monday afternoon, Nancy arrived at the local café half an hour early for her appointment with Emily. She wanted to feel relaxed and prepared for the difficult conversation ahead.

She needed to wrap her mind around how to proceed with the timid, downtrodden, and broken soul that was Emily. Living with a verbally abusive and oppressive husband had led her to a debilitating feeling of powerlessness. Any one of us, Nancy thought, could find ourselves in the same position. We all needed kind words and encouragement.

Nancy looked out the café window and saw Emily parking her car. Instead of the downtrodden sadness Nancy expected, Emily bounced into the booth seat opposite Nancy and smiled at her with sparkling eyes. This was a different Emily than the one Nancy had met just a few days earlier.

"You look cheerful," said Nancy. "How is everything?"

"Good," Emily replied. "I haven't stopped thinking about our last conversation. What a blast of fresh air. Swept out the cobwebs. I'm glad you stopped by our house. Did you ever find your dog?" She spoke so fast she was breathless.

The dog. "It wasn't my dog; it belonged to a friend, and, yes, I heard it's now back home safe and sound." The white lie couldn't be helped.

"Great!" Emily grinned. "I'm s-s-so excited."

She did look excited—and happy. Quite a different woman. A server hovered. Nancy glanced at the menu and gave her order for a hamburger and iced tea and watched Emily do the same, adding French fries. Nancy arched an eyebrow. *Well, well, well.*

Emily saw Nancy's expression. "M-m-maybe I'll eat it all; maybe not, but when I think of l-l-leaving my prison. . ." She grimaced. "I need a break. I was hanging around for the kids, b-b-but one's in college, and the other one's a senior in high school. They'll be f-f-fine if I take a sabbatical, won't they?"

Nancy smiled. "Certainly." Emily's stutter was much less pronounced, and the food she had ordered was a sure sign she was taking control of her life.

"I thought c-c-calling it a sabbatical was less threatening," Emily said. "For the boys, I mean. I'm not r-r-really running away from home. I'm just taking a vacation...by myself."

"Good for you." Nancy sipped her iced tea. Emily also wasn't fluttering her hands nervously much anymore. A miraculous cure, but Nancy had noticed that kind of cure before. Hope and a new attitude made such a difference. A friend had once told Nancy that when she left her husband, she stopped biting her fingernails for the first time in her life. Nancy was seeing a similar transformation in Emily. "What do you plan to do?" Nancy asked.

Emily giggled. "T-t-talking to you was the k-k-kick in the

pants I needed. Made me question the f-f-fix I've gotten into when it's no good for me." She smiled at the server as the hamburger and fries were set in front of her. She immediately picked up the burger. "I'm h-h-hungry," she said. "I skipped lunch at home with M-m-mike. Anyway, he's used to that." She frowned. "You know, I never stuttered when I was a kid. It just c-c-came on gradually, l-l-living with M-m-mike."

And no wonder. The way he dominated and verbally abused her would intimidate anyone.

"I'm hungry, too," Nancy said to be companionable. What did Emily have in mind? Nancy knew from experience differ- ent people interpret words differently for good and bad. *Emily could have taken my words in any direction. What had she de- cided?* Nancy waited.

Emily grew quiet as she ate the hamburger, her mind else- where. She nibbled on the French fries, nodding to herself and smiling at Nancy.

"What I want in a nutshell," she said, laying the hamburger aside, "are self-respect and the ability to support myself. I want to be independent and that means being able to leave a bad s-s-situation. I'm the family scapegoat, you know. I get ridi- culed for everything I think, say, and do. M-m-mike is ashamed of me. Now that he's a c-c-county commissioner, he thinks he's way above me. I didn't recognize how bad it had gotten until I viewed it from your eyes." She paused and glanced at Nan- cy. "I know you s-s-saw our little act in the grocery store. Me following the boss man around and him criticizing my every move."

Nancy blushed. "I was picking up a few things…"

Emily waved that away. 'Doesn't matter. My friend Donna hates the way he treats me. She's been trying to get me to leave him for years. The boys have kept me there." She shook her head. "The boys and my fear. I didn't think I could get by on my own. Mike's brainwashing."

"Sometimes you need a little perspective." Nancy sipped her iced tea. She felt uneasy, knowing she may have sparked a big change that might lead to disaster. Then she tossed that feeling aside with the knowledge that the real disaster for her and her sons lay in staying in a bad situation.

"That's right," said Emily. "I've been thinking about that." She looked Nancy in the eye. "I'll die if I stay in that house."

Nancy nodded. "I agree. I've always held a job because I don't like feeling trapped."

Emily pursed her lips as she stared out the window of the café. "Trapped is exactly h-h-how I feel." Her gaze came back to Nancy and she smiled. "I have to f-f-find my way alone." She visibly relaxed as if the hard work was over. "M-m-mike won't like it, and he'll put roadblocks in my way." She shrugged. "I need to make my plans without him. That m-m-means leaving the boys, too. That will be tough, but they need to learn a few hard lessons that I can't t-t-teach them unless I leave."

Nancy nodded again, carefully noncommittal. It needed to be Emily's idea, but she silently applauded Emily's decision

"I'll always love them, you know, but they follow their dad's lead in disrespecting me." She looked at Nancy as if for approval. "I don't want them t-t-treating their wives the way they treat me. They should know there are consequences."

"There are always consequences," said Nancy. "Will you

file for divorce?"

Emily shook her head. "I'm c-c-calling it a sabbatical. I just want to g-g-get away for awhile. I know Mike will twist things, call me names, and involve the kids."

"He will involve the kids anyway," Nancy noted. "I suppose he could sue you for desertion or divorce you."

"He has already done his worst." Emily's eyes suddenly teared. "I hope the boys are old enough to make up their minds about their parents. I've been to every school event and ball game for them and made sure they were able to participate in any activity that interested them. I hope they will remember that. I hope they will miss me." She paused and stared into space a few moments, then she looked sadly at Nancy.

"How demoralizing for you," Nancy said. "Mike could hire a lawyer and claim custody of the boys." *Could he? Nineteen was too old, wasn't it? And the other one was less than a year shy of eighteen.*

"In a way, Mike has already done that." Emily wiped away a tear. "He's torn me down in front of them again and again. He has taken the power in the family, so they'll insist on staying with him rather than me if we split. And he'd win. He owns a business, and he's a county commissioner. I don't have a chance against all that." She paused and stared out the café window for a moment.

Nancy held up a hand. Emily needed a reality check. "Wait a minute, Emily. Both your sons are grown men."

"That's right, Nancy. And both those boys are going to college. Mike can afford the tuition. I can't. I'm all right with him paying the bills."

Then her voice turned from bitter to thoughtful. "I could leave tomorrow, but that would be foolhardy. I'm not prepared."

Nancy waited, feeling better now, hearing that Emily's plans weren't precipitous. She was using her brains, but how much preparation would Emily think she needed? This is where she could equivocate indefinitely, never feeling prepared enough. What would Emily do?

"You know what the business schools say." Emily smiled and winked. "Make your plan and work your plan. That's what I've been doing since I last talked with you." She pulled a small notebook out of her purse. "I've got it right here." She waved it at Nancy. "It's my journal. I keep it with me all the time." She flipped past the first few pages, glancing at Nancy. "I've got grocery lists up front in case Mike happens to open the book. I don't want him or the boys to find out what I'm planning."

Using her finger to mark her place in the book, she paused and glanced at Nancy. "I must have been subconsciously planning to leave for years."

"What do you mean?" asked Nancy.

"You don't know m-m-much about me, except that I'm a pitiful drudge."

"I never thought that," said Nancy, "but I saw the way your family treated you, and you looked sad."

Emily waved Nancy's protest aside. "Yes, I am. Mike got me pregnant when I was seventeen. Then we got married. He was six years older than m-m-me." She shrugged. "I thought I was so grown up and…and sophisticated, m-m-marrying an older man." She shook her head. "That's the kind of fool I was. I didn't even graduate from high school."

"Oh no," Nancy reassessed Emily's chances of making it in a world where education gave one opportunities.

"You're right," said Emily, "A couple of years ago I began seeing the writing on the wall." She grinned and picked up a French fry. "That's why I got my GED."

"Good thinking," said Nancy. Listening to Emily was like riding a rollercoaster with all its ups and downs. "What will you do for money?"

Emily nodded. "I've been thinking about that. Here's my plan. Any ideas and suggestions are welcome." She snapped her fingers and began to smile as she read from the notebook. "First step: Obtain my own private bank account and m-m-mailing address." She grinned at Nancy. "I scoped that out, and I've already set up a private m-m-mail box at a mail drop and UPS store in town. This morning, I established my bank account." She grinned. "I do the household accounts, and I've been paying myself a salary. I have $5,000 in my new bank account. I also have a credit card in my name, using the m-m-mail-drop address." She grinned. "Make your plan. Work your plan."

Nancy smiled and nodded. *Maybe Emily was going to get out.*

"Tomorrow morning, I'm driving into Charleston to purchase a laptop." She reached into her purse and pulled out four beige-colored cards. "I was going crazy sitting at home, so I've been taking computer courses," she said. "These are certificates of course completion." She spread them out like cards. "Word, Excel, Publisher, PowerPoint. I think they'll come in handy."

"Wow. These are excellent skills for job hunting." Nancy was impressed. Emily was smart—and resourceful.

"I've been taking the courses during the day at the community college," Emily said. "Mike and the boys don't know anything about them."

Nancy looked at Emily with new respect. She was a go-getter. "You may not have had a plan," she said, "but you've been working one anyway."

"You bet." Emily collected the certificates and the notebook and returned them to her purse. "It's funny, you know. I never had any plan to leave. I was just taking courses because I wanted to. I knew Mike wouldn't support me in this." She paused to reflect. "I guess I worried that if he left me or had a heart attack or something, I'd better be able to do something to support myself and the boys."

Nancy nodded. "That could happen."

"Since I talked to you, all the bits and pieces I've done the last few years, the GED, computer courses, it's like all that came together at once and became part of a plan."

"What's next on your list?" Nancy asked as the server collected their plates and left the bill.

"Don't l-l-laugh," Emily said. "This might seem, well, ridiculous...for me, I mean." She gripped the glass of tea so tightly her knuckles turned white.

Nancy tried to look as receptive as she could, hoping not to show surprise at whatever Emily might say next. "I think you can do anything you put your mind to," Nancy said to open the door.

Emily stared out the café window. "I need to get away from this place. Far away."

"You won't be really on your own until you do." *How far*

away? Was Emily thinking Paris? London? Rome?

Emily bit her lip, took a deep breath, and blurted, "And...I want a college degree." She sat back and studied Nancy's face.

She's looking for me to shoot down that idea, thought Nancy, but she nodded at Emily. "Yes. You're college material. No doubt about that."

Emily visibly collapsed in her chair and burst into tears. "I-I-I thought y-y-you'd laugh at me. A c-c-college degree. At my a-a-age."

Nancy reached forward and patted Emily's hand. "Of course not. Every part of your plan I've heard from you has been eminently practical, doable, and sensible. Tell me how you're going to get the degree and where you want to go."

Emily pulled a tissue out of her purse, blew her nose, and wiped her eyes. "You think I c-c-can do it?"

"A lot of other people have done it. Why not you?" Nancy sipped her tea.

Emily shook her head, took a deep breath, and haltingly said, "I'm looking into online universities first because I'll have to work." She paused and waited.

Nancy realized Emily was seeking approval. "That's a good way to begin."

Given this go-ahead, Emily added, "I'll see if I can get a student loan."

"Good idea," agreed Nancy. "You could look into certificate programs, too, that would be shorter and train you for a job." She thought a moment. "Or you could take one or two courses at a time while you work."

Emily laughed. "Slow and steady wins the race, right?"

Nancy saw that she seemed much more relaxed and assured now. "Right. Do you know what you're aiming for? I mean, in terms of a career."

"Vaguely. Maybe social work. I want to help people like me who make mistakes that trap them." Emily nodded to herself. "Or maybe some kind of criminal justice work."

"Good choices." Nancy finished her tea and picked up the bill. Emily started to protest, but Nancy waved that away. "You treat me when you've got that degree," she said. "You told me before you wanted to be a private detective."

"That's where the criminal justice c-c-courses come in." Emily shrugged. "There's so much I want to do, and I'll probably change my mind along the way, but social work could lead to any number of careers, including in the criminal justice system."

"True. I know several people at Whisperwood who are retired social workers and could probably give you a lot of advice. Let me know if you'd like to talk to them."

Emily grinned. "Thank you for not making fun of me, like…" She tossed her head. "Maybe I'll take you up on talking to the social workers eventually, but first let me keep on working my plan."

"You're well on your way. Even having a plan is a huge step forward, and it's all exciting news." Nancy smiled at Emily and reached over to squeeze her hand. "Congratulations."

"Wait for the congratulations until I've accomplished something."

"It's a deal." Nancy paid the bill, and as they walked out, she asked casually, "By the way, do you know any reason Mike would have a problem with someone at Whisperwood?"

Emily reached her car and stopped to consider but shook her head. "I have no idea. M-m-mike doesn't confide in me except to brag." She paused. "He has been pretty pleased with himself about s-s-something lately," Emily added. "Whatever it is, he thinks it will set him up for life. Some big project."

"I wonder what that could be." Nancy waved the question away. "Whatever it is, it's nothing for us to worry about."

"I haven't p-p-paid much attention to what's he's been up to," Emily said. "I don't care. The only things he says to m-m-me are put-downs, but he can say what he wants. Soon, I won't be around to hear it." She grinned.

***

Computer Courses Start Soon

Whisperwood resident Karen Woodside, retired computer technology instructor, will start teaching beginning-level courses in the Microsoft Office programs of Microsoft Word and Microsoft Excel (a spreadsheet program) on September 8. Each course will be four sessions of two hours each. Word will be taught on Tuesday and Thursday mornings; Excel on Tuesday and Thursday afternoons.

The charge is $25 for each course. Register at the lobby reception desk.

The Whisperwood Breeze,
Whisperwood Retirement Village Newsletter

Chapter 8

As Nancy walked into the dining room that evening, she realized it was abuzz with rumors. It seemed almost everyone had a story about Bill, and many of them generated affectionate laughter. Looking across the room, Nancy also saw faces that were not amused; some were even grim. Were they also missing Bill or saddened by the thought of their own mortality? Or were they victims of Bill's insatiable curiosity? Were they afraid Bill had discovered some distasteful secret about them?

The four 90s Club members sat at their places, sober looks on their faces as they surveyed the dining room. Nancy noticed several pairs of eyes turned speculatively toward their table. Were they curious about the 90s Club's sleuthing activities now that another murder had rocked Whisperwood? Or were they worried about protecting their reputations?

Louise shook her head. "I've heard Bill ridiculing the local politics, and I told him he should get out of town, but I was joking. I didn't think anyone would murder him."

Neither did I," added George, smoothing his bright blue trousers. "He must have riled someone pretty bad."

"He'd ruffled a lot of feathers." Fitz took Nancy's hand. "It's not our fault. We don't have a crystal ball. Even if we urged Bill to be careful, he would have laughed at us and ignored our advice."

"The only thing we can do is find the killer," said Nancy, her eyes still roving around the dining room. She couldn't say what exactly she was looking for, but one of these people could be a murderer.

George sat back and patted his stomach. "Don't jump the gun on this. We don't know how he died. Could have been natural."

"I don't think so," said Nancy.

The next morning, Suzanne called Nancy and asked her to drop by the office when she could.

She must have news about Bill Myers, Nancy thought. She dropped the book she was reading to head immediately to the lobby. Suzanne stood outside her office and waved Nancy in. Closing the door behind Nancy, Suzanne sat at her desk while Nancy took the visitor's chair.

"What happened to Bill?" Nancy asked.

"The attending physician thinks Bill Myers was suffocated." Suzanne picked up a paper clip. "The autopsy is expected to confirm this as the cause of death."

Nancy's mind snapped into gear. Signs of suffocation were obvious to a doctor. It would show in the eyes and on the pillow or whatever was used. "I see," said Nancy. "He was murdered."

Suzanne nodded, her hands fiddling with the clip. "And now the sheriff is involved, and there will be an investigation."

Nancy grimaced. "Of course."

Suzanne searched Nancy's face. "Do you have any idea who could have murdered him?"

"No, no," Nancy said, pushing the idea away with her hands. "It's just that we've noticed some odd things going on around him, that's all. He was fine the night before."

"What kind of odd things?"

"Bill knew how to antagonize people, and he was nosy. He was dabbling into local politics, too, questioning the county commissioners and generally making himself a gadfly there and here at Whisperwood." Questions about Bill's daughter, his home health aide, Mike Johnson, and Axel flitted through Nancy's mind. She thought of the grim people in the dining room the night before. Talk of Bill's exploits had not amused them. She glanced at Suzanne's worried face and decided to keep these thoughts to herself. *Wait and see.*

"He didn't trouble to be popular," Suzanne said. "He came in here and bothered us, too, but I know how to handle that." Suzanne sat quietly for a moment, hooking and unhooking a chain of paper clips, before she looked up and said, "He didn't cause us any problems, but you seem to have suspicions about people here who might have wanted to murder Bill."

Nancy shrugged. "Bill liked to find out about people. Most of us have secrets we'd prefer to keep buried."

"I suppose so," said Suzanne, "but right now my biggest fear is that the residents will be terrified they'll be murdered, too, and we'll have a run of people wanting to move out."

"This wasn't a random murder. The killer targeted Bill and would have seen Bill's face as he covered it with the pillow. Unless there's another murder by suffocation, it's not a serial killer. You need to keep the residents well-informed on what's happening and what you're doing about it. The first thing would be to hire more security guards until the murderer is caught."

"I can do that," Suzanne said, "but we've got to catch the killer as soon as possible. I don't know how good a detective this sheriff is…" Suzanne added another clip to the chain. "I haven't been in this area very long."

Nancy rolled her eyes when Suzanne mentioned the sheriff, having seen him bungle simple incidents in town. He was an elected local man with little experience in law enforcement. The county didn't have a town big enough to hire a police force, and the crime rate was low. The sheriff's office took on any police duties needed. "I think he has assigned Detective Yost to the case, and he'll be okay. I met him in the case we solved at Lilac Inn earlier this year."

Suzanne nodded. "Do you think he'll work with you?"

"Yes," said Nancy, "I do." Maybe, she thought.

"Okay. You see a lot of what's going on around here. People talk to you. If you hear anything that will help catch the murderer, I presume you'll pass it on to me and the detective."

"Of course." Nancy smiled. "We'll be glad to help. This is our home."

Suzanne nodded. "Please limit yourself to observations around Whisperwood only. You could get hurt. You know the residents, but don't let them catch on to what you're doing."

"The 90s Club is already on the job." Nancy rose and turned to the door. "We'll let you know what we find out."'

"Not the 90s Club, please, Nancy. Just you and keep it to observation only. Pass on the rumors you hear to me, but let the detective conduct any interviewing and actual law enforcement." Suzanne's voice was firm. It was an order.

Nancy nodded to show she'd heard, but she had no intention of agreeing to Suzanne's request. The 90s Club worked as a team.

"One more thing." Suzanne stood. "Be careful, please, about what you say, and don't ask any questions. I don't want the residents any more upset or worried or scared about being killed in their beds than they already are."

"I know it's a delicate situation, and I'll do my best," said Nancy as she left. Once back in her apartment, she roused Fitz, who was napping, and then she immediately called Louise and George. "We need to meet," she said. "My place."

"I'll make the coffee," Fitz said, heading for the kitchen.

Nancy hurriedly cleared off the couch and dining table. She was a terrible housekeeper—all her friends knew that—but now that Fitz was living with her, she had hired the housekeeping staff to keep her place clean and neat, but no amount of cleaning kept Malone's catty dander from clinging to walls and furniture. This made her apartment difficult for George and his allergies.

George arrived first, looking like a road worker in his neon green polo shirt. He sniffed the air as he walked in and nodded at Nancy. "I used my inhaler before I came. I'll be okay."

Louise followed in a few minutes, relying on her cane. The word "Pesticides" with a red diagonal line across it was the slogan on the customary button pinned to her khaki vest. "What's up?" she asked, tossing her braid over her shoulder.

Nancy checked the hall before she closed the door behind

them. "The Bill Myers murder," she said. "The sheriff is here investigating."

George sat back and nodded. "Sorry about ol' Bill."

"Me, too," said Louise, laying her cane at her feet. "Even though dying is SOP in this place, and Bill was in poor health, he wasn't ready to go yet. As Nancy said last night, we've all been getting strange vibes as we've talked to the people here."

"I agree. Bill had his fingers in several possibly dangerous pots," said Nancy, "but I've been worried about Bill since we heard his daughter and her husband had taken control of his money, and a home health aide was overly friendly with him. What's her name? Does anyone know?"

"Sure," said Louise. "I see her in the halls every day. Read her name badge. Tammy Swann. She seems nice enough."

"We all can imagine why she was with him alone in his apartment after dinner," Nancy said. "She wasn't wearing a uniform and it didn't sound like she was working. Is she a fortune hunter?"

"So what if she is," said George. "Better his money go to her than that vulture of a daughter."

"Whatever. Right now that's irrelevant." Nancy scribbled a few words in a notebook. "We have another possible suspect," Nancy said. "I saw Mike Johnson, a county commissioner, come barging in wanting to throttle Bill who was ready to accuse Mike of embezzlement. And you know Bill loved digging into people's lives."

"We have three suspects right off the bat," said George, raising the white eyebrows that matched his thinning white hair. He counted them off on his fingers. "His daughter, son-in-law, and that county commissioner."

"Don't forget he was a nosy old cuss," said Louise. "Always wanting to know about the people here—more than was good for him, I'd say. Who doesn't have secrets? I even found him chatting up Suzanne's assistant. Maybe he found something incriminating or scandalous in the front office."

Fitz shook his head. "Bill didn't have enough sense to keep his mouth shut."

"All we know right now is that he was suffocated," said Nancy, nodding at Fitz. "The security guard checked on him when the peg on his door showed he hadn't gone out that morning."

George raised an eyebrow. "An unattended death is the usual situation here, but it calls for extra attention from the authorities." He suddenly sneezed and drew out his handkerchief. "Allergies kicking in," he said.

Nancy moved a box of tissues closer to him on the coffee table. "They'll be doing an autopsy. Suzanne is worried about the residents being upset." Nancy shrugged. "There is one other thing you need to know." She hated to tell them this.

"What's that? They want us to load the guns we don't have?" Louise quipped.

"Suzanne asked me to work alone, to keep all of you out of the investigation."

"You've got to be kidding," Louise said.

"No way," added Fitz, folding his arms. "We work as a team."

"Who does she think she's dealing with?" asked George and banged his fist on the coffee table.

Nancy nodded. "I've talked with her. She has only been here a few months, but she knows I used to be a private detective, and that the four of us have solved several mysteries while at Whisperwood. She still told me to limit my activity to observation and squelching any scary rumors. I think she'd prefer not to deal with us at all."

"She's got another think coming," said Louise. "That's not how we operate."

"You're darn tootin'," added George with a huff.

"Good." Nancy nodded approvingly. "You know where Suzanne stands, so we'll keep her out of the loop. We're all agreed, then, on helping Detective Yost nail the killer in whatever way we can."

"You betcha," said Louise.

"Detective Yost knows us and what we can do," added Fitz.

"You're right." Nancy paused. "I'm in the lobby a lot. I'll remind him that we met during the murder investigation at Lilac Inn. No use dealing with the sheriff. We know from past experience, he will be smarmy and useless."

"He's only interested in collecting overdue taxes anyway," added Fitz. "And getting reelected."

Nancy shrugged. "They want to keep us out, but we will only be doing our duty as citizens to keep our eyes open for suspicious activities and alert the law as appropriate."

"Suzanne and the sheriff need us." Louise flexed her muscles in show. "All of us."

"Sure they do," muttered George.

"They do need us," Nancy said with a warning glance at George. "I listened to Suzanne, but I didn't agree with her suggestion. We work as a team. Everyone at Whisperwood knows that. "

Fitz nodded. "It might go better for us if we pretend to agree, let Nancy be the visible investigator, and the rest of us work in the background."

"I like working in the background," Louise said. "There's only one thing wrong with the idea."

"What's that?" asked George.

Louise frowned. She reached over to Nancy and hugged her. "It makes Nancy a target for the killer."

***

Notice to Residents
Security Peg Check-Up

Whisperwood has added two extra security guards to patrol the grounds and the halls. As an extra safety measure, the guards will check to make sure the pegs and locks outside every apartment door work properly. As you know, the guards flip up the pegs late each night and check them every morning. If the resident has not opened the door that morning, the peg will still be up. In that case, the guard knocks on the door to make sure the resident in that apartment is all right. Whisperwood is such a safe and secure place to live that some residents never lock their doors, but we urge all residents to make sure their doors are locked at night and when they are not home.

Suzanne Craddock, Assistant Administrator
Whisperwood Retirement Village

Chapter 9

That evening, feeling overfull and stodgy after dinner, Nancy cajoled Louise into walking up the stairs to the fourth floor to find out what might be going on at Bill's apartment. Nancy was itching to look around inside if she could find some way around the crime scene tape across the door.

"The sheriff's deputy isn't guarding the place anymore," Louise observed.

Nancy studied the door. "I guess they're depending on the tape and sign." She pointed to the sign taped to the door that said, "Crime Scene. No Entry."

But someone had beaten her to the tape. It had been discreetly sliced with a razor blade at the cracks around the door, so it could be opened while keeping the tape in place. Nancy wouldn't have noticed this if she and Louise hadn't stopped at the door and spent a few minutes thinking about Bill. Once Nancy realized she could open the door without disturbing the tape, she wanted to get inside the apartment. She tested the door, but it was locked.

Who had sliced the tape? Why? It could have been his daughter Megan, who would feel she had the right. Or someone else concerned about Bill's files. She turned to Louise. "Got your credit card?"

"What? You're not going in there, are you?" Louise asked. "I can get a credit card, but using it to open doors is George's department."

"We don't have time," said Nancy. "Can't you smell the smoke?" She pointed to curls of gray wisps snaking out from under the door.

"Omigod!" shrieked Louise. She ran to her apartment and disappeared inside. Within a minute she was back with a credit card. "I called Security, but I don't know how to use this to open a door," she moaned. "I don't have a criminal background where I'd learn stuff like that."

"Neither do I, but I can do it." Nancy took the card and slipped it between the flimsy lock and the door jamb.

The lock gave. Nancy rushed in.

On the floor next to the desk, a small fire blazed, fed by files from the desk and sheets of newspaper. She immediately pulled one of the emergency cords to make another call to the security guards. Louise ran to the kitchen. She picked up a pitcher, filled it with water, and ran back to the fire to pour water on the flames. By the time the guards arrived, the fire was out, and Nancy and Louise were stomping on the ashes.

"What happened?" asked a guard.

"You're not supposed to be in here," said the other.

"We were walking by and smelled smoke," said Nancy.

"We saw it coming out under the door," added Louise. "My apartment's down the hall."

"The tape was already cut." Nancy pointed out the slits in

the tape. "We were able to get in and put out the fire. It was set on purpose, and whatever was in the pile they ignited was burned up." She stared at Louise, willing her to go along with this idea.

"Yeah, they probably got what they came for," said Louise, glancing at Nancy.

"We better call the Sheriff's Office," said the first guard, "and the Fire Department. They'll want to investigate."

The other guard looked around the apartment. "This is where that old guy was killed."

"Detective Yost in the Sheriff's Office is investigating the case," Nancy said.

"Yeah, we know him." The guard was already on the phone.

The second guard pulled a notebook out of his back pocket. "I need your names and room numbers, please," he said, pen ready. "Then you can go. They'll contact you if they want to talk to you."

Nancy and Louise gave him the information, and he ushered them out. Nancy followed Louise into her apartment. Speaking softly so their voices wouldn't carry into the hall, Louise turned to Nancy. "Why did you want them to think the firebug was finished with that apartment and wouldn't be back?"

"We don't want them posting a 24-hour guard there," Nancy whispered back. "We need to get in and look around."

"We do?" asked Louise.

"Regardless of what I told the guards, the arsonist may not have gotten what he or she went after. The firebug counted on nobody finding that fire until it had done a lot more damage."

Louise pursed her lips. "We still have a good chance of

finding whatever they wanted to destroy."

"We'll have to wait until Yost has gone over the apartment." Nancy went to the door, quietly opened it, and looked into the hall. "The guards are still in Bill's apartment. I guess they're waiting for Yost to show up."

"I don't get it," said Louise. "Whoever broke in could have taken their time to find what they wanted and then leave. They didn't have to start a fire."

"Maybe they didn't know exactly what they were looking for so they tried to get rid of all of the files and ruin his computer as well.

"Then it could have been anyone," said Louise.

Nancy nodded. "Someone must have a terrible secret, and Bill knew it."

***

Reminder to All Residents
No Smoking Allowed

Whisperwood does not permit smoking anywhere in the buildings or the grounds. This is for the good health of all our residents and staff. Smoking kills. The buildings at Whisperwood are all constructed of concrete and non-flammable materials to minimize damage from fires, but your papers, clothes, and furniture are vulnerable. We urge all residents and staff to take special care with matches, candles, and other lighted items to protect themselves, their belongings, and the rest of us.

Suzanne Craddock, Assistant Administrator,
Whisperwood Retirement Village

Chapter 10

The next morning, Nancy watched the sheriff's detective Dwayne Yost arrive and head for the executive suite of offices to the left of the lobby. The secretary ushered him through the suite to Suzanne's office at the back and tapped on the door.

Suzanne invited the detective in and closed the door, shutting out a sea of curious faces, including Nancy's. After a few minutes, Suzanne opened the door and took the detective to a closet-sized room next to her office in the suite. Nancy surmised he'd been given space to use for whatever he needed. It had room only for a small desk and two folding chairs.

Nancy waited for Suzanne to return to her office, then she rapped on Suzanne's door and entered as Suzanne looked up from a stack of papers. Her reading glasses dropped to her chest. She tucked back a stray hair. "The detective is here," Suzanne grumbled, "as if I didn't have enough to worry about."

Nancy nodded. "He must have come in last night to investigate the fire. Did he say anything about it?" she asked.

"I talked to him. You know how they are. Wouldn't tell me anything." Suzanne looked frazzled.

"I've worked with him before, but he might not remember

that," Nancy said. "Would you introduce me to him? Tell him how I can help as a resident here—to give me some status. He might brush me off, but he'll at least know who I am."

"Good idea." Suzanne nodded and confirmed Nancy's surmise. "I've given him a space with a desk where he can set up his laptop and do interviews if he wants." She led Nancy to the room where the detective sat, staring at the photos in his wallet. He stood when Suzanne entered.

Nancy smiled and stepped forward. "Are those photos of your family?" she asked.

Dwayne grinned. "My baby daughter. She was born two days ago." He opened his wallet again and showed them the photos.

"What a beautiful baby," cooed Nancy and passed the photos to Suzanne.

"She certainly is. And your wife is, too," said Suzanne. "You're one lucky man."

"Don't I know it," said Dwayne. "Now what can I do for you?"

"Corporal Dwayne Yost is the detective in charge," Suzanne said to Nancy, then turned to the detective. "Corporal Yost, let me introduce you to one of our residents here. Nancy Dickinson. She's a retired detective and knows the people and what's going on here. I think she can help."

The detective was still glowing with pride as he put his wallet back into his pocket and gave a perfunctory smile, then looked more closely. "Ms. Dickenson. I remember you, ma'am. That murder at Lilac Inn, right?" He grinned and shook hands with Nancy. "A pleasure, Ms. Dickinson. Please sit down."

Nancy nodded, glad he'd decided to be friendly. Maybe he realized how helpful she could be. Some law officers she'd met would balk at her involvement and disregard everything she said. Maybe he understood that solving this case depended on knowing the situation and the people here. She could make his job a lot easier.

Suzanne melted away.

Nancy waved in Suzanne's direction. "She overstates the case, I'm afraid, Detective Yost. I haven't worked as a detective for many years. However, I am a trained observer and may be of help to you because I'm acquainted with many of the residents. My friends and I all knew the victim quite well. You might remember Louise Owens. The two of us discovered the fire last night in Bill Myers' apartment. Were you able to find out how it started?"

"It interrupted my beauty sleep," said Yost. "With a new baby in the house, I don't get much. The fire caused minimal damage. The rug and some papers were ruined." He gestured to his laptop. "They scanned your statement and sent it with a report to me this morning. No incendiary material was used. The arsonist counted on a match and the papers in the waste can. Someone must have been desperate to pull that stunt. Glad you saw it in time, ma'am."

"We are, too." Nancy sat back and relaxed. "We think someone was trying to destroy the evidence, and it would have been. Most residents go to their rooms after dinner and stay there. The fire could easily have burned everything in the apartment if Louise and I hadn't come by."

The detective pursed his lips and nodded with a slight smile.

"What evidence do you think the arsonist wanted to destroy?"

"Bill was an old newspaperman, always digging into people's backgrounds," said Nancy. "It was a hobby that could be dangerous. He was working on an article of some kind to sell to the Charleston newspaper."

Dwayne nodded. "I'm sure you have heard by now that the autopsy results show Mr. Myers was a homicide, death by suffocation, and we are investigating it and the fire last night in his apartment."

"That was fast work." Nancy nodded. Sometimes autopsies took months.

"No backlog, for once," said Dwayne.

"We had heard Bill was murdered." Nancy considered telling him about the home health aide but decided to withhold that information for now. The aide would make too easy a target to blame for the murder. Then she thought about Bill's daughter and her husband and their usurping of Bill's bank account but again decided against saying too much. They must have had strong reasons for such an extreme action. Bill probably was reckless in his spending. Anyway, that information was easily available from other sources.

Yost leaned back in his chair and regarded her with a faint smile. "Yes, ma'am. Is there anything else you know that might be useful?"

Nancy listened carefully to his tone. Was he being sarcastic? She could give him something real to chew on. "Bill had a dispute going with a county commissioner. Mike Johnson is his name. I don't know any more than that."

The detective nodded. "We're well aware of Mr. Johnson's

position and activities as county commissioner."

Nancy couldn't tell from the detective's bland tone how he meant that. "I'll ask around to see if I can learn anything from the residents that will help the investigation," she offered as she rose to leave. "They're more likely to talk to me than to you."

He shook his head and waved at the chair. Nancy sat down again.

"Wait a minute here," Dwayne said. "Going around asking questions might turn dangerous. Remember, you're dealing with a killer. We don't want you or anyone else getting hurt trying to play detective. Leave that to us."

"But—" Nancy began.

Dwayne interrupted. "We know about your background and your help with the murder at Lilac Inn, but we can protect ourselves. You can't. We don't want you to get hurt." He pulled a notepad toward him and picked up a pen. "Now tell me what else you know about Mr. Myers. How did you feel about him?"

Nancy was careful in what she said, not wanting to cast undue suspicions on the aide or Megan and Don. Her response was vague and noncommittal.

"Thank you. I understand the situation." He folded his arms and sat back, regarding her without expression. "And what did this Mr. Myers mean to you, Ms. Dickenson?" he asked. "I gotta ask. Were you involved with him?"

The question flabbergasted Nancy. "Not at all," she sputtered. "I gave him rides to the grocery store occasionally and enjoyed chatting with him, but that's all."

"I'm going to be asking everyone this question," Dwayne said. "What were you doing last Saturday night?"

"A concert was held in the auditorium," Nancy said. "I attended that and then went back to my apartment where I spent the night. My friend Fitz was with me. We live together."

"I see." He made a note. "You and your friends were the star performers in the Lilac Inn case, but this is different. I repeat. Stay out of my investigation, Ms. Dickenson. Do not ask questions or do any detecting. I will do all the checking of residents necessary." He ran his fingers across the desk as if drawing a line.

He came around the desk. "And thank you for coming in. It's nice seeing you again." He shook her hand and ushered her out the door.

As she walked back to her apartment, Nancy considered his repeated warnings. He was a new father and a member of the community. He probably would like to be friends, but in his profession, he had to suspect everyone. *Even me.* He said he didn't want her to get involved because detecting was dangerous. But if she were the killer, she could muddy the waters by planting red herrings through suggestions she might make about the other residents.

She remembered several cases she'd worked in which the helpful citizen turned out to be the culprit. She was also at the fire, and arsonists liked to watch the fires they set. She had the feeling that offering to help put her name prominently and high on the suspect list. She shook her head at the irony.

***

That afternoon, Nancy was searching online for any information she could find about Megan and her husband when she heard a faint, timid knock on her door. Opening it, she faced the home health aide she'd seen giggling with Bill Myers. The woman looked about twenty-five and had long, bleached blond hair, a freckled face, and coral red lips. She wore jeans and a T-shirt instead of the aides' standard uniform of flowered top and blue slacks. *She must be off-duty.*

"I'm sorry to bother you," the young woman said, "but I need to talk to someone…"

Nancy invited her in and stepped aside, gesturing the young woman over to the sofa. The woman sat, teetering on the edge, her hands tightly clasped.

"I've seen you in the hall," said Nancy. "You're one of the aides."

"That's right. I've seen you, too," She licked her lips nervously. "And I know you are a detective. I need a detective, but I can't pay much."

"Retired detective," Nancy said automatically.

"You still know what to do. I'm hoping you'll help me. My name is Tammy Swann." Her voice shook, and she swallowed as if she were nervous. "Mr. Myers up on the fourth floor was one of my people."

"Would you like a cup of tea?" Perhaps tea would calm the young woman.

She looked surprised. "Tea? Oh, okay. That would be nice." She sat back and glanced around the room. Malone eyed her from his perch on the windowsill. His tail flicked back and forth. "I can't stay long."

Nancy made tea for both of them and set the cups and sugar on the coffee table. "I was sorry to hear about Bill Myers," she said. "Is that why you're here?"

Tammy took a deep breath. "I don't know what to do," she said. "I'm worried I'll be blamed for Mr. Myers' death, and I'll lose my job. The man from the Sheriff's Office asked me a lot of questions. I'm afraid."

"Why would anyone blame you?"

"I don't know, but his daughter and her husband are making trouble, and now the police are saying Mr. Myers was murdered. You knew Mr. Myers, and you seem like a nice person. People say you are a good detective; you know how to find out things. I need your help."

"What kind of trouble are they making?"

"People are looking at me funny. I hear them saying I killed him…for his money." Tammy was trying hard not to cry. She hid her face as she sipped the tea.

Nancy blushed, remembering her own concern. "Why would they think that?"

"I don't know. I just tried to do the best job I could for Mr. Myers and all my clients, but his friend, a lawyer, has told his family about a missing will. I know nothing about that. And his daughter, I know she hates me. She told everyone I exercised…I don't know what they call it…"

Nancy supplied the words. "Undue influence?"

"That's it. Me, I don't have any influence over anybody, but now people look at me funny. I hear the rumors. People are saying I made Mr. Myers give me money in his will. Why would Mr. Myers do such a thing? I treated him like I do all my clients. Just the same. I don't want any trouble with this job." Tammy pulled a tissue out of her pocket and wiped her eyes.

Nancy didn't know what to say. Tammy had lied, though.

She was certainly friendlier with Bill than she let on.

"You must believe me," said Tammy. "You knew him. He often talked about you. No one can find the will. If they did, they would see I had nothing to gain. You're a detective. If you would search for it, you might find it." She held out her hands, palms up. "Then everyone would see how crazy it is that I would kill Mr. Myers for his money. His daughter and her husband can go home and leave me alone."

Nancy patted Tammy's hand. "When did you first hear about this will?"

"Mr. Myers, he joked about such a thing, but I never believed him. Now, this lawyer says it must be found. I am sure the daughter and her husband will inherit whether the will is found or not."

"I think the lawyer must have a copy of the will," Nancy said.

Tammy shook her head. "Mr. Myers wrote it himself. That's what the problem is. He asked the lawyer about doing that. Then he hid it. He was a joker sometimes, you know?"

Nancy nodded, remembering Bill's insistence on making out the will by himself and hiding it. Somehow, she and Axel were supposed to figure out where. "He was a character." And a fool who didn't know where the game should stop.

"Mr. Myers told you what he'd done? Did he give you any hints about where he hid it?"

"Of course not. Even if he had, I would think he was still joking and not paid any attention."

"And Mr. Myers never showed any signs of preference towards you?"

"He always asked for me to help him." Tammy shrugged. "I have many people who prefer me to the other aides. I work hard." She paused as she studied Nancy. "There is something else, but I haven't said anything about it to anybody. It is not a nice thing…"

"Uh oh," thought Nancy. Had that old goat come on to this poor girl?

"You see," Tammy said slowly, "Mr. Myers is my grandfather."

Whatever Tammy might have said, this was the furthest from Nancy's mind. "Grandfather?"

Tammy nodded. "Yes. He and my grandmother had an affair. It was all over long ago, but he knew I worked here, so when he moved here, he asked for me. He told me this and then apologized for not being around for me when I was growing up. That's what he said, but my grandmother would not have wanted him there. We didn't need him, but that is why he said he left money for me in his will. A lot of money."

"I see," Nancy said, still reeling. "That means his daughter isn't his only relative, and it makes finding the will important for you."

"I would like the money, yes. I have a right to it along with his daughter and her husband. Mr. Myers was very nice to me, but people are saying I killed him because he was leaving me money in his will."

"Perhaps he explained your relationship in the will," Nancy said.

"I don't think that matters." Tammy shrugged. "The police will think I killed him anyway." She brightened. "But if he didn't leave any money, then I have no motive."

Nancy shook her head. "Even if he didn't leave you any money, if you thought he did, that would constitute a motive."

Tammy stared at Nancy for a moment. Then she flicked her hair. "Anyway, I always treat my patients as if they were extra special—and they are to me. But I'm not looking for any reward. I trained for this job. I work hard. It's not my fault that Mr. Myers is my grandfather."

"What about your grandmother or your mother. What are their thoughts on Mr. Myers?"

"My grandmother died years ago. My mother knew Mr. Myers was her father, but she hadn't seen him in a long time. She told me about him, and he knew about me."

"Have you seen her birth certificate?"

Tammy shook her head.

"I'm sure we could obtain one if we need to," Nancy said. "The will needs to be found, though, to clear up these issues."

"I think so, yes," Tammy agreed, "But I don't need the money, and I don't like people spreading rumors about me."

Nancy regarded Tammy thoughtfully. Was she really scared she'd be accused? Was Bill really her grandfather? Had Bill really told her he'd left her a bequest in a will? Who else would know? Was there a hidden will?

Tammy seemed to waver between worrying that she would be accused of murder for money and protesting that she didn't expect any inheritance and should be freed of suspicion.

"I can't promise anything," Nancy said. "I'll see what I can do." But she'd caught a glimpse of Tammy's dreams the morning she'd seen Tammy preening in the sunshine. Tammy didn't need the money, but she'd certainly like it.

"Oh, thank you, thank you." Tammy clasped her hands as if in prayer and headed to the door. She stopped, reached into her purse, and handed Nancy a note. "My phone number. I am home most evenings." She winced. "Maybe most days now if I am fired. I don't know. I don't want to lose my job. None of this is my fault."

"Don't worry. Carry on as usual, and I'll try to get to the bottom of it," said Nancy. She walked with Tammy to the door and watched her hurry down the hall.

This was an interesting turn of events. She walked to her laptop and looked up Tammy on Whisperwood's website. The young woman was shown in a photo with the other home health aides, each of whom was accorded a brief biographical paragraph. Tammy's said she was born and brought up nearby and received her training at an applied medical school in Charleston, West Virginia. Before Whisperwood, she had worked at a rehabilitation center outside Charleston. Nancy could see no resemblance to Bill.

Nancy looked up the phone number for the center and asked to speak to someone in Human Resources. A sweet young voice came on the line. "How may I help you?"

"We're checking our files here at Whisperwood Retirement Village and found that we don't have a reference from you for one of our employees who used to work for you. Her name is Tammy Swann."

"Is there a problem with the employee?"

"Not at all. This is just a procedural thing to complete our files. I was checking and found that the reference from you is missing. According to her application, she worked for you from January through July last year. As I say, I'm just trying to complete the file, that's all."

"I see. Just a moment, please."

A brisk, more mature voice came on the line. "You need a reference for Tammy Swann? I believe we sent you that reference months ago"

"It's missing from the file," Nancy repeated. "We need to have it for our records."

"All right. I'll have my assistant fax you a copy. What is your fax number?"

Nancy provided her fax number, which was anonymous. An email address would be harder to fake. They wouldn't send such a document to her personal email unless she could furnish a reasonable explanation for why they should. She wrote a note to herself: Make up an email address that is anonymous but business-like. It could be useful in the future.

Two hours later, she heard the fax machine grind out a new message. The document was, as Nancy expected, brief and noncommittal, providing only confirmation that Tammy Swann worked at the rehab center from January to July last year. No commendations, no ratings of how she performed. No information of the kind Nancy wanted, but it was what she expected, and it did confirm Tammy's employment there. The reference was bare bones, but most human resources staff were afraid of lawsuits.

***

That evening, the 90s Club met in the Whisperwood Pub for dinner rather than the dining room. They ordered drinks immediately—for Nancy, a chardonnay; Louise chose beer. Fitz sipped a martini, and George looked with disgust at a glass of water. Just as quickly, they ordered from the Pub menu's light fare.

"This is a nice change," Louise commented, surveying the cozy room with its brick fireplace, even though no fire blazed in the summer months. The green badge on Louise's collar said "Green Peace" in white letters.

"Guess I'll have to watch you ladies, what with all the alcohol," George said. He wore a red sports coat and pink polka-dotted bow tie with navy blue slacks.

"You wish," snorted Louise, winking at Nancy.

"I like it here," said Nancy, sipping the wine.

"What is this meeting and change of venue about?" George asked.

"Remember what I said about staff not fraternizing with us inmates here?" Nancy peered at them over her glass.

"Inmates?" George sniffed at the word. "Are we talking about Bill Myers?"

"Yes. His home health aide came to visit me today, nervous and upset. Bill's daughter has accused her of killing Bill for his money."

"He didn't have any money." George banged on the table. "His daughter had control of all his accounts."

"That's what we've been told," said Louise. "Anyway, his aide has been super nice to me lately. She comes over and helps me out even when I don't request her services."

"What do any of you know about Bill's daughter?" asked Nancy.

"I'm glad she ain't mine," said George. "Of all the busy-body, controlling, self-centered females, she's got to be at the top of the list." He leaned forward. "She didn't even want to wait for Bill to die. Had to get her paws on his money now."

"We've talked about this before, but why would she do that and how come Bill didn't fight it?" Nancy asked. "He seemed sound of mind to me."

"I guess Bill was a spendthrift, and they're living beyond their means. They need Bill's money now," Fitz said in his Jamaican lilt, running a hand across his white, tightly curled hair. "Not content with waiting, Luv."

"I've done some online searches on Megan's financial situation," Nancy said. "She married a sports promoter. He makes a lot of money, but they have an expensive lifestyle. Condo in the Watergate; active in social and civic affairs, country club memberships. They move with a fast crowd."

Louise set down her beer. "Did Bill get any kind of stipend? You need some pocket money for little odds and ends."

George snorted. "He complained to me about it. She put him on a piddling allowance that wouldn't even buy him a candy bar. She told him he didn't need any money since he gets his meals here and can put anything he buys at the Whisperwood market on the monthly bill. And then she took away all his booze." George thumped the table and sat back.

"Do you think he did hide money and a will somewhere?" asked Nancy.

"Sure. He was a wily old thing." Louise said and grinned. "If he hid anything, it's in an old clock."

"Oh?" George looked at them. "He told me that time was

on his side."

Louise nodded. "That's what I mean."

"He was always hinting about clocks and time," said Nancy, "but surely he wouldn't stoop to such a hackneyed idea. That was trite a hundred years ago." Clocks seemed to follow me around, she thought. Her first case, years before she even had a license, involved a square-faced mantel clock that she was later given as a souvenir after she solved that mystery. A few months ago, she had encountered another mystery involving an old clock and its secret. Maybe clocks were written into her destiny.

"He was a newspaperman. He could do better than that," said George, "even if he let that daughter of his twist him around her finger."

"He had a clock radio in his apartment. Otherwise, he wore a wristwatch." Louise glanced around, caught the server's eye, and gestured to her glass.

"Tammy is afraid that if they find the will and she does inherit anything," said Nancy, "they'll think she killed him."

"Bill could have written her into the will," said George. "She's a sweet young gal and he was livid with his daughter."

"Would he have told Tammy he was leaving her a bequest?" Nancy asked. "How else would she know anything about that?"

"Maybe she hinted at it and is hoping he did." Louise shook her head. "Bill gabbed too much, but his lawyer wouldn't talk to anybody but his client. He's supposed to keep that stuff confidential."

"There's something else," Nancy said. "Tammy told me Bill was her grandfather. He and her grandmother had an affair that resulted in her mother's birth. Tammy's mother knew who her father was."

"Wow," Louise said. "That's a new wrinkle. Bill would have a good reason to leave his daughter or granddaughter money then."

"That means Megan isn't the only possible heir as kin." George pursed his lips in thought. "If it's true, Bill probably told his lawyer. It certainly complicates the situation."

Nancy sipped the chardonnay. "I happened to pass by Bill's door when Security had just discovered his body. No crime scene tape and no forensic people around. They were surprised to see me and closed the door in my face."

George stopped with his glass halfway to his lips. "Anyone dies here, a staff person whisks the body away quickly and quietly. They put an oxygen mask on his face and pretend he's still alive. Use the freight elevator. An ambulance or funeral home van is standing by in the basement garage. Don't want to disturb the residents, you know."

Louise laughed. "I've often wondered how they do it. I've never seen a body transported through the halls here or even a hearse come around the building."

"They probably transport the person by ambulance," said George. "That's common enough. We don't even notice those."

"I suppose they thought at first it was just another old person dying as expected," said Nancy. "Then the doctor noticed signs of suffocation, and now the sheriff's office is investigating his death as a homicide."

George sat back and nodded. "I've been listening to the rumors for anything that will help us."

"Me, too,' said Louise, "and I saw that detective poking around. I remember him from the Lilac Inn case."

"I talked to him a short while ago," said Nancy. "Noncommittal as usual, but I told him I was ready to help and am keeping my eyes and ears open." She grinned at the others. "You know I mean all of us."

"We know that, Luv," said Fitz, "but he told you to stay out of the investigation, didn't he?"

Louise's eyes sparked. "They always say that. Think they're such hotshots when they know nothing about any of us."

Nancy shrugged. "I pay no attention."

"Business as usual, I say," added George. "That is, our business. We'll have to be circumspect."

"They called in a physician to pronounce him dead, and he's the one who noticed the signs of suffocation." Louise sipped her beer thoughtfully. "They must have sent the body for autopsy to the West Virginia Medical Examiner's Office in Charleston."

"The autopsy has already been completed, and it confirms suffocation," said Nancy.

"Fast work," said Louise.

"I'm glad they have a medical examiner and not a coroner," Nancy added with a shiver.

"Why? They're the same, aren't they?" asked George.

"If I were going to murder anyone," Nancy said, "I would do it in a state with a coroner. A coroner is elected and could be anyone who throws his hat in the ring."

"Oh, yeah. That's right. I'd like to run for the job if West Virginia had a coroner system," said George.

"Any yahoo, including the burger flipper at McDonald's, could be elected," said Louise. "Even you."

"That's true," said Nancy. "A medical examiner has to meet certain standards such as having a medical degree and other special certification. Also, a list of criteria is established to mandate autopsies."

'George wiped his mouth with his napkin. "I'm glad Bill is in good hands, but I'll bet you a dollar his daughter did it. Or maybe her husband. They sure wanted their hands on his money."

Nancy nodded. "They aren't the only possibilities," she said. Looking at them all, she added, "It's a new case for the 90s Club, and we better get crackin'."

***

An Invitation to Residents
MEET YOUR NEIGHBOR

Whisperwood will host a "Meet Your Neighbor" afternoon tea and social hour on Wednesday at 3 p.m. in the lobby. Refreshments will be served, Please sign up at the Reception Desk. To help you connect, you'll have a name tag where you can add your occupation, hobby, or other interest to help you meet others with similar interests while mingling. We look forward to seeing you there!

Mary Ann Hopkins, Social Director,
Whisperwood Retirement Village

Chapter 11

Nancy sat side by side with Axel on the couch in his apartment as they leafed through the album yet again. Nancy worked to pull memories out of Axel. She found the photos intriguing. They presented a picture of European life in the thirties, back when wagons were pulled by horses, and wells and outhouses were common.

"I used to visit a friend's farm when I was growing up," said Nancy. "Long time ago. They had a well and outhouse, too. At home in the city, we had an indoor bathroom with flush toilet."

Alex laughed. "You were lucky. I grew up using the outhouse and well on the farm in England. We had a slops bucket in the kitchen for wastewater."

Nancy laughed. "Despite the primitive conditions, I loved spending weekends and summer vacations at the farm, even with its outhouse fifty feet from the kitchen door."

"Modern conveniences for me, thank you," Axel retorted. He pointed to the horse-drawn covered wagon featured in a number of the photos. "That's our horse." He put his finger on the horse's neck. "We called her Cobby, I think."

"Why Cobby?" The name sounded British to Nancy.

Axel shook his head. "Have no idea."

"Do you remember moving around a lot with that wagon?" asked Nancy.

Axel shook his head. "I don't know. Too young to remember, although I do think we lived in the wagon. Maybe we couldn't move, you know. There'd been a huge depression. We must have been very poor. Maybe my sister said something about that to her kids." He spread his hands helplessly.

"What did your parents do?" asked Nancy. Axel had been sent to England when he was five. How much would a five-year-old remember?

"Musicians? Entertainers?" Axel thought a moment. "Someone had a dancing bear." He leafed through the album to find the bear photo. "I don't remember much."

"So the bear was a part of the entertainment." Nancy studied the photo thoughtfully.

"He was with another family...in another wagon. There were lots of us. We all had wagons. And horses."

"Do you remember the house you lived in?"

Axel shook his head. "I slept in the wagon...with my sister and my mama and papa."

Nancy was developing a theory about Axel's background and everything fit, but she kept her revelation to herself for now. Axel should come to it himself. It might shock him. "Your parents must have been terrified to send you away. This couple on the farm in England, they weren't religious, you said?"

Axel nodded. "Even my family in England was afraid of Hitler and the bombs. Of course, a war was going on, but I'll never forget listening for planes and for that weird whistling sound that meant a bomb and then we'd all run for cover.

"When I was in Belgium as a little boy, I didn't understand what was happening. We didn't have much to eat, and everyone was afraid of the soldiers. My father made connections somehow—I don't know how he did this—but he was put in touch with the couple in England who would take us. The couple wanted children but had none—my Mama said this to me—so this old couple would adopt us for awhile until my parents could come for us." He sighed.

Nancy felt the tragedy in Axel's voice. "And they never did," she said softly.

He pointed to the album. "My Mama hid this old album in my suitcase to keep safe in England until we could be together again. And now it is all I have left." He shook his head. "And my sister's kids, of course."

Nancy closed the album. "I'd like to meet them. Your sister may have mentioned any memories she had of her earlier life to them. She was two years older. She might have remembered more than her little brother."

"I'll see what can be arranged. They live in Maryland outside of Washington. They are busy, so we may have to drive there."

"That would be fun." Nancy loved a long drive with the chance to explore. She rose. "By the way, I've ordered a DNA kit for you. That might be the biggest help. I haven't done it myself, but a friend told me that once you receive the results, you can request that the company forward an email to the list of people related to you and then hope they reply."

Axel grinned. "DNA test! I've heard about them but thought they were a useless gimmick."

Nancy shook her head. "Not at all. People who've taken the test are finding relatives they never knew they had in unexpected places." She picked up the album as she stood.

"I can see that happening," Axel laughed as he walked her to the door, "but I would love to meet any relatives."

Nancy smiled. "Of course, you would."

She held up the album. "I'll keep this a while longer if I may."

"Find out whatever you can, even if they were born, like the old saying goes, on the wrong side of the blanket. I don't care. I'm sorry I don't remember much."

Nancy returned to her apartment. As she approached, she saw Tammy Swann hovering outside the door. Tammy hurried up to her. "I hoped to see you. The police are here, and I am so afraid. Did you find out anything? Do they know who killed my grandfather?"

Nancy paused. Noncommittal seemed like the best response. She had no information. "I'm sure you have nothing to worry about."

"But the will. It hasn't been found?"

Nancy studied her. What was behind that question? Fear? Or avarice? "I don't know," she said. "I'm sure you're worried about nothing. Bill probably left everything to his daughter anyway."

Nancy saw Tammy's disappointment flash across her face, but she smiled. "Yes, yes, you are right. I am sorry Mr. Bill is dead, but no one can think I killed him." She nodded to herself.

"And I didn't set any fire in his apartment," she added. "Who would do such a thing? You don't think it burned up the will, do you? Could someone, maybe his daughter, have tried to set it on fire? Maybe they were afraid of what Mr. Myers might do."

"The police are looking into it." Nancy unlocked her apartment door and stepped inside. "They'll find out who murdered Mr. Myers and discover his will, too."

"Thank you, Ms. Dickinson. I'm probably worrying about nothing. You are right." She turned and hurried back down the hall to the lobby.

Tammy didn't set the fire, thought Nancy. She thinks Bill left her a significant bequest. No matter what she says, she wouldn't risk burning up the will, if there is one.

That evening, the 90s Club met at their usual table fifty-six in the dining room. Louise carried a bag and set it on the table with a loud clunk.

"What have you brought?" asked Nancy. You never knew what Louise would think was worth sharing with friends. At least whatever was in the bag wasn't moving.

George unfolded his napkin and laid it across his lap. "It can't be flowers." His laugh wiggled the red and yellow-striped bow tie that matched his yellow and red-striped suspenders.

Louise frowned at him. "Shows how much you know. It is flowers. Sort of. I've brought a bouquet for each of you." She pulled a small Mason jar out of the bag and placed it in front of George. The golden syrup inside glowed. She handed a similar jar to Nancy. "Honey from my hive. What do you think of that?"

"I'll be darned," said George. "Did you get all this honey

out of your hive by yourself?"

Louise shook her head. "That's hard and heavy work. A couple of local beekeepers helped me in exchange for most of the honey. I mean, how much can I use anyhow? They took two supers off the hive, extracted the honey, returned the supers, and gave me ten of those jars filled with honey from my huge workforce of bees." She pointed to the jars. "Lots more where that came from. I got thousands of employees."

Nancy dipped a spoon into the jar and sampled the liquid gold. "Delicious," she said.

"Yep." Louise grinned. "Flowers from the landscaping here mixed with pine pollen, my guess." She looked up at the server hovering by their table. "Teriyaki salmon," she said.

The other three gave their orders and the server left, nodding at the manager to take their wine orders. Nancy asked for pinot noir, George declined as usual, while the others opted for chardonnay.

"I've been thinking about Tammy Swann's problem," said Nancy. "She's worried that if the will is found, and she does inherit a bundle, she'll be accused of influencing him, and then she'll lose her job."

Louise tapped her lips thoughtfully. "If she doesn't inherit, then she has no problem."

"She could still be accused of murder," added Nancy, "if they think Tammy expected to inherit, whether she did or not."

George tapped a spoon on his glass for attention. "I got some news."

They looked at him. "What?" said Louise.

"I heard his daughter Megan and her husband are anxious

to find the will." George sat back with a smile. "You'd think the lawyer would have a copy, but Bill wrote it himself and kept it. They don't know where he hid it, and they've been turning his apartment upside down trying to find it."

"Have you met them?" asked Nancy.

George shook his head. "No, but I found out they live in D.C."

"How do you know that?" asked Louise.

George grinned. "I got my sources and keep my ears open."

"So that's what's been going on in his apartment," said Louise, nodding to herself. "Makes sense now."

Nancy looked at her. "What's been going on there?"

"The detective put more crime scene tape over the door but didn't post a guard. I saw Bill's daughter Megan rip the tape off, and I think the two of them are ransacking his place," Louise said. "I hear all kinds of noises when I go by. Makes sense if they're searching for something."

"Like a will," added George.

Fitz looked up. "Do you think they've found it?"

Louise shook her head. "Their search is still going on in there."

"We need to discover the will first," said Nancy. "Bill told me we should be able to find it behind an old clock. That is, Axel and I should. I have no idea what that means."

"If Tammy Swann inherits, that makes her a prime suspect," said Louise.

Fitz nodded. "And the detective won't look any further. He'll charge her."

"I don't think Tammy has talked to anyone but me about

her expectations," said Nancy slowly.

Louise flicked her braid. "If the detective doesn't know, and Tammy isn't mentioned in the will, they probably won't think about her as a suspect. She is only a home health aide, after all.

"We want to learn the truth and to identify the murderer," said Nancy, "but I'd like to protect Tammy from a quick judgment that she's guilty."

"Bill was wily, you know, and a joker." Louise stared into her wine glass. "He'd do something clever with the will. Of course, he'd think you would be the logical person to bait. His daughter doesn't strike me as being that bright."

"Or as imaginative as her dad," added Nancy.

"Mean, though," said George. "Taking all his money the way she did."

Nancy summed it up. "We need to get into Bill's apartment. When do you think the sheriff will allow her to start moving his things out?"

"Whisperwood has some rule about how long the family can hold onto a unit here. Anyway, I'm sure he was paid up until the end of this month. If they want to keep it longer, they'll be paying a stiff monthly fee. His daughter will want to get that financial burden off her hands pretty quick. We'll have to move fast." Louise drummed her fingers.

"Tonight then." Nancy looked at them for agreement. "Almost everyone is tucked into their apartment by nine."

"Visitors have to leave by ten," added Fitz, "and the security guard comes down our hall on the first floor about 2:30 a.m., then he goes up to the next floor. What time does he get to your floor, Louise?"

"I'm a night owl, so I hear him." Louise glanced at her watch. "About 3:15 a.m. He holds to that schedule. All of them do."

"They're not expecting skullduggery," said George. "They're just flicking the peg up on each door."

"I like that feature," said Louise. "If the peg is still up after eleven a.m., they check on you to make sure you didn't kick the bucket during the night. I don't want to be decomposing for days before someone thinks to ask about me."

"We'd check on you way before that," said George, putting an arm around Louise.

"I agree, but back to business," said Nancy. "I heard them, too. His daughter and her husband were here this afternoon. I saw them come in and followed them up, then I listened outside the door. There was a lot of moving and cursing going on."

Louise laughed. "I didn't know you were out there."

"We don't have time to waste," said Fitz. "If we can get into Bill's apartment around nine this evening, we'll have about six hours to search."

"Most people return to their apartments after dinner," added George, "unless they're taking a class or there's a special event. We'll have to be quiet, but we should be able to do it without being heard."

Louise nodded. "I'm two doors down from Bill. We can meet at my apartment. The locks are flimsy. We can open Bill's door with a credit card like Nancy did with the fire."

"The locks in this place remind me of an apartment I had years ago." Nancy rolled her eyes. "The lock was like the ones here, so flimsy a neighborhood kid got in. I found him raiding the refrigerator when I came home one afternoon."

Louise laughed. "Bill's daughter Megan stopped by my place this afternoon. She looked at my furniture as if she were calculating its value. All she sees are dollar signs."

"If she saw mine, she'd want to throw it all out," Nancy said, "but your antique and vintage pieces are beautiful." And totally out of character for Louise, but Nancy knew she had inherited most of it and was saving it for her daughter.

"Fortunately, Megan and her husband Don didn't stay long," added Louise. "She asked me if Bill had given me anything to keep for him." Louise shivered. "She had cold eyes. She looked mean. And Don, he sat there flaring like a cobra. He said she was looking for some keepsakes of her Dad's for sentimental reasons. Made a point of telling me Bill had nothing valuable in case I might want anything of his."

"Yeah, I'll bet. I saw her in the hall and did my best to be friendly and charming as you know I am." George waved his fork. "She was too high and mighty to respond. She acted suspicious of me and my motives, like I was out to rob her."

Louise nodded. "That's how I felt. I told her I didn't have anything of Bill's, but she persisted, asking if maybe Bill had given me an envelope . . . "

"The will," said Nancy.

"Then she asked if he'd given me a box or a book."

Fitz sat back and folded his arms. "Maybe her husband knew Bill had stocks or bonds they can't find."

"She stopped by my table in the lobby the other day," said Nancy. "I told her I didn't have anything that belonged to him. She gave me her phone number in case I thought of something."

George looked up. "That for sure means they didn't find it."

"Yes," said Louise. "I wish I'd thought of more questions to ask her."

"What we want to know," Fitz commented, "is who killed him, and that would be a tough question to ask his daughter."

George twirled his wine glass. "Especially since it could have been her."

"I'm sure Dwayne has talked to her," put in Fitz.

"Megan, Don, and Tammy want the will." Nancy said. "They wouldn't start a fire that might destroy it."

"But who did?" asked Louise. "And why?"

"If Bill died without a will," added George, "West Virginia law says next of kin gets all of his estate except for taxes due. Tammy wouldn't have a case."

"But the lawyer knows Bill wrote a will," Nancy said, "and it might include Tammy as a beneficiary. Without the will and with a possible additional legatee, the legal process would be slow."

"And we think Don and Megan need the money now," said Fitz.

They finished their dinner and went up the elevator to Louise's apartment. At nine p.m., the halls were empty of residents, and the hall lights were dimmed. George pulled a sheaf of credit cards out of his wallet and fanned them before selecting one. He waved at the group, silently opened the door, and left for Bill's apartment. Two minutes later, he knocked on Louise's door. They scurried into Bill's unit and immediately stopped and stared.

Axel Cooper, surprised in the act of rifling a drawer in Bill's desk, gaped at them.

"What are you doing here?" asked Nancy.

Axel closed the drawer. "How embarrassing," he muttered and shrugged. "I'm not a thief. What are you doing here?"

George stepped forward. "You first."

Axel wrung his hands. "You know how Bill was," he said. "Always nosy. He told me he was checking into my background because he didn't like being pulled off my little project. He wanted to know what I was afraid he'd find." He turned to Nancy. "You know, I asked you to take it on instead of him. Bill was nosing into my life, and I didn't trust what he planned to do with whatever he turned up."

"He was too curious," agreed George. "What are you searching for?"

Axel shrugged. "The folder he'd put together on me. Maybe he somehow turned up the answers I was looking for. That's all." He looked from one face to the next, and then seemed to recall where he was. "What are you doing here? You've no more right to be here than I do."

"That's true," said Fitz.

"We're trying to help the investigation," added Nancy, "by finding Bill's will. His daughter and son-in-law have been searching, too, maybe others." She glanced meaningfully around the room.

Only the spot on the floor where the fire had been was cleared and cleaned. All of them surveyed the damage.

"I didn't do this," said Axel, gesturing at the overturned furniture.

The recliner lay on its side, and the searchers had stacked

books in piles on the floor. They had unscrewed the seats of the dining room chairs and unfastened the seat covers. Drawers hung open in the kitchen and bathroom. In the bedroom, some-one had folded the bedding and piled it in a corner. They had slid the mattress off the bed frame and overturned it. Pillows were stripped, the bureau pulled away from the wall, and the drawers removed from the bureau and overturned.

"I didn't do this," repeated Axel.

"Neither did we," said Louise.

Nancy picked up a book from the floor amidst piles of newspapers and magazines. "I guess this means there *is* a will and maybe a stash of something somewhere," she said, "but how many people are searching other than us?"

"What do you mean?" asked Louise.

"The four of us plus Don, Megan, and maybe even Tammy are searching for the will," Nancy said.

"Sounds right," said George, "but what about him?" He stared at Axel whose face had turned red.

"Yes. And how many others would like to know what kind of information is buried in Bill's files? Who would want to de-stroy those files?"

Fitz whistled softly. "Someone in that bunch set the fire."

"You're looking for a will?" asked Axel. "I can't imagine his daughter didn't find it."

"I don't think she did," said Louise.

"Not yet, anyway." Nancy opened the refrigerator, checked the ice basket, and unwrapped the frozen food containers. She ran a knife through the sugar and flour in the canisters. George and Louise stared at the furniture. Axel watched them.

"We've been outdone," said Louise,

"It must still be here," said Nancy. "We need to rethink about where to look." She glanced at Axel. "Bill told me you and I would know where he hid it."

Axel snorted. "That's a laugh. I have no idea. Couldn't get away from him fast enough."

"We might as well call it a night," said George. "We're getting nowhere."

Nancy nodded. "I'm going to search the common areas in the buildings here. Bill must have meant something by all those references to an old clock. There isn't any such thing in his apartment."

Louise agreed. "I'm going to find out who last saw Bill alive, and then see if his daughter visited Bill the day or evening before his death."

"The murderer had to be present to suffocate him," added Nancy. "No long-lasting poison was used that would confuse the timing for alibis."

"He died late Saturday night." George scratched his chin. "Bill wouldn't have missed the concert that night."

Louise chimed in. "The dining room and pub were closed by the time it let out."

"Fitz and I were there," said Nancy. "But we didn't see him, Did you?"

"Briefly as we were going in," Louise said. "But I didn't notice anyone else in particular. I'll check on it, though."

"We can compare our findings at dinner tomorrow," said Nancy, slipping out into the hall.

Axel followed her with his walker. "If you find anything

he had on me, let me know, please," he said as he hobbled toward the elevator. "It would only be personal stuff. Nothing criminal."

"See you tomorrow," whispered Fitz, waving at Louise and George and taking Nancy's hand. They stepped quietly to join Axel at the elevator.

She was sure the will had not yet been discovered, but finding Axel in Bill's apartment was a surprise. Who else had a reason to know what Bill was up to? What were they doing now to find and destroy any damaging information?

***

Insomniacs Club a Boon for Night Owls

Have trouble sleeping? Why fight it? The library and the club room are open around the clock. No need to toss and turn in a hopeless attempt to sleep. Join other insomniacs for a game of bridge, Scrabble, conversation, and companionship. Groups gather in the lobby, library, club room, and classrooms on the lower level.

The Whisperwood Breeze,
Whisperwood Retirement Village Newsletter

Chapter 12

Nancy finished breakfast and was reading the newspaper when the phone rang. With the prevalence of scam and telemarketing calls, she usually let it go to an answering machine. When she heard Emily's voice leaving a message, she quickly picked up the receiver.

"Nancy! You're home. Great! You won't believe what I've been doing. I'm glad I met you! When I drove home after talking with you at the café, my heart was lighter than it has been for years."

Nancy could hear the excitement in her voice, but before she could respond, Emily babbled on.

"I was so excited that the very next day, I drove to the nearest computer shop and bought a laptop computer with all the Microsoft Office programs." She stopped to take a breath. "Good thing I pay the bills. Mike won't like this." She chuckled. "If he ever finds out, that is."

"Terrific," Nancy began, but Emily interrupted.

"We have WiFi at home because the kids need it. I've been using the library's computers. About time I got my own, wouldn't you say?"

Nancy nodded. "Certainly is."

"But Nancy," Emily turned serious, "I have a request to make. It's important or I wouldn't ask."

"I'll be glad to help," Nancy said. Emily was making big moves. She was serious about getting out. Nancy was pleased that Emily was making moves instead of talking about making them. What worried Nancy was that she had encouraged Emily to make these risky changes in her life.

What if Emily failed? How responsible would she feel if she had ruined someone's life? It didn't take long for Nancy to decide that whatever happened, Emily was right to leave her home. Seeing how happy Emily was with the decision, the fact that she was eating again and not stuttering much—all that was proof enough. If Emily failed and blamed Nancy, that was fine. *I wouldn't have done anything differently.*

"What do you need?" she asked.

Emily turned hesitant. "Would you mind if I left my laptop with you? I don't want Mike to see it. He'll ask questions."

"Of course, you can." Nancy's first response was usually positive and supportive no matter what was asked. If she could help she would.

Emily breathed a sigh of relief. "It won't be for very long."

"What do you mean it won't be for very long?"

Emily giggled. "I'm getting out, Nancy. I'm leaving on September first. Isn't that wonderful?"

"All right..." Nancy said cautiously. "Where are you go-ing? Do you have money? A job?"

"I'm not a dummy," Emily said resentfully. "I've saved up five thousand dollars in my own account. And I've been doing the family books for years. I know what things cost, okay?" This time she sounded truculent. "I know what I'm doing."

"Of course you do," said Nancy. For just a moment, she wondered if Emily could have any ulterior motives for confiding in her, but what could they be?

"I signed up for a couple of online college courses," Emily said, "and they begin in two weeks. I'll be gone by then, but in the meantime, I'll have to come over to use my laptop, but don't worry," she rushed to say, "I'll take it out to the lobby and work there. You won't have me underfoot."

"There are plenty of quiet places to work around Whisperwood." Nancy smiled. Emily was thoughtful, kind, and smart. Her husband didn't know what he was losing. "Not a problem, but…"

"But what?"

"Your husband was here last week, angry and looking for Bill Myers. Then sometime early Sunday morning, Myers was murdered. The sheriff's detective is here investigating."

"Wow." Emily paused and then said, "I'm sure Mike had nothing to do with Mr. Myers' death, but why would Mike have any interest in anyone at Whisperwood?"

"Mike sounded like he was upset because Bill was looking into the commission activities."

"Hmmm," said Emily. "I had been doing Mike's bookkeeping, but now that the business is successful, he has an accountant manage the finances and the taxes. I always thought Mike was at least honest. I don't keep up with what he does as a commissioner. Just lost interest in him, I guess."

Emily sounded as puzzled as Nancy about Mike's appearance at Whisperwood.

Nancy let Emily ponder this a moment. "I only mentioned Mike's visit to suggest you might want to stay out of sight when you're here. He'll probably be back. You can work in my apartment."

"You're right. I'll take you up on that. Okay if I drive over there right now?" Emily sounded anxious as if she wasn't used to asking for favors. 'I'll watch out for Mike."

"Fine. Why don't you stay for lunch here, too?"

"That would be nice. I'd love to. I'll mess around with the laptop until lunchtime, then."

Nancy hung up the phone. She had encouraged Emily to change her situation, and Emily had taken that advice.

Emily could have confronted her husband and kids, told them how she felt, and demanded different treatment. Would that have worked? From what she'd seen of Mike, probably not. She would have suffered further disparagement. Men like Mike would deny any problem at all and then want to know what was wrong with her.

Could Emily have asked for a divorce? Definitely. Why didn't she? Nancy pondered the question. Emily probably hoped that Mike and the boys would change their behavior if they were confronted by a wife and mother who didn't need to put up with their abuse. She could leave and make a living on her own.

But could she? Nancy admired Emily's courage for wanting to find out.

An hour later, Emily arrived with her new laptop.

"You can work in my apartment," Nancy said, "but you

might like this better. Nancy took her up to the library on the fifth floor, noticing that Emily greeted people along the way with no trace of a stutter. She looked radiant.

"The library is quiet and as private as you need," Nancy said. "You can use my apartment if you'd rather, but Malone might be a nuisance." Nancy ushered her into a room filled with shelves and books.

"Only the residents come here," Nancy added.

Emily surveyed the walls of books and the table and chairs against the back wall. "This is perfect," she said.

"If anyone asks, tell them you're doing something for me," said Nancy. "Not that anyone will, but just in case."

Emily flung her arms around Nancy in a hug. "Thank you."

"I'll leave you to it, then," Nancy said, walking to the door. "Meet me at the Pub at noon for lunch."

Emily was already setting up the laptop. "Great! See you then."

Nancy left her there, wondering what kind of business Mike had had with Bill. Was Mike worried about what Bill would do with whatever information he had? Could Mike have somehow set the fire? How could Nancy find out? Whatever it was would make Mike a possible murder suspect.

When Nancy met Emily in the Pub for lunch, she asked a few more questions. "I'm still wondering why Mike wanted to see Bill," she began.

Emily shrugged, her eyes on the menu.

"Did he have any extra cash?" Nancy asked. "Maybe he sold Bill something."

Emily looked up. "I have no idea. The garage is doing very

well, though, but he has an accountant who handles the business finances."

Bill didn't own a car. "What about late night meetings?"

Emily laughed. "He has some evening meetings. Commission stuff. I don't think he's having an affair, if that's what
you're thinking."

"No, no." Nancy laughed with Emily. "I just wondered if
he and Bill were collaborating on something." Clearly, Emily
did not know much about Mike's activities with his business or
the commission. Nancy took the conversation into more congenial waters.

That evening, Nancy, Fitz, and Louise arrived first for dinner and claimed their usual isolated table. George poked along
towards them, matching his pace to that of the man at his side
who stooped over a walker. "This is Dr. Tom Gerrard," George
said. "You've probably seen him around the building. I invited
him to join us. You might be interested in what he has to say."

"Welcome," said Nancy with a smile. Louise pulled out
a chair, helped Tom into it, then folded the walker and set it
against the wall. A server approached the table, gave them
menus, and poured water into glasses.

"I've already filled Tom in on our little project," said
George, perusing the menu. He turned to Tom. "Tell them what
you told me."

Tom picked up his napkin. "I know you people are looking
into Bill's murder, and I'd far rather trust you than that sheriff
or his detective.

"Smart man," said Louise with a laugh.

"I've known Bill a lot longer than most people here," Tom

began. "We used to visit each other a lot. He was an investigative reporter in Washington for years. When he retired, he worked for one of those political action groups. He knew a lot of movers and shakers, and he knew their dirty little secrets." Tom paused and studied the group at the table, all of them hanging on his words.

"He had been looking into the backgrounds of people here, too," Nancy said.

Tom chuckled. "He couldn't help himself. It's a wonder somebody didn't bump him off long before this."

George waved his fork. "Wait till you hear this. Go on, Tom."

Tom glanced at George and nodded. "Bill was writing his memoirs, but in it, he was going to expose some of those secrets and unsavory incidents in the lives of the rich and famous in D.C. He called it his *magnum opus*."

They all absorbed this information silently. The server brought their dinners.

Once the server disappeared, Nancy spoke. "I didn't know about the book project. Thanks, Tom."

"Who did know about it?" asked Fitz.

"He'd talked about writing such a book for years, but most people took it as just talk." Tom picked up his fork, ready to tackle his meal.

Fitz glanced at Nancy. "There was a concert here that Saturday night."

"Concerts bring in visitors and relatives of residents," added Louise.

"Anybody could come in," George said. "The receptionist

doesn't try to get all the extra visitors to sign the book."

"I wouldn't pay attention to any strangers in particular because there would be too many." Nancy glanced thoughtfully at the doors marked "Exit." Those doors were locked to prevent anyone from coming in, but they could go out.

George shook his head. "That greatly expands the number of suspects."

"Depressing," said Nancy glumly.

Louise broke in. "Bill had dinner with his friend John Davis and his wife on Saturday night. John is an old newspaper buddy who lives here. He might have noticed something. Afterward, they went to the concert together and later to his apartment for a drink. He was fine then and found dead the next morning." She glanced at Nancy. "I discovered something else, too."

"And what was that?" asked George, pushing vegetables to one side of his plate.

"John Davis told me he had suggested to Megan and Don that they take charge of Bill's bank account. John said Bill was losing his memory. Megan was always the responsible one ever since her mother died. Bill was a spendthrift who couldn't keep a dime for more than two minutes."

"John thought Megan and Don were all right," added Louise, "that they cared for Bill and were trying to help."

Fitz sat back, frowning. "Is that right?"

"That's the size of it," Louise said.

"I found out something, too," said George. "I talked to the Hansens—you know them, up on the third floor. Tammy worked for them, too, and she was always hinting about how poor her family was and how she needed more money. They didn't like that very much since we all pay enough for her services and tipping isn't allowed. They asked for a different home health aide. But," George paused and held up his hand, "they saw her here on Saturday evening—passed her in the hall."

"Saturday evening?" Fitz sat up. "Hardly any of them work on weekends. What was she doing here?"

"Are they sure it was Tammy?" asked Nancy.

"Yup. And they know it was Saturday because they'd just left the concert in the auditorium and were surprised to see her." George paused to sip his wine. "They thought she was surprised to see them, too."

"She may have come for the concert," said Fitz.

"If she could come here on Saturday evening, she could come any evening," Nancy added. "She could stay as late as she wanted if she was careful."

"That's right," Louise said. "She could use the back door that's open all the time. Probably everyone on the staff knows about it."

Tom suddenly joined the conversation. "Are you talking about Tammy Swann, the home health aide?"

They all turned to him. "Do you know her?"

"Sure. She calls me her favorite patient," Tom blushed. "She's always asking me to tell her about my travels. She even suggested she go along as a companion on my next trip." He glanced at Nancy and winked. "She picked the wrong pigeon. I'm not taking any more trips in this lifetime."

"She must have been joking," Louise said.

Tom shrugged. "Could have been, but I don't think so. If she could have bundled me up and put me on a plane with her, she probably would have done it." He gazed out at the other diners thoughtfully. "She could have been practicing, you know. A lot of people at Whisperwood are in much better shape than I am and travel quite a bit."

George laughed. "Guess we better be careful what we say around her."

"I've got a bad feeling about all this," said Nancy.

"Me, too," agreed Fitz.

"Bill died sometime after the concert on Saturday night and before eleven the next morning," said Louise.

"I still think we need to find the will and the stash if there is any. Then decide what to do from there," Nancy said.

"Your nosy button kicking in again?" George asked.

"It's always busy," Nancy retorted. "But even if Tammy didn't inherit anything from Bill's will, she might think she did. She'd still have a motive for murder."

"But where could the will be?" asked Louise. "Bill only had one bedroom, one bath, just like mine."

"What we're looking for are flat pieces of paper. What can you do with flat pieces of paper? Where would you hide such a thing?" Nancy frowned.

"You could slip them piece by piece into a roll of toilet paper. Nobody would look there," said Louise. "Or stash them in a jar in the toilet tank."

"Roll them up and put them in the shower curtain rod," said George.

"Or the drapery rod," added Nancy.

"Under the linoleum in the kitchen?" Louise suggested.

"Under the parquet floor in the hall? What's under those

floors anyway?" asked George.

Nancy answered. "Concrete."

Louise cast her eyes around the dining room. "The will could be taped on the back of a bookcase."

"What about under the backing of a painting or photo?" asked Nancy.

"Or the dishwasher? You can turn those front pieces around, you know," said Louise."Tape the will inside the panels." She sat back, folded her arms, and looked for the server. "I'm ready for dessert."

"Me, too," said George. "How much imagination did old Bill have, anyway?"

"He was a retired newspaper man. What do you think?" Nancy said.

Louise looked at her. "What about that stack of old *New York Times* newspapers by his chair?"

"They were next to the pile of old *Time* magazines," said Nancy, "but I don't think they'd been gone through. Let's make one more foray, check the places we've mentioned, and bring the newspapers back to Louise's apartment."

Three heads nodded while Dr. Tom looked on placidly.

George tapped on his chair arm. "Can't do it tonight," he said. "I'm waiting for a phone call from my sister."

"And I'm tired. Been working outside on my hive and the garden all afternoon," added Louise. "Tomorrow night okay?"

Nancy glanced at her watch and bit her lip. She was ready to search Bill's apartment again now, but working with the group was a better idea than going it alone.

"That should be okay," Nancy said. "I heard Megan and

Don arguing in the hall about when they could come back and empty the apartment."

"Have to get the sheriff's okay first," said George.

Nancy nodded. "They seem to be in and out, but mostly during the day. We've got plenty of time to nose around at night."

"Tomorrow night okay with everyone?" asked Fitz.

"All right," said Louise.

They looked at George. "Well, sure," he said, "but Louise should keep an ear out for any strange noises down the hall toward Bill's apartment."

"Will do," said Louise.

"I'm in," added Fitz.

"So tomorrow at nine p.m., we'll meet at Bill's door," Nancy said. Three other heads nodded around the table. "Who do you think we'll surprise in his apartment this time?" she asked.

***

Emergency? Press That Button!

Feeling sick? Hurt? Need help? Press the emergency button in your apartment. Buttons are on the wall in the bathrooms, bedrooms, living room, and kitchen. Make sure you can find them quickly in an emergency. Paramedics are on call 24 hours a day, every day. They are here to help you. Don't hesitate to press that button for help. The life you save might be your own.

The Whisperwood Breeze,
Whisperwood Retirement Village Newsletter

Chapter 13

Bill Myers' newspaper buddy, John Davis, lived on Whisperwood's top floor, the sixth. Residents called these apartments the "penthouse suites," although they were the same as other apartments in the building. Nancy usually walked up the stairs but not to the sixth floor. She knocked on the Davis' door at eleven o'clock the next morning, figuring John would probably be up and about by then.

His wife Evelyn opened the door, and her eyes widened as she saw Nancy. "Whatever it is," she said, "we didn't do it."

Nancy laughed. "Of course not. We all know you are two outstanding citizens at Whisperwood." She winked. "May I come in?"

"Of course. We've been expecting you to drop by," Evelyn said. She stepped aside and gestured. "I'll bet this has to do with Bill Myers. John will enjoy talking with you." She ushered Nancy into the living room, where John was reading a newspaper.

He laid the newspaper aside and greeted Nancy, gesturing to the paper. "Checking for errors, you know."

"Somebody's got to keep watch," Nancy said.

"You bet." He waved at an armchair. "Take a load off."

"Coffee? Tea?" asked Evelyn.

"Thank you. I'd love a cup of tea if it's no trouble," said Nancy, taking a seat. Evelyn disappeared into the kitchen.

"What can I tell you about Bill?" asked John with a grin.

"I know you two were friends," she began.

"That's so." John shook his head. "I'm gonna miss that guy. Now I hear they're calling it murder."

Nancy nodded. Whisperwood's gossip line was on the job. "Detective Yost is investigating the case, but the 90s Club is helping."

"Savvy bunch, your 90s Club. You've reaped a bunch of successes. The sheriff ought to be darned grateful to have you on his side."

"We've been lucky," Nancy demurred. "Anyway, since you were close friends, do you have any idea who wanted to kill him?"

"Ol' Bill was a snoop, excuse me, investigative reporter. They put him out to pasture, but they couldn't stop him from investigating. It was in his blood. So, yes, probably a heap of people here are glad he has moved on, one way or another if you catch my drift." John sat back, hands across his ample stomach, ready to talk.

Evelyn brought in the tea. For them this morning, Nancy was the rather grim entertainment.

"Can you think of specific people who might have been threatened?" Nancy asked.

John squinted at Nancy. "You, for one, but all he could find on you confirmed what you've told people here. Nothing sus-

126 The 90s Club & the Clue in the Old Album

picious at all."

"That's good. I am relieved," Nancy said wryly. "Who else?"

"He was intrigued by Axel's story," John added, then he snapped his fingers. "Wait a minute, there was someone else Bill was investigating."

"Who was that?" Nancy asked.

"Some woman here, but I have no clue who he meant. He was keeping it under wraps."

"He didn't tell you anything?"

John shook his head. "Afraid I'd scoop him, he said, but it was something big. That's all he'd leak to me." John shrugged. "I'm out of the game now and wasn't that interested, to tell the truth. He was bored and depressed. I figured he was making a mountain out of a mole hill."

"Did he tell you about his memoirs?" asked Nancy. "He said he was writing them and going to expose a lot of dirty secrets."

John laughed. "Everybody in D.C. says they're going to write their tell-all memoirs." He looked at Nancy. "But you know what? A book is hard to write, much less get someone to publish it. I'd be surprised if he even began writing it."

Nancy mulled on this possibility. Bill had never mentioned writing a book to her, but he could have threatened someone enough with just the idea of it that they killed him. Maybe she could find clues to what it was in his files, as long as they were looking for the will anyway. Another possibility might be even more promising. "Do you know Mike Johnson, one of the county commissioners?" she asked.

John grimaced. "Now there's a piece of work for you. Bill made no secret about investigating him." He pointed toward the balcony behind him. "We have a beautiful view out that way, looking over woods and a stream and seeing the mountains in the distance. It's the reason we bought into this place."

Evelyn had sat quietly, but she seconded his comment. "It's scenic and peaceful, too."

"Mike Johnson's doing some finagling to get a bunch of his cronies to buy that acreage and mine it as a quarry. Can you imagine what that would do?" His voice rose in anger. "I'll bet he's got his hand out on similar projects, too, but I'm only interested in that quarry."

"They would strip the land down through the bedrock with huge machines," added Evelyn. "Make our backyard ugly and noisy."

"How was Bill investigating that?" asked Nancy.

"He had been examining the county financial records and watching Johnson's activities closely."

"Johnson's only one of the commissioners. There are two others. What do they think?"

"The other two are on the fence, but they're all elected, and if the quarry means jobs, they could be swayed."

"There are other ways to prevent this quarry."

"That's my angle," said John. "We've put together a committee to lobby the state legislators on turning that area into recreational park land with hiking, skiing, horseback riding, and other activities, including a lodge and cabins." He smiled. "I'm also suggesting we develop a hospitality training center there. We're talking clean jobs, professional jobs, jobs people can be proud of."

Nancy nodded. "It could even be an experimental ecotourism site." Louise would love that idea.

"Don't forget that Whisperwood has one thousand residents, and most of us vote. In this rural county, that's a huge voting bloc. Whisperwood also employs a lot of the locals. I've organized a committee to visit the county commissioners to put forth our objections and remind them who we are."

"Sounds like you've got a powerful plan," said Nancy, setting aside her tea cup. "Is there anyone else you can suggest as to who might want to get rid of Bill?"

"Sure," said John. "His daughter inherits his millions..." He laughed. "Just joking, but Bill does have a substantial estate. His family had money, and he was an only child. He inherited it all."

"Don't forget that home health aide he was fooling around with," added Evelyn. "We're all wondering if he put her in his will. He could have, you know, he was so miffed at his daughter."

Nancy realized that most people didn't know Tammy was Bill's granddaughter if, indeed, she was.

"How will you figure out which one did it, Nancy?" asked Evelyn.

Nancy looked at her. "I don't know," she said. "Bill made a lot of enemies." But she was thinking that if Bill died with a substantial estate, how did that jibe with his daughter's assertion that he was a spendthrift and needed oversight on his spending? Unless, of course, she wanted all of his estate, not just the part left over.

***

Announcement to Residents
Sign Up Now for Blackwater Falls Trip

A day trip is planned for Sept. 23 to scenic Blackwater Falls State Park in the Allegheny Mountains of West Virginia. The Blackwater Falls is a 62-foot cascade where the Blackwater River leaves its leisurely course in Canaan Valley and enters the rugged Blackwater Canyon. This excursion leaves at 9 a.m. and returns at 5 p.m. Cost: $50 per person including lunch. Reserve your place now! Reservation forms are at the reception desk in the lobby.

Chapter 14

For several days, Emily had been finding nooks and crannies around Whisperwood to settle in and use her laptop. Neither the staff nor the residents paid any attention. Nancy found her by chance one afternoon at the table in the back of Whisperwood's library and noticed her troubled expression. Makeup partly obscured a large bruise on Emily's cheek. "What happened to your face?" Nancy asked.

Emily sighed. "I tried to cover it up. I stood up to Mike last night, and he slapped me, hard. First time that's happened, but I just realized how much I hold back on telling him what I think." She shook her head. "Always keeping the peace, that's me." She sipped from the coffee cup beside the laptop.

"I'm so sorry…" began Nancy. She was stunned.

"Don't be. It was a revelation." She drummed her fingers on the table. "I need to get serious about leaving and just go. I've been obsessing over the details."

Nancy sat in the easy chair across from Emily. "Where do you want to go?"

Emily closed the laptop and frowned. "I've opened my mind to the possibilities. I could go anywhere. Miami. San

Francisco. Baltimore. All exciting places, but none of them speaks to me. Then I turned serious. This isn't going to be a joyride. I'm not a frivolous person, Nancy."

Nancy nodded. "I never thought that."

"Thank you." Emily smiled. "I have three serious tasks I want to accomplish. First, I'm adopted, and I've often wondered about my birth mother. I want to find her and connect her personal history with mine. She was from Savannah, Georgia, so I'm planning to go there."

"Savannah is a large city," Nancy said. "You ought to be able to find what you need."

Emily nodded. "Second, I want to earn a college degree, and third, I want to know I can make my living by myself. I never again want to be dependent on anyone else. Mike will never forgive me for leaving him, but I hope the boys will. I just cannot continue to live with people who tear me down every step I take."

"You do have your feet on the ground," Nancy said, nodding in approval but wondering if Mike's abuse was escalating and Emily needed to leave as soon as possible. "You've carved out a tough road for yourself, but all of your goals are doable. I have complete confidence in you." Brave words, Nancy thought, but doubts persisted. "Perhaps you should see a lawyer," she added. "Find out how you can protect yourself whatever happens."

"I've thought about that." Emily stared thoughtfully at the bookshelves. "I told you I'm leaving a letter of explanation and love for the boys and for Mike, too. I'll tell them I'm taking a sabbatical, and I'll give them my email address. They'll be able to contact me whenever they want to. I won't be abandoning them, but Nancy, you know they are basically adults now. The oldest is 19. He's in college. The other one is a high school senior. I'll handle Mike's reaction when I return."

She'll be a much different person then, thought Nancy.

Emily shoved back her chair and paced back and forth. "It won't be easy. I know that. I need to find a place to live in my new town and that might take all the money I have. I've heard apartments require the first and last month's rent, plus a security deposit."

"That adds up to a daunting sum," Nancy said. "Maybe you can find a boarding house, cheap motel, or a roommate."

"I thought I'd look around." Emily shrugged. "Find people to ask."

"I don't think I know anyone in Savannah," Nancy said. Her mind ran through a list of friends and contacts she knew around the country. She shook her head. "I'll ask my friends."

Emily smiled. "That's all right. I'd rather do this on my own, anyway, to see if I can."

"You can always come back here. I'll help however I can."

"Thanks, Nancy." Emily managed a tentative smile. "I'll need a job or at least an income. I have computer skills but no references, and I don't want anyone I know here to learn where I am." She glanced at Nancy and grinned. "Except you, Nancy."

"You may have to settle for minimum wage jobs until you get settled."

"Sure, I'm not above working in a McDonald's or as a waitress somewhere. My friend Donna was a waitress, and she told me her boss was always complaining about servers who didn't show up. I can probably get a job doing that. Worst case, I can put a note on community bulletin boards that I'll clean apartments or houses. I can charge better than minimum wage that way, too." Emily looked at Nancy. "What do you think?"

"I think you'll do fine," Nancy said. "Your plans are solid. With your computer skills, you can get a better job in an office."

"Office work is Plan A for now. Restaurant server and cleaning are Plans B and C. And I'll keep my spending minimal," added Emily. "I don't need to buy clothes or much of anything. If I do, it's Goodwill for me.

Nancy laughed. "I shop there myself sometimes."

Emily's smile broadened. "For the first time in years, I'm too excited to sleep. I've been thinking of the things I once dreamed of doing. Maybe I can't do them all at once, but I can make them happen eventually."

"Use me as a reference if you need one," Nancy said.

"Thank you. I won't let you down."

"Since you'll be searching for your birth mother, maybe I can help." Nancy pulled a notepad out of her pocket. "I subscribe to a genealogy website. I'll order one of their DNA kits for you. I'll need your mail drop address."

"I'll email it to you right now. I can pay you whatever it costs," said Emily. "I'd heard about them but wasn't sure how they worked." She tapped quickly on her keyboard. "There. Sent."

"What do you know about your mother?"

"Nothing. Who was she? Why did she give me up for adoption?" Emily shrugged. I can guess the easy answers, but I want more than that. Even though it had nothing to do with me, I still feel lacking inside, like maybe I wasn't good enough." Emily laughed. "Ridiculous, isn't it? It's still there, though."

"I understand," Nancy said, "but don't forget the people who adopted you did choose you, and you're special to them."

Emily nodded. "My adoptive parents are good people. Lewis and Elaine Struthers. They lived in Savannah when they adopted me. He was in the Navy. They tried to have children and were thrilled to take me in when I was three years old. They adopted me officially a year later."

Emily shook her head. "They wanted me to forget all about being adopted and refused to think of it themselves. I can't go to them for any information. I don't want to hurt them."

"You could go and live with them," suggested Nancy.

Emily frowned. "No way. You must be kidding. Bad idea, Nancy. I want to move forward, not backward. Anyway, they live in Biloxi, Mississippi, now."

Nancy abandoned that idea and suggested another. "Do you know your birth mother's name?"

"Yes, it's on my birth certificate. Ashcroft. My parents didn't want me to see it, but I needed it to get a Social Security card. Anyway, I was glad to have it. What if I wanted a passport? I looked up Ashcroft online but didn't find anyone who might be my mother."

Emily had become more self-assured as she spoke. "I'd like to travel, see the world. Mike wasn't interested."

"The biggest help will be the DNA kit," said Nancy. "It will probably turn up a horde of relatives for you. Will Mike have any reason to think you'd go to Savannah?"

Emily frowned, some of her new enthusiasm ebbing away. "Good question. What have I told him about my upbringing and adoption? Not much." She stared out the window in thought. "Anyway, he never asked. I can't think why he married me." Emily sighed. "I suppose it speaks well for him. He didn't run away when I found I was pregnant, but he certainly hasn't been interested enough in me to want to learn more about who I was and where I came from."

Nancy nodded. "Would the Struthers think of suggesting Savannah if he asked them for your whereabouts?"

Emily laughed. "No, and he wouldn't ask because he knows they hate him. They blame him for ruining my life. I sent them a wedding announcement, and they forgave me and love their grandsons, but Mike keeps away when they visit. Better for everyone."

Nancy leaned back in her chair and smiled at Emily. "Seems like Savannah is a good choice. It's too far for you to run into anyone you know and large enough to have job opportunities."

"That's what I thought." Emily rapped her knuckles on the library table as if to underscore her determination. "I'm moving up my departure date. Leaving the day after tomorrow."

"Good for you," Nancy said. She had wondered if Emily was one of those people who talk about leaving but never put words into action. The day after tomorrow sounded firm and positive. She needed to get away from Mike. If he slapped her yesterday, what would he do tomorrow?

"You have my email address." Emily quickly tapped on her laptop keyboard. "I'm sending you my new cell phone number. The mail drop will forward things to me, but we can always text each other or use email."

Nancy smiled at Emily's fast work on the keyboard. "How do you plan to get to Savannah?"

"My friend Donna is driving me to Martinsburg, which has a commuter train into D.C." Emily stretched her arms out wide. "From there I can get a train to just about anywhere in the country."

"Just about anywhere," Nancy repeated with a grin. "Some people never find out about that train."

"When I get to Savannah, I might buy a bicycle to get around." A reminiscent smile brightened her face. "I haven't biked in years "

"Wonderful." Nancy applauded. "You have an exciting adventure ahead."

"I'm scared, too," said Emily, her chin high. "Anything can happen."

***

Genealogy Expert Offers Seminar

Welcome new Whisperwood resident Marylou Pierce, lecturer and author of books on genealogy. Want to find out more about your family history? Here's your opportunity to learn how. Attend Marylou's free lecture in the auditorium, 11 a.m. Wednesday.

The Whisperwood Breeze,
Whisperwood Retirement Village Newsletter

Chapter 15

The next morning, while Emily sat at the dining room table working on her laptop, Nancy ordered the DNA kit to be sent to Emily's mail drop. Then Nancy began searching genealogy databases for references that might help her find Axel's family.

A search for Jewish Holocaust victims did not turn up any identifying material that matched the meager information she had on Axel's parents. Axel and his sister had been formally adopted by the farm couple who took them in, but there had been no siblings and further exploration of that couple's lineage would not be helpful to Axel.

Nancy tried searching Axel's birth name and birth date, also with no result that could be tied to Axel's story. It was as if Axel and his family had never existed. When he and his sister were adopted, they took their adoptive parents' last name, but Axel knew his birth name and date and that of his sister's. This was the only concrete information she had, and it led nowhere.

The reason was obvious. The Nazis had invaded Belgium. The country, like all of Europe, was bombed mercilessly, and many of its buildings—and records—destroyed. Axel and his sister were smuggled over to England before the invasion when Axel was five and his sister, seven. Their parents disappeared. Nancy found no record of his family before, during, or after the war. What had happened?

An easy answer was that his parents were forced into concentration camps and murdered. Or they could have been killed in the bombings. Axel had no memory of any of the rituals of Judaism. He was too young when he'd been adopted. Could he have forgotten or was his family part of another ethnic or cultural group arrested by the Nazis? Nancy had a theory, and everything she had heard and read was confirming that theory.

Nancy called Axel. "When can we arrange a visit to your sister's children?" she asked. "Do they live nearby?"

"My sister's children? Of course, you can visit them," said Axel. "We will go together. Make a day of it, okay?"

"Where do they live?" Nancy asked again impatiently.

"Okay, okay. Hold your horses, Nancy," Axel said. "My nephew, Danior, works for the Department of Agriculture and lives in Beltsville, outside Washington."

Nancy made a note. "You have a niece, too, don't you?"

"Yes, yes. A niece, Lavinia. We call her Vinnie. She is a schoolteacher, and she lives near Columbia, Maryland. Just a minute, I can give you addresses and phone numbers, but let me call them when I hang up and tell them what I'm doing. They'd like to know more about our family, too. Then if they agree, which I'm sure they will, we can set up a time to visit. Okay?"

"That sounds fine," said Nancy. "We'll go on a jaunt. I can drive." She hung up and thoughtfully glanced at her calendar.

She looked up and saw Emily watching her.

"I couldn't help hearing your conversation," Emily said. "Are you sure you want to drive that far? I mean at your age?"

Nancy frowned. The young made such assumptions. "I drive all over the place. No problem." She refused to add that she often took back roads to avoid the breakneck speeds on the Interstates. She preferred country roads anyway. And she didn't drive Interstates at night.

"But..." Emily shook her head.

"We'll be fine," said Nancy crisply to stop further objections. "Do it all the time. No problem." Before Emily could add any more ageist pronouncements, Nancy asked, "How are your studies going?"

"Classes haven't started yet," Emily said. "I'm lining up my new life." She looked pleased. Nowadays, a smile constantly hovered on her lips. "You know what's funny?"

"No, what?" Nancy asked.

"Mike wants to know what's wrong with me because I'm smiling a lot." Emily laughed. Nancy joined in as she walked to the kitchen and made a pot of tea. She held up a cup to Emily.

"Thanks. I'm ready to relax a bit." Emily straightened her legs and leaned back in the chair.

Nancy set a cup at Emily's place and sat on the couch next to Malone, who lay on his back, clawing at Nancy's sleeve to pull her hand over to scratch his belly. Nancy obeyed. Nobody messed with Malone.

Emily smiled. "I've been looking up places to stay and job opportunities in Savannah. I'm hoping I can line up an apartment to share with a roommate. My money will last longer if I can't find a job right away."

"Any luck in your search?"

"You're going to laugh," said Emily.

"I won't laugh."

"I've never held a real job, but I thought to myself, why settle? What would be an interesting job where I might learn something?"

"Good thinking," said Nancy.

"And I decided to try to get a job with a detective agency."

Nancy could see Emily was holding her breath for Nancy's reaction. Well, why not try for a job with a detective agency? They all needed office workers. Emily would move on if she didn't have any luck with them. Or if the work became tedious. Detective work wasn't all glamour and excitement. Far from it.

"I'm not laughing," said Nancy with a smile. "Go ahead and see what you can find. If you strike out, move on to your next idea."

"That's what I thought." Emily sat back, a satisfied smile on her face.

"You're a good person," said Nancy, "and you work hard. I can see that. Any employer would be glad to have you."

Emily sat silently for a few minutes, her mouth trembling as if any minute she would burst into tears. Finally, she managed to say, "I didn't expect such support and encouragement," she said. "That's all."

What a sad life Emily must have led, Nancy thought. "Be sure to send me your address when you get a place. I ordered the DNA kit for you to be sent to your mail drop, but someone should know where you are."

"You're right. The mail drop will do for the time being. I'll get one in Savannah, too. Then the one here can forward mail to wherever I am. I am extremely excited about the DNA kit." Emily gulped and blinked rapidly.

"You might find you have a slew of relatives, and…" Nancy laughed. "You hate all of them."

"At least they won't be after my money," Emily retorted, "since I don't have any."

***

Travelogue Series Begins Tuesday

Matthew and Lorraine Henson will discuss their world travels in a series beginning next Tuesday at 10 a.m. in Classroom C, lower level. Each lecture will cover one of the many cities or countries this adventurous couple has visited, including Egypt, Turkey, Greece, Peru, Australia, New Zealand, Cambodia and Vietnam, and China.

The Whisperwood Breeze,
Whisperwood Retirement Village Newsletter

Chapter 16

That afternoon, Nancy ran into Bill's daughter Megan buying a soft drink in the small convenience store off the lobby. Nancy greeted her with a nod and since she hadn't seen her since Bill's death, stopped to add, "I'm sorry for your loss." She was touched to see tears hovering in Megan's eyes. And a little surprised since she had heard both Megan and Don speak harshly of Bill, but he was her father, after all.

"I miss him." Megan turned away and surreptitiously brushed a hand across her eyes. When she turned back, her composure had returned, and her manner bordered on coldness. "He was a handful these last few months," she said. "You probably noticed it." The words were a question.

"How so?" asked Nancy.

"We were worried about his drinking," said Megan, "and the way he was spending money. How long could he keep that up before he wouldn't be able to pay the fees here?"

"He seemed all right to me," countered Nancy. "He was active with his investigations although he seemed depressed sometimes."

Megan nodded. "His depression concerned us."

"He did have friends here," Nancy added.

"Maybe so, but he annoyed most people. Snooping into their past. Everybody has secrets. That's probably what got him killed." Megan's eyes reflected the venom of her words.

"We'll miss him," said Nancy. "I always enjoyed chatting with him."

"Of course." Megan looked her up and down. "You're a Nosey Nellie yourself," she sneered. "Retired detective indeed."

She flounced off down the hall. What an unpleasant woman, Nancy thought.

At dinner that night, Louise started the conversational ball rolling. "I saw that detective from the sheriff's office nosing around Bill Myers' apartment today."

"That's Detective Dwayne Yost trying to find any evidence he might have missed," said Nancy. "He's already been through it a couple of times."

"That apartment is contaminated by now." George sat back and twirled his wine glass. "They don't know about Axel or us, but they've got to know Megan and Don have been all over the crime scene. Do you suppose Dwayne has gone through Bill's files? He could have been looking for the will, too, though, if Don and Megan told him about it, which they probably did."

Louise and George grinned at each other. "I hear them rummaging around his apartment, cursing so they haven't found the will," said Louise. "That will be up to us."

Nancy told them about her visit with John and Evelyn Davis. "We also need to look into Bill's files and find out who he was investigating. Besides Axel and Mike, that is."

"Dwayne must have done that," said Louise. "I saw him take Bill's computer."

"I suppose there's some police resource that can get into his computer files," said Nancy, "but I doubt if our rural county would allocate funds for it. He may have to go to a state lab and that will take time. Then whatever Bill has in his files will need interpretation by someone here. Dwayne doesn't know Whisperwood and the residents the way we do. He's at a big disadvantage."

"Dwayne may have his computer," said George, "but I'll bet Bill hid a back-up flash drive around somewhere. We need to look for that."

"Dwayne's been asking people for alibis," said Louise. "Even me."

"Me, too," added George, "but I don't see how he'll get anywhere with that. We'll all say we were in bed in our apartments. Alone. No witnesses."

"That's true. Even if it was confirmed by someone else…" Fitz smiled at Nancy, "he couldn't trust them not to protect each other. Anyway, tonight's the night."

"Yep." Louise took a sip of wine. "Time to find the will."

"And the list of suspects Bill was investigating," added Nancy.

"The 90s Club is on the job." Fitz raised his glass. All their glasses clinked together in a salute.

After dinner, the 90s Club trooped up to the fourth floor and followed Louise into her apartment two doors down the hall from Bill Myers' place.

"George, you've got your credit card?" Nancy asked.

"Sure do. I'll text you when I'm in."

"First, everyone put on these latex disposable gloves," said Louise.

"Good idea," Nancy said, taking a pair and sliding them onto her hands. "We should have been wearing these the last time."

Two minutes later, the three intrepid detectives followed George into Bill Myers' apartment and began another intense search. Nancy checked the shower and drapery rods and bookcase; George looked for cracks in the linoleum and parquet floors and took off the dishwasher front; Louise removed the backs from paintings and photos.

Nothing.

It wasn't only the will they were searching for, Nancy reminded herself. Bill was snooping into the lives of several people here. Who were they? Would they have a motive for murder?

She shuffled through the papers on Bill's desk. Most of them were unpaid bills, but none of them were overdue. Advertising brochures and the current issue of *National Geographic* and *Smithsonian* magazines comprised the rest. Nancy sat in Bill's chair and stared at his desk, a mahogany antique with two rows of small drawers at the back. She pulled out one after the other, finding paper clips, pens, Post-It note pads, and miscellaneous other office items. As she suspected, one drawer in this ancient desk was shorter than the others. She pulled it out and found another behind it. *Aha! The proverbial secret drawer.*

At first, she thought it might hold the will, but instead, she found Bill's flash drive. She held it up as she turned to face the others. "I've got his flash drive."

"Hallelujah," said George, stepping across the debris to take it from Nancy. "Now we're getting somewhere."

"It was hidden in that secret drawer," Nancy said. "Maybe that drive is where he backed up the files on the people of interest and his book manuscript, if there is one."

"We shouldn't need a password to look at this," said George. He glanced at his watch. "I'll open it on my computer and email the files to Nancy and Louise."

"I'm done here for now," said Louise, standing up with a groan.

"All right." Fitz had begun gathering up a pile of newsprint. "I'm taking the newspapers and magazines stacked on the floor to Louise's apartment so we can go through them."

Louise led them into her unit and had Fitz set the pile of newsprint on the dining room table, dividing them into four batches. They each took one and began leafing through the pages.

"We know we're looking for a will," Nancy said, "but if you see any odd word or phrase scribbled anywhere in the pages, point that out to us. It might be a password in case we need it."

After an hour of silence but for the turning of pages, Nancy caught her breath. She looked at the others. "I've found something."

She held up a section of the *New York Times*. Tucked into the fold between two pages was a sheet of standard letterhead with Bill Myers' address at the top. Below that was a typed statement with Bill's signature at the bottom alongside a caricature of Bill's laughing face. The statement read: "Looking for my will? You'll discover it behind a traveling clock. Nancy and Axel can find it if they're smart enough. And now I've given you enough clues."

"What a clown," said George in disgust. "Why couldn't this be the will instead of another incomprehensible clue?"

"He's added something at the bottom," said Nancy. "It says, 'Time is on my side. My real treasure is in another old clock. Seek and maybe ye shall find.'"

"Oh, brother," said Louise. "What do you think, Nancy?"

"He made that reference to time and clocks to me several times," Nancy stared at the newspapers. "And that's the *New York Times*. "Times. Get it?"

Fitz pointed to the *Time* magazines. "Then there are those."

Louise groaned as she rose to her feet and stepped into the kitchen to wash her hands. "He thought Nancy knew about a traveling clock." She turned to Nancy. "Do you?"

"He said Axel should know, too." Nancy stared at the note. "I've been thinking about that, and I have a glimmer of an idea where the will is."

***

Do You Have a Will?

Attorney William S. Page will conduct a seminar next Saturday morning, 10 a.m., in the auditorium on the importance of making a will. In West Virginia, if a person dies without a will, the entire estate goes to the nearest surviving relative. Is this what you want to happen? Do you want to make sure your wishes are carried out properly when you die? Be sure to attend this important seminar.

The Whisperwood Breeze,
Whisperwood Retirement Village Newsletter

Chapter 17

Nancy eagerly called George the next morning. "Did you get into Bill's files?" she asked.

A glum-sounding George answered. "I've been trying, Nancy, but that flash drive is password-protected."

"What? A protected flash drive? I never heard of such a thing," Nancy said.

"Neither had I, but I Googled it and sure enough, you can buy all kinds of programs to protect your flash drive." George sighed. "Who would have thought Bill was that computer-savvy?"

"He was surprising."

"I've been trying to think of possible passwords, but no luck so far and I get kicked out after three tries, so I have to wait before I try again."

Nancy stared out the window as she considered this new wrinkle. "I didn't see anything that might have been a password on his desk."

"I'll keep trying. Ask Fitz. He might have an idea." George said.

"I'll be out of town this weekend, but I'll tell him about the problem before I leave."

Setting up meetings with Axel's nephew and niece had been quickly accomplished. The next day found Nancy and Axel on their way to the Washington suburbs. They made it an overnight trip. Nancy left Fitz in charge of Malone, and the two of them warily eyed each other as Nancy left early for the four or five-hour trip from central West Virginia to central Maryland. She had mapped out the trip using back roads and less-traveled portions of the interstates.

Axel was thrilled to get away from Whisperwood. "I've been living here for five years, and it's fine. I like it here, but a change of scenery keeps a body alive, I say."

Thanks to Nancy's planning, the trip was an easy one, and by two p.m. they were pulling into the driveway of Axel's nephew Danior in Beltsville, Maryland.

He came out to greet them, wearing jeans and a short-sleeved khaki shirt. A pen and the top of a small notebook poked out from a pocket protector. "Been looking forward to seeing my Uncle Axel again," he said, hugging the old man. "And you must be Ms. Dickinson. Nice to meet you."

He ushered them into a two-story colonial house on a tree-lined street.

His wife Alma came in from the kitchen. She also wore jeans with a white blouse and sweater. The day was a bit cool.

Danior invited them to sit in the living room, while Alma brought in plates of cookies and coffee cake and got their drink orders. Iced tea all around.

"Danior is an unusual name," said Nancy. "Where did it come from?" She had already searched the Internet for the name and found it was of Gypsy origin, which opened up a new line of inquiry for Nancy.

"Mom said it was her father's name," Danior said. "That's all I know."

The odd table in front of her emitted a loud buzzing noise. As Nancy peered through its glass top at the box-shaped object underneath, she realized that it housed a beehive. A tube ran from the hive through a window and outside. Fascinated, Nancy watched bees hurrying to and fro through the tube and outside into the open air. She immediately felt comfortable in this unusual living room. Louise would love this, she thought.

"You like my furniture?" asked Danior with a grin. "I'm an entomologist at the USDA facility here in Beltsville. I work with bees."

"I made the cakes and cookies in front of you with honey,' added Alma. "Please help yourself."

"Don't mind if I do," said Axel.

"Let me tell you," Danior said, sitting back with legs crossed, "I'd sure like you to find out who we are and where we came from. I feel like I live in a hole with no connections anywhere. Except you, Uncle Axel." He tossed Axel a fond glance.

"We're so pleased to have you both visit us," Alma added. "We've tried finding the family on genealogy sites with no luck."

"Yeah, me, too," said Axel. "That's why I asked Nancy here for her help. She's a genuine detective who knows how to do those searches."

"Retired a long time ago," put in Nancy. She always said that when the subject came up to defuse any high expectations or nervousness. Some people were thrilled to meet a detective; others feared intrusions into their privacy.

Danior nodded with a friendly smile. "Have you found out anything?"

Nancy shook her head. "Not yet. That's why we're here. We need more information."

"That's the truth," laughed Axel. "Your mother, my sister, was a couple of years older than me. That means she was only seven and I was five when we were taken to England, but she might have told you about some memory she had, some tidbit of information that will help us learn what happened."

"It was a long time ago," said Alma, looking at her husband.

Danior sighed. "I've been racking my brain trying to think of anything she might have said. She mostly talked of the family and farm where you grew up in England. What she remembered earlier than that had to do with horses and living in a wagon. Sounds like they might have been vagabonds. She loved horses, though."

"Did she mention any Jewish connection?" asked Nancy.

Danior shook his head. "Not at all. She and Uncle Axel were raised with the farm family who weren't religious. Probably Church of England. Didn't know anything much about her life before that."

"Was there anything else?" asked Axel. "Any clue to our father's occupation?"

Danior sat silently for a few moments. "Barrel-maker. Because of the family name, Cooper or Kuiper, you know. And blacksmith," he finally said, snapping his fingers. "Mom said someone was a blacksmith. We had horses, and horses need shoes, so that makes sense. And there were lots of cousins and aunts and uncles who lived together—not all in the same wagon, of course."

"Did you know Danior was a Gypsy name?" asked Nancy.

"What?" Danior exclaimed and glanced at Axel who stared back at him, mouth open.

"Were we Gypsies?" Axel said wonderingly. "I never thought of such a thing. Never in a million years."

"Did you ever have your DNA tested?" asked Nancy.

"Nancy ordered a kit for me," Axel put in with pride. "That's how we'll find out for sure."

Danior shrugged. "I thought about doing that, and I probably will when I get around to it, but I don't think it will tell us much about my grandparents or aunts, uncles, and cousins."

"At least it will tell you where your family came from," Nancy said, "and might turn up relatives you could contact."

Danior scratched his chin. "That's true, I guess. "Sorry. I don't remember anything else. Maybe the longer I ruminate on the question, the more I might remember what my mother told us, but I don't think she knew much more than Uncle Axel. She told us her early life was mostly a big blank in her mind."

"It must have been traumatic," said Nancy.

Danior nodded. "One thing's for sure. I am gonna take that DNA test now, just to see what comes up." He grinned at his wife. "Me, a Gypsy."

She laughed.

Nancy glanced at her watch and stood. "I guess we should move along to Axel's niece."

"Wait. Before you go, would you like a quick tour of the USDA research station here?" Danior picked up his keys and wallet and headed for the door. "I'll drive. Won't take too long. You ought to know what your tax dollars pay for." He winked.

Nancy never turned down a chance to learn something new. "We'd love to."

"I like knowing what the family is up to," said Axel, following Danior out the door.

"I'll go, too,' said Alma, grabbing her purse.

For half an hour, Danior drove them through the farm-like setting where agricultural research was underway, pointing out his colorful beehives, the greenhouses, the barns, fields, and buildings where the researchers worked.

"Reminds me of the farm in England," said Axel, "but nothing in this landscape makes me think of Belgium. I wonder why."

"Mom said the same thing." Danior glanced at Axel. "Hitler's invasion was underway, and you were terrified when you were put on that boat. That's why you don't have many memories."

"Hard to believe we're just off the Washington Beltway," said Nancy as they returned to Danior's house.

Nancy and Axel thanked Danior and Alma and left Beltsville for a thirty-minute drive up I-95. After they exited the interstate, they drove west and eventually stopped at a five-acre tract in a rural area. The tract was fenced, and two horses grazed in the pasture. Several chickens pecked the grass by a small barn next to a two-story, white frame house. A middle-aged-woman wearing jeans and a gray sweatshirt sat on the front steps. She rose to greet them as Nancy parked in the driveway. "Danior called me to say you were on your way here," she said as she hugged Axel. "So glad to see you again, Uncle Axel. What did you think of his beehive?"

"Loved it," said Nancy. Axel was noncommittal about the hive but hugged his niece warmly.

"You're a sight for sore eyes, Lavinia," he said. "You look like your mother."

She glanced at Nancy. "Call me Vinnie, please. Come on in." She led the way into a living room with light wood floors and south-facing windows. The afternoon sun streamed in, making the room uncomfortably warm. Vinnie turned on the air conditioner.

"Iced tea okay?" she asked as she pulled off the sweatshirt, revealing a white T-shirt.

She laid a plate of chocolate chip cookies on a large, square coffee table made of rough plywood in front of the couch. "Put your feet up," she said and left to get the iced teas.

She passed the glasses to Nancy and Axel, then sat in an armchair and stretched her legs out with her feet on the table. She saw Nancy's surprise. "It's only a board with legs," she said, "You can spend the night here, can't you?" she asked. "I have plenty of room. Bedrooms and baths to spare."

Axel looked at Nancy. "That would be very nice," she said. "If you're sure we won't be any trouble."

"Of course not. We'll have plenty of time to see what memories we can dredge up." She laughed. "And I love sitting around with friends at breakfast."

"Me, too," said Nancy.

"It's lovely to see you again. I miss your mother," said Axel. "Nancy is helping me find our family history. She thought it would be useful to hear what you remember of things your mother might have told you about the early days."

Vinnie leaned forward, glass in hand, facing Axel and Nancy on the couch. "Since I talked with you, I've been trying to remember what Mom might have said about her childhood. She wanted us to send you the old album." She looked at Axel with a question in her eyes.

He reached into the satchel and pulled it out. "I brought it, yes." He held it up.

"Mom tried to remember, too, you know, but she was only seven when you were bundled onto that fishing boat. And you were…five?"

Axel nodded. "She didn't remember anything?"

"She remembered tambourines," said Vinnie. "She loved to shake them to the music. Music is what she remembered. And horses. She loved horses." Vinnie paused and added, "And so do I."

"I also remember the music," said Axel. "Someone played the accordion. Somebody else played a violin…maybe a fiddle…I don't know."

"This was Belgium before the Nazis invaded," mused Nancy. "Horse-drawn wagons were still on the roads…but mainly by farm families? Would others have a car?"

Vinnie opened the album, leafed through several pages, and pointed to a photo. "This must be their wagon. People are sitting on a bench in front, and behind them, it looks like one of those covered wagons that went out west."

"Maybe their idea of a camper," said Axel. "I remember horses being around. A lot of horses."

"One more thing," said Vinnie. "Mom said her mother told her to take care of the album and keep it secret. No one in their family liked her mother having a camera and taking pictures. Mom gave up trying to figure out why it should be secret years ago."

"I never heard that," Axel said, a puzzled expression on his face. "But get this. Nancy found out that Danior is a Gypsy name."

Vinnie sat back in surprise. "Gypsy? How interesting."

They spread the album out on the dining room table. Axel and Vinnie sat side by side to leaf through it. Nancy pulled out a pad of paper and a pen. "Go ahead. Talk out loud about the pictures and anything you remember. I'll take notes."

"Look at this man. What kind of weird costume is he wearing?" Vinnie pointed to a tall, thin man with a handlebar mustache who was flexing his muscles. His clothes looked like an old-fashioned bathing suit. He showed his teeth in a full grin.

"One of our relatives clowning around," was Axel's assessment.

"Maybe so, but they all look like they could be Gypsies. Let's move on," said Vinnie.

They had concentrated on the photos of people, but town scenes and landscape photos filled several pages, then Vinnie turned a page to a photo showing two toddlers, both in sweaters but one wore short pants and the other a skirt. They were staring at the camera curiously. The photo was larger than the others and behind them stood a gothic tower with a large town clock embedded in stone.

"That might be you and my mother," said Vinnie, tapping a finger on the toddlers. "Are there any others?" She perused each page. "That's one of you hiding in the wagon."

"And that's probably us in the group photo," said Axel. "But none of this is telling us much."

Nancy's thoughts remained on the photo of the town clock. "Didn't you say Bill borrowed this album for a couple of days?" she asked. She ran her fingers across the photo. As she thought, it was slightly thicker than the others.

"That's right." Axel shook his head. "A mistake. I should never have let him see it. I got it back as soon as I could."

They spent another hour going through the photographs but finally laid it aside. Axel gave up trying to read out to Nancy several faded cryptic notes on some of the photos. The cramped handwriting was too difficult to decipher into possible names.

Axel closed the album with a sigh. "I was hoping we would find out more," he said.

"Too bad your parents didn't send you away with better information," said Nancy, thinking of a possibility that had occurred to her. She itched to get her hands on the album to pursue this idea but not with Axel watching. She might be wrong, after all, and he might object to what she'd have to do to find out if she was right.

"I suppose they thought they would join you later," Vinnie said. "The question is why didn't that happen?"

"I'm beginning to think we could have been Gypsies," said Axel, "even though my name is an ancient Jewish one."

"Danior was named after our mother's father, you know,"

said Vinnie. "I figured out that much."

"If we were Jewish or even Gypsies, then we can guess what probably happened to them," said Vinnie, "but Mom never did or said anything to indicate that as a possibility. And you and Mom grew up in England."

"Did your mother ever try searching for her family?" asked Nancy.

"She wondered if her parents lived through the war and were looking for her." Vinnie sipped her tea thoughtfully. "She contacted organizations that worked to locate displaced persons and found several possibilities, but they didn't pan out."

"What else can we do?" asked Axel in despair. "Are we at a blank wall?"

"Not yet," Nancy said firmly. "Let's see what we get with a DNA test."

***

Improve Your Memory

Memory lapses like forgetting a friend's name or where you put your car keys are probably familiar to most of us, but there are exercises to help us remember. Come join us on Friday at three p.m. for tea and cookies and a fun time of playing games designed to help you sharpen your memory. Held in Classroom B on the lower level. Social director Mary Ann Hopkins will lead the session.

The Whisperwood Breeze,
Whisperwood Retirement Village Newsletter

Chapter 18

Nancy and Axel returned to Whisperwood the next afternoon. Nancy dropped Axel and his walker at the entrance. As he reached for the album, Nancy asked, "May I keep it a few more days?"

"Sure," said Axel, beginning his slow shuffle toward the elevators. "I know where you live." He grinned back at her and waved.

Fitz visibly brightened when Nancy came in the door to her apartment. He hugged and kissed her and then stepped aside, so Malone could deliver his complaints. After a session of petting and several kitty treats, he was appeased enough to stalk away and sniff her overnight bag.

"How was your trip?" asked Fitz.

"Enjoyable but not too useful. Axel's nephew and niece were happy to see their uncle, but it's looking as though the events that put them on a boat to England were so traumatic neither Axel's sister nor Axel remember much that occurred earlier. Anything happen while I was gone?" she asked.

"Nothing happens when you're gone, Luv," he replied and grinned. "Glad you're back."

She blew him a kiss and opened a note she was given at the reception desk when she walked in. It was from Emily.

Dear Nancy,

I'm on my way! I stopped by Whisperwood to say goodbye, but they said you were gone for a couple of days with a friend.

I left letters for Mike and each of the boys, explaining what I was doing and assuring them I loved them. I told them I was simply taking a sabbatical, but said nothing about where. Sabbatical! Like I was a professor or something, but that's what I'm doing. You never met my best friend Donna, but she knows about you. I didn't tell her where I'm going, either. She'd probably blab it to Mike if he confronted her. I don't want him barging into my life and wrecking my plans. He's done enough.

Last night I fixed sweet potato casserole with marshmallows—the boys' favorite—to go with a pot roast and green peas. I made it special for them.

I took a large serving and ate every bite—my doctor would be happy! No one noticed, and for once, Mike didn't comment on my scarecrow looks. No one thanked me, and I noticed that. After I cleared the table, I surprised myself by eating another helping of sweet potatoes by myself in the kitchen. It was my choice, and no one else's business.

My mind is buzzing with ideas and plans. I'll keep you posted on what happens. Right now I'm on my way to catch a train to Savannah. I'll be looking for a job and a room, but the adventure has begun!

Love and thanks,

Emily

Nancy sat back with a smile. Emily's exuberance bounced off the note. This was a different Emily from the defeated woman hunched over grocery bags that Nancy had first seen. She sent a congratulatory reply by email and urged Emily to keep in touch.

Then she petted Malone, who lapped up the attention, and set his food bowl down for him. He always made a show of ignoring it with a disdainful look at first, then eating it sneakily after she left. Nothing was ever quite good enough for Malone.

Fitz walked over and kissed the top of her head. "Time for dinner."

Nancy glanced at her watch. "Let's go."

Louise and George were already seated at their favorite table, Number fifty-six.

"How was your trip?" asked Louise.

"Enjoyable. We learned a few things about Axel's background, but no one knew very much." Nancy shrugged. "The DNA kit I ordered for him will probably be the best bet."

"That won't tell him what happened to his family," grumbled George, tucking his napkin into his collar.

"The one I ordered provides a way for people to contact each other if they wish," said Nancy, perusing the dinner menu. "Once Axel gets the results, he can send an email to the company to be forwarded to the other people identified as related. We hope he'll get a lot of responses."

Louise nodded. "I would think that anyone searching for their past through DNA links would be eager to learn about their relatives."

"I would think so. Any news about the Myers' investigation?" Nancy asked.

"Wait a minute." George held up his hand and nodded at the server, who had arrived to take their orders. They all had their favorite menu items and relayed them quickly.

"Anything else?" the server asked, gathering the menus. Receiving no answer, he left.

George glanced around the table, picked up his glass, and said in a loud whisper, "Coast is clear."

"The sheriff's detective stopped by my apartment and interviewed me," said Louise. "I was as charming as I can be in asking questions, but he stonewalled me."

"Did you talk to your neighbors?" asked Nancy. "Does anybody know anything?"

Louise nodded. "One of them said she heard people in his apartment several nights ago rummaging around." She glanced at Nancy with a wry smile.

"She must have heard us," sighed George. "Good thing she didn't see us."

"And a good thing we don't rummage apartments for a living," said Louise with a wink at Nancy. "We'd be found out for sure."

"Speaking of that," said Nancy, "did you get into Bill's flash drive, George?"

He shook his head. "We've all been trying to think of a password, but nothing's worked so far."

"How aggravating," Nancy said. "I've got another idea. Can all of you drop by my apartment after dinner? I need witnesses, and I might have something to show you."

"Don't tell me you found the will," said Louise.

Nancy smiled and picked up her fork. "Maybe."

Even Fitz looked surprised at that, but Nancy refused to say more until they gathered around her dining room table after dinner. Nancy opened Axel's album to the page with the large photo of Axel and his sister, two toddlers, and the town clock.

"I see a clock," said Louise. "She ran her hand across the photo. "This photo feels thicker than the others." She glanced at Nancy. "Are you thinking what I'm thinking?"

"Axel let Bill take this album for a couple of days to see if Bill could use his investigative background to come up with information about Axel's family," explained Nancy. "I'm wondering, what if…?"

Fitz nodded. "Bill could have hidden a will behind the photo."

"Bill told the lawyer about the will," Nancy said, "and told me that Axel and I would find it behind a clock."

"Axel should be here, then," said George.

Nancy shook her head. "He'd want to tell everyone about it. We need to be more careful."

"I said it was thicker than the others," Louise said, running her fingers around the edge of the picture. "We can easily pull it out of the corner pieces that secure it to the page. It feels loose as if it has been lifted before."

"Careful. I don't want to damage anything," said Nancy.

"Don't worry," said Louise. "I'm an old hand at this, but I need a sharp knife with a thin blade."

Nancy brought a paring knife from the kitchen and handed it to Louise. She gingerly lifted the top edge of the photo out of the corner hinges that held it in place. Then she used the tip of the blade to pull out a thin piece of onionskin paper. She picked it up and unfolded it as everyone gathered closer to read it.

"It's a simple, hand-written will," said Fitz.

"Bill wanted everyone to keep guessing," groused George. "We know he talked to a lawyer about how to make this sort of thing legal but didn't want anyone to know till he was dead and gone."

"Who gets Bill's money?" asked Louise, stepping back from the table.

Fitz whistled as his eyes scanned the document. "Tammy gets $100,000. Bill doesn't say anything about being her grandfather. He just says he owes it to her."

"I wonder what he meant," Louise said.

"Because he's her grandfather?" suggested Fitz.

"I don't believe it." George pursed his lips. "Maybe he liked her or her companionship and wanted to give her a helping hand."

Fitz shrugged. "Whatever. Then he gives sizeable amounts to a couple of journalism schools. The rest goes to Megan."

Nancy nodded. "So now we have a different problem."

"What problem?" Louise put her hands on her hips. "Seems straightforward."

"I don't think so." Nancy fanned herself with the will.

"Why not?" asked Louise.

Nancy laid the will on the table. "I'm worried about the repercussions."

"What repercussions?" asked George.

"What we've been afraid of all along," Fitz said slowly. "Bill was murdered. If the police and Megan learn the contents of the will, Tammy will be the one everyone points fingers at, whether or not there's any supporting reason to believe she's guilty."

"I believe there is a reason," said Louise. "One hundred thousand smackers from a guy she worked for."

"Who she says was her grandfather," Fitz added.

"Megan will refute that and make sure everyone knows about the huge bequest," said Nancy, "to a lowly home health aide. She'll make it sound very suspicious."

"It is suspicious." Louise nodded. "Even if she didn't kill him, Tammy will probably lose her job here since they'll figure she violated their rules and fraternized with a resident."

"I've seen people railroaded before," Nancy said. "Tammy doesn't have powerful friends or the money to mount an effective defense."

"Ahem," put in George. "She could be guilty."

Nancy nodded. "I know."

"We can't keep the will hidden," said Louise.

"I suggest we hold the will for a few days until we see if Dwayne finds evidence to charge anyone else for Bill's murder. You can bet they're looking hard at Tammy, with or without the will. I just want to even the odds for her and give her a fair chance."

"We do that, I'm sure we'll be breaking some law." George looked worried.

"We're not destroying the will," put in Louise. "We're only delaying its discovery for a couple of days."

"I'll hide it in the newspaper." Nancy slipped the will between the *Times* newspaper sheets, folded the newspaper, and put it in her desk drawer. "I'll give the newspaper to the lawyer or executor of the estate when we're ready. I'll tell her Bill loaned the newspaper to me, and it took me a few days to read it."

Fitz folded his arms and looked at Nancy with a slight smile. "Could have happened that way."

"Sure it could," Louise said.

George shook his head. "I think it's as illegal as hell. We'll all go to jail."

"Let's take a vote on Nancy's suggestion," said Fitz. "I'm in favor. It won't hurt to hold it back awhile until we see how things shake out."

"Anyway, Tammy told Nancy she doesn't want his money," added Louise.

Nancy shrugged. "If we take her at her word, we could even destroy the will. Not that I would, but then Megan would inherit the estate, and Tammy's life would remain the same— as she says she wants."

"Come on," said George, "I don't believe Tammy doesn't want the money."

"Tammy could take the case to court since she says she believes he's her grandfather. It could be proven or not by DNA tests." Fitz stepped back to pet Malone, curiously nosing the album.

"Or we could look up her mother's birth certificate," added Louise.

"Sometimes the father's name is left blank," said Fitz.

"Without any confirmation, we can only take her at her word," Nancy said firmly, but she thought of the glamour poses she'd seen Tammy affect as she sat in the sun. Tammy had dreams that only money could make come true.

"More busybodiness," grumbled George, "but you got a point, so I'll go along."

Louise sniffed. "Whenever rich people notice anything missing, whether it really is or whether they forgot it some-where, the person they accuse first is the maid or some oth-er vulnerable service person who doesn't have the resources to defend herself." Louise's eyes sparked as she stood on her soapbox. "I wouldn't work as a maid for anything. Just ask-ing for abuse." She folded her arms. "So yeah, give the lady a break."

***

Staff Scholarships

We at Whisperwood are fortunate to have a hard-working staff dedicated to providing excellent service to us, whether it's in the dining room, medi-cal center, the grounds, or in our apartments. Please remember that Whisperwood has a no-tipping policy, but all employees receive a holiday bonus in Decem-ber, and the high school students on staff are eligible for scholarships in June. Donations to these funds may be made at any time. Just add any amount to the monthly fee and specify "Bonus" or "Scholarship." Thank you.

Suzanne Craddock, Assistant Administrator,
Whisperwood Retirement Village

Chapter 19

Dear Nancy,

I arrived in Savannah late the day I left home. I booked into a cheap motel near the historic downtown area and lay awake the rest of the night. I have done it. What are Mike and the boys doing now? Mike probably groused about missing his dinner. I'm sure he bought a pizza. Now he's thinking how he'll punish me when I crawl home. I know I'm taking a big risk. They think I'm a nitwit. At first, I thought Mike was joking when he put me down and made fun of me. I laughed along with him. When I realized he wasn't joking and protested, he made fun of my protests. The kids followed his lead.

This morning as I sat drinking tea, I realized that I felt relaxed. My stomach wasn't tied up in knots the way it was all the time at home. Having a doctor warn me about anorexia was the wake-up call I needed. Then you showed up at the door. You opened it for me. This morning I ate a full Grand Slam breakfast at Denny's. I find myself smiling all the time.

Your friend,

Emily

Nancy finished reading Emily's email with her own smile. Emily was indeed on her way. She replied to the email with an "atta girl" note of encouragement, adding how much she enjoyed learning how Emily was doing. She sent the email and closed her laptop.

She glanced at her watch and walked to the lobby to check her mailbox. Each resident at Whisperwood had mail and message boxes lining the walls in a small alcove off the lobby. The DNA kit she'd ordered for Axel had arrived. The message box, intended for communications among residents and staff, contained a long letter. That usually meant an important message from Whisperwood's assistant administrator, Suzanne Craddock.

Nancy read the letter quickly, noting with impatience the euphemisms as Suzanne attempted to avoid alarming the residents. She submerged the facts of Bill's passing under a sea of vagueness, but all she could do with the bare fact of the sheriff's investigation was to bury it in the last paragraph with the sheriff's request: "If anyone has any information that will help in the investigation, please call the sheriff's office at 304-555-9260."

Too little, too late, was Nancy's first assessment of this letter. Suzanne obviously didn't know how to handle the situation and stewed over it for days before finally deciding to send this rather bizarre note. She had a lot to learn. Too bad the head administrator, Harry Doyle, was out of town. He would have tackled it head on, knowing the residents would have heard of the murder within hours and be out spreading rumors and fear among them. Dwayne hadn't made an arrest so far. All the obvious suspects seemed to have motive, means, and opportunity. He probably found it difficult to narrow all that down to one culprit.

Nancy was glad the 90s Club was with her on withholding the will for a couple of days. Nancy suspected Tammy was guilty of conniving to get Bill to change his will in her favor. She also thought Tammy was the underdog here. How desperate were Megan and Don to claim Bill's estate?

As she mulled over Tammy's position, two other residents wandered into the mailroom and read the message from Suzanne.

"Hey, Nancy," said Carl Rucker, "Says here, if I'm readin' this right, that they're finally getting around to tellin' us Bill Myers' death was murder. Is that right?" Nancy knew Carl was a retired physicist who liked to affect a country manner and speech.

The other elderly gentleman, Brian Cook, peered at Nancy curiously.

"I don't know," Nancy prevaricated. "Did you know Bill well?"

"Hell, yeah," said Carl. "That old buzzard was tough as nails. Surprised the hell out of me when he died."

Brian nodded. "Me, too. Mind you, he looked kinda poorly the last week or so, but he just got over a case of flu."

"What do you think happened?" asked Nancy.

Carl scratched his head. "Don't know." He glanced at her. "Seems like it might be up your alley, don't it?"

Nancy shrugged and gestured to Suzanne's letter. "Both of you played poker with Bill. Do you have any thoughts about what happened?"

Carl nodded. "Yep. That daughter of his shoulda been horsewhipped. We had to start betting for pennies so's we could include Bill since she cut him off his money. Bill complained about it and swore he'd get even. I'd put my money on her."

"Thanks, guys," Nancy said as she left. Neither of the men knew anything worth sharing to the detective. Nancy took the elevator to the fourth floor. No one was in the hall as she walked slowly by Bill's apartment, pausing at the door to listen, but she heard nothing. She pulled a notepad out of her pocket and wrote down the names of the people living in adjacent apartments. She'd met all of them except the new resident who had moved in across the hall. The nameplate on the door said "Darlene Robinson."

She needed to talk to Darlene, but she wanted her questions to seem like a casual interest. She glanced at her watch. Time to set up her laptop in the lobby. Maybe she could pull some information out of the detective when she saw him, but she didn't have much to offer in exchange.

She took the stairs to the second floor and down the hall to number 205. DNA kit in hand, she knocked on Axel's apartment door. She heard his walker thumping its way to the door, then Axel opened it, surprised to see Nancy standing there.

"What's up?" he asked.

She waved the DNA kit. "It's arrived. Let's get this done and in the mail."

She stepped past Axel and went to his dining room table where she opened the box. Inside were a small vial, return packaging, and a sheet of instructions. "Here we go," she said.

"What do I have to do?" asked Axel. He sounded scared and uncertain. "No needles, are there?" he joked.

"Nothing to worry about," She picked up the vial. "All you have to do is spit into this, then we seal it up and send it back."

"I don't see how that will tell anybody anything." Axel sat at the table, staring dubiously at the vial.

"Neither do I, but they know what to do." Nancy pushed the vial closer to him. "Just spit into it."

Axel did as requested, shaking his head between deposits. "Never heard of such a thing," he muttered.

Nancy sealed the vial, placed it as instructed in the return package, and waved goodbye to Axel. "I'll mail it today. I can hardly wait to see the results," she said.

"Me, too." Axel followed her to the door, still shaking his head. "Wait, Nancy." Axel reached out a hand to stop her before she opened the door. "Any news on Bill's murder?"

"The sheriff's detective is working hard. I'll mail this, and see if I can get an update from him."

"Don't tell him about…you know."

Nancy did know. Axel was worried about being caught snooping around Bill's apartment. "My lips are sealed," she said as she stepped out into the hall. Who else at Whisperwood was worried about what the deputy might find?

Nancy dropped by her apartment and picked up her laptop. On the way to the lobby, she stopped in the small convenience store off the lobby. It also functioned as a gift shop, since the many visitors often forgot a gift and felt one was called for. She bought a card and baby booties and used the shop's gift-wrapping service. Then she hurried to the lobby to set up her table.

With her laptop open and ready and no one in the lobby, Nancy stepped over to the administration offices and found Dwayne at his laptop in the closet-sized room.

"Brought you something," Nancy said and handed the gift over to him. "Just a little present for your new baby."

Dwayne took it and grinned as he opened it. "Booties!" he exclaimed delightedly. "Keep her little toes nice and warm." He looked up at Nancy. "Thank you." He brought in a chair. "Have a seat."

"Thank you," Nancy said, feeling cheered at Dwayne's reaction. "What's her name?"

"Angela." Dwayne pulled out his wallet. "Got some new pictures." He pulled out an accordion-fold of photos and Nancy oohed and awed at each one. "Beautiful child and a beautiful name," she said and returned to her table, leaving behind a beaming new father.

She was in time to catch Bill's neighbor, Darlene Robinson, as she stepped out of the elevator. Identifying her was easier than Nancy had thought. Darlene still wore the name badge given to new residents to help them make friends.

Darlene stopped by Nancy's table. "Are you signing people up for something?" she asked.

"I'm the help desk," Nancy replied with a smile. "Nancy Dickenson. You can ask me about Whisperwood, but I mainly tell people how to avoid frauds and scams." She waved her hand. "At our age, we're all targets for scammers."

"Wonderful," said Darlene. "I almost got taken last year by a phone scam. Somebody claimed to be my grandson. I happened to know exactly where my grandson was at the time, so

I gave that scammer an earful."

"Good for you. That scheme is ever-popular." Nancy gestured to a nearby armchair. "Have a seat."

Darlene sat as she glanced at her watch. "I can only stay a few minutes."

"You live across from Bill Myers' apartment, don't you? On the fourth floor?"

Darlene looked surprised. "I do. How did you know?"

"My friends and I wondered if you heard or saw anything that might help solve his murder."

Darlene's eyes widened. "His murder? Oh, my."

Now I've done it, thought Nancy. I *should have been more careful what I said.* "There's an announcement in your mailbox, but don't get upset. The sheriff is investigating, and the security guards are out in force. Let them know anything you might have observed."

"I'd heard something about it." Darlene sank back against the chair. "Just gossip, I thought."

At this point, Louise arrived and took the other chair. She noticed Darlene's name tag and introduced herself. "I'm your neighbor on the fourth floor."

"Did you know about the murder?" Darlene asked.

Louise glanced at Nancy and immediately sized up the situation. "Don't worry. Bill antagonized everyone here. Somebody got fed up, I guess. Anyway, the detective and the security guards are taking care of the situation."

Nancy followed up. "Did you notice anything strange on Saturday evening a week ago?"

"Saturday? I'd just moved in and I was dog tired. It must

have been late Saturday night because I heard him go into his apartment around nine." Darlene thought a moment." I had trouble sleeping. New place, you know. Later, around one a.m., I heard light footsteps and then the elevator opened and closed. For some reason, I thought the footsteps were those of a woman, and she didn't weigh very much." Darlene looked from Louise to Nancy. "Do you think that will help?"

Nancy immediately thought of Tammy, who was thin and of average height. "You ought to tell the detective," said Nancy. She peered at the administration offices. "He's in now. Go on over and tell the office assistant you need to talk to him."

"All right," Darlene said uncertainly. "If you think it might help."

As she tottered away, Nancy stared thoughtfully at her laptop. Could those light footsteps have been Tammy's? Or Megan's?

The front door opened, and Mike Johnson stalked in, his face red and angry. He approached Ashley at the reception desk and banged his fist on it. "I need to see that busybody Nancy Dickenson," He barked. "Where is she?"

Ashley glanced at Nancy.

"Uh oh," thought Nancy as she stood to meet the man. Louise also rose to follow Nancy in confronting Mike. "I'm Nancy Dickenson," she said, keeping her voice calm and quiet.

"What do you mean by filling my wife's head with nonsense?" He leaned toward her, his hands drawn into fists.

Nancy faced him, eyes narrowed, but she waved at the easy chairs. "Let's sit down and you can tell me what this is all about."

"You know what it's about," Mike shouted, pointing his finger at her face.

"You stop that," said Louise. "Come on, Nancy. You don't have to listen to this bully."

"Bully! Do you know who I am?" Mike's face turned even redder.

"Yes, I do," Nancy said calmly. "You're a man who intimidates and insults his wife and squashes her dreams."

"What dreams?" he sneered. "You tell me where she is, right now."

Nancy turned away. "She'll be back when she's ready."

She left Mike sputtering at the reception desk, packed up her laptop, and she and Louise walked toward the hall. Nancy felt Mike's rage boring a hole in her back, but several couples had entered the lobby and forced him to bury his anger under the congenial politician façade.

She stopped a moment and turned around to see Mike exit through the front door. Ashley grinned at Nancy with a thumb's up.

***

Welcome Our New Residents

Three new residents joined us this week. Be sure to welcome them when you see them around the building. Ask them to join you for dinner or your favorite activity here.

Darlene Robinson hails from Berkeley Springs, WV, where she ran a Bed & Breakfast establishment and was active in many civic activities. She loves animals and hopes to volunteer at our local shelter.

Roger and Maryann Carlson grew up in West Virginia but lived most of their lives in Georgia, outside Atlanta. Roger is a railroad hobbyist and looks forward to helping set up the toy train tracks during the Christmas holiday. Maryann is a retired teacher and loves to sew. They are pleased to be back in their home state of West Virginia.

The Whisperwood Breeze,
Whisperwood Retirement Center Newsletter

Chapter 20

From the clues in the old album and the memories of Axel and his family, Nancy had begun to form a theory about Axel's family, but she needed to surf the web for more information.

She had visited the Netherlands, Belgium's neighbor, in the 1960s and had seen horse-drawn wagons. Before World War II, they must have been even more plentiful. But the horses in Axel's photos were pulling covered wagons that looked as if they were lived in. Were Axel's family vagabonds?

Or could it be the people in his family were traveling entertainers? There were musicians in the photo.

That afternoon, she called Axel. "I've got a few ideas to discuss with you," she said.

"Sure. Come on by," he said and laughed. "One thing I got is time."

Before she left, Nancy checked her email and found a message from Emily.

Dear Nancy,
From the time I was a young girl and devoured the

Nancy Drew mysteries, I've dreamed of being a private eye. I've been looking into that possibility. That was your career. I'll listen to any advice you have.

I meet the basic state requirements for a P.I. license. I'm old enough and a U.S. citizen, and I haven't been convicted of any crime. Having no job at all means I don't hold a position that would be a conflict of interest.

Step 2 will pose the problems. I have to obtain a certificate of training from a school that provides criminal justice education. I'm already enrolled in a beginning online course in criminal justice. But I also need experience with the police or a private investigations agency. How am I going to get a detective agency to hire me without any experience?

Your friend,

Emily

Nancy replied quickly, complimenting Emily on her good work, reminding her of her computer skills, and suggesting that she had excellent management and organization skills from running a household. Then she logged off and walked up the stairs to meet Axel.

"Have a seat," he said, gesturing toward the living room and hobbling behind her on his walker. "The DNA results back yet?" he asked.

She shook her head. "Not yet, but I've been doing some web-surfing and want to see what you think." She sat on the couch.

"I'm ready." He folded his walker and sat in an armchair as he waited for her to begin.

Would he be ready for this? Nancy wondered. "From our visit to Lavinia, I get the idea that your family loved horses."

"That's true." Axel nodded. "I used to ride a lot on the farm growing up."

"You're a musician, and some of the people in your family photos seem to be musicians as well."

Axel nodded. "I even remember good times and a lot of music when I was a small child."

"The album includes photos of horses and covered wagons." Nancy took a deep breath and spoke slowly, watching for Axel's reaction. "We know Danior is a Gypsy name. Have you thought any more about the possibility of being from a Gypsy family?"

"You suggested that, but really, Gypsies?" Axel shook his head. "Hard to believe. Do they even still exist?"

Nancy waited a moment before adding, "Gypsies, or more properly Roma, were originally from India and traveled all over Europe, often working as musicians or circus and carnival performers. They also were horse traders, weavers, brick makers, and other such occupations. Does any of that sound familiar?"

Axel nodded reluctantly. "Gypsies lived in wagons and traveled," he said. "Wagons like in the photos."

"Hitler attacked the gypsies, just like he did the Jews," said Nancy. "The Roma were discriminated against and victims of vicious prejudice all over Europe and here in America, too."

"If my family were Gypsies or," he winked at Nancy, "Roma, then that's the reason I couldn't connect with the Jewish religion. I wasn't Jewish."

"That's right, but your family knew the German Nazis were

after them. That's why they got you out of the country."

Axel nodded. "And that's why we never heard from them again. The Nazis killed them. Maybe killed them all. I wondered what had happened to my parents. For years, I hoped they'd show up on my doorstep."

"One other thing I learned," said Nancy, "and it's sad. Because of the rampant discrimination against them, the Roma lifestyle is usually at poverty level, typified by poor health, little or no education, and widespread illiteracy."

"Oh boy. Sounds terrible." He shook his head. "I had a much better deal, then, growing up in England."

"And you're alive," said Nancy.

"That's true," Axel agreed.

"Think about all this, and then let's see what the DNA kit says," Nancy added as she left and returned to her apartment. As she hoped, Emily had sent another email. Most emails tended toward brevity. Nancy felt Emily's longer messages reflected her excitement and need to talk to someone.

I'm at a Denny's for lunch. I've made friends with a server named Denise. She said she'd ask around about a place to stay and to come back tomorrow. She might not find anything, but servers would know about cheap places to live, and they work all over town. Meanwhile, I tried craigslist.com where I found eleven listings. Most of them were for sharing an apartment and several offered a room in a private home. I responded to five of them.

I visited the mail drop office here to meet the staff, and I've opened a bank account. I also made forwarding arrangements with the mail drop at home.

The next item on my list is the hardest. Finding a job with a P.I. agency.

I spent the rest of the afternoon polishing a resume. Thank you for reading the draft and for your suggestions. I am so grateful for your help and encouragement. With only a GED certificate and some computer training but no experience, I need all the help I can get. Wish me luck.

Emily

Nancy spent a few minutes replying to the email with more words of encouragement. After a few pats to appease Malone, she left her apartment for the gym. Passing through the lobby, she encountered Madge and Helene Burwell, sisters noted for their venomous gossip. Nancy tried to stay clear of them, but this time they used their stolid overweight bodies to block her way.

"We were hoping to see you," said Madge. Lipstick bled into the wrinkles of her smile.

"We're afraid to sleep in our beds," said Helene. Her sharp eyes raked Nancy from head to toe. "Have they arrested her yet?"

"Arrested who?" asked Nancy, afraid of the answer.

"Why that home health aide," said Madge. "She did it. Poor Bill."

"He was such a nice man," Helene added.

"No one has been arrested," Nancy said. "I'd be careful about accusing anyone. You could be sued for slander."

"Nonsense," said Madge, the nastier of the two sisters. "I heard Mr. Myers left her money in his will.

"Where did you hear that?" asked Nancy.

"It's what everyone's talking about," sniffed Madge. That means she has a good motive, and she could easily get into his apartment. She had him wound around her finger, but she didn't fool me."

Nancy stepped around the sisters and continued to the gym, inwardly seething. No doubt Tammy was being tried in the court of speculation. *I'm glad we hid the will. Inheriting $100,000 is one big motive whether she knew about it or not.*

But hadn't she immediately thought of Tammy when Darlene mentioned light footsteps?

***

Gym Extends Hours

Due to increased demand, the gym will now be open from 8 a.m. to 10 p.m. although no attendant will be available after 6 p.m. Get in shape! Lose those extra pounds! Take advantage of Whisperwood's convenient and well-equipped gym.

The Whisperwood Breeze,
Whisperwood Retirement Village Newsletter

Chapter 21

At dinner that evening, Nancy brought up the list of suspects to the 90s Club. "I ran into Madge and Helene in the hall today," she said. "They told me Tammy should be arrested for murder and are probably passing that idea along to everyone they meet."

"Of course, they would," groaned Louise. "You know how they are. Tammy is their perfect victim. Vulnerable. She wants to keep her job, so she's not likely to fight back."

"If those old bags could," grumbled George, "they'd organize a lynching mob."

"That was my thought. Tammy came to me for help," Nancy reminded them.

"Good move on her part." Louise sniffed her wine.

Tom had joined them again that evening and nodded his head. "Madge complained about one of the servers here, and that poor girl lost her job. Nobody wants to work any table where Madge and her sister are sitting."

Louise frowned. "That pair of gorgons are despicable."

"Who's on our suspect list now?" asked Fitz.

"Tammy is on mine," said George.

"Bill's daughter and son-in-law, Megan and Don," added Louise.

"We have to rule out Axel," said Nancy, "even though he was worried Bill had found some kind of incriminating evidence against him. What that might be, I can't imagine."

Louise nodded. "He's such a mild, pleasant man, but he's not very strong and too short to hold a pillow over Bill's head."

"High on my list is Mike Johnson, one of our esteemed county commissioners. Bill had uncovered some malfeasance on Mike's part." Fitz laid his silverware across his plate and sat back.

"That's right. Bill told me he had enough on Mike for him to lose the next election," added Nancy. "There may be others here or elsewhere who are afraid of what Bill uncovered."

"Like the high-ranking Washington types he was exposing in his memoirs," Fitz said. "If such a memoir exists."

"How do we find that out?" asked Louise.

George raised an eyebrow. "Never fear. Help is here,' he said. "Just before I left for dinner tonight, I hit on the password. Guess what it was?"

Don't mess with us," said Louise. "What was it?"

"What you'd think. *Investigator*."

Nancy laughed. "Of course. Should have been the first word we thought of."

George looked wounded. "Easy for you to say. I've been messing with that flash drive for days."

"At last we can get into those files," Nancy said.

"What files?" asked Tom. Their easy-going chatter seemed to fascinate him, although he didn't say much.

Nancy glanced around the dining room. No one seemed interested in their conversation or was even looking their way. She spoke softly. "We think Bill may have uncovered small-town corruption here. He had a big fight with Mike Johnson several days before he was killed. We want to know if Bill had any evidence of bribery or other coercion regarding the proposed quarry."

George nodded. "Bill was an investigative reporter. He'd love to bite into something like that."

"That's what we thought," said Louise.

Tom had been watching the conversation with amusement. "If that's the case, it would be an excellent motive for murder."

"One of many we're finding," George quipped.

"I'm anxious to look at those files," Nancy added. "Can you get them to us tonight?"

"Sure. After dinner."

"I've got a class." Tom signaled the server for his walker. "Anyway, I'm not fit for a life of crime. Fill me in later."

"How about brainstorming other possible suspicious characters at Whisperwood?" suggested Fitz. "Who else would Bill have his eyes on?"

"There's the Whisperwood bookkeeper and the treasurer on the board. I'd consider anyone who's got his finger in a money pit," said George.

"I've never met the bookkeeper," said Fitz. "Any of you know him or her?"

"I've met her," said Nancy. "Ginger Springale. Doesn't say much. Sticks to her job."

"I've talked to the Board treasurer," said George. "He looks like a businessman. Tall, distinguished-looking man—exactly like you'd want a treasurer to look. Elected on appearance alone, I'd bet. Style, no substance. Doesn't seem too bright to me, but all he has to do is rubber stamp the statements Suzanne and the bookkeeper put in front of his nose."

"That's not good enough," said Nancy, "but we all get copies of the reports and statements. I guess we're all accountable if we don't raise questions and pay attention."

George picked up his napkin and laid it by his plate. "Let's get out of here and go look at that flash drive. My apartment."

"About time," grumbled Louise. "You can't hog it all to yourself, you know."

"You try to come up with some random word that Bill would think of for a password," George retorted.

They left the dining room and headed for George's apartment. He unlocked his door and stepped aside to let the other three enter. They trooped over to his computer on a desk in his office, actually the second bedroom, and waited while George turned on the computer, plugged in the flash drive, and opened it with the newly found password, "Investigator."

He scrolled down the list of files and looked up at Nancy and Louise. "All these files have people's names on them. I recognize some of them as residents," he said as he sat back. "Take a look."

Nancy leaned over George's shoulder to glance at the file names. "He's even got a file on me. What on earth...?" She laughed. "I can hardly wait to see what's in that file."

"We're all in his files," said Fitz. "He was trolling."

Bill has files on a lot of people here at Whisperwood," said

Nancy. "When you're casting a wide net, then you're bound to come up with something."

Fitz studied the list. "I don't see anything that looks like a manuscript."

"If he ever did plan to write such a book, it probably never got beyond the planning stage," Louise said. "He might have juicy stuff in the paper files still in his apartment."

"I don't care," George said. "I'm not going after them. I'm done with a life of crime."

"We'll leave those to Dwayne." Fitz folded his arms. "Whenever they hack into Bill's computer, they can compare those files with the paper ones. If they haven't found the murderer by then, that is."

"I'll keep an eye on Bill's apartment," Louise added. "And we can all be extra friendly to strangers who seem to be wandering around by themselves."

Nancy turned to George. "It's getting late. While we're here, you can forward those files to me and Louise." We'll all work on them."

"I think we've lucked into some pretty interesting material," Louise said. "I'm surprised we only found Axel in Bill's apartment foraging around his desk."

"I think Bill was a wacko," George muttered as he hit "Send."

***

Message to Residents
Everyone Needs a Good Night's Sleep
Please consider your neighbors and keep noise to a minimum after ten p.m. and before eight a.m. We

have received complaints about late-night furniture moving, loud televisions and music, and other nuisances. Thank you.

Suzanne Craddock, Assistant Administrator,
Whisperwood Retirement Village

Chapter 22

The next morning, Nancy sat at the card table in the lobby, logging into her laptop. This was not her usual day to field questions from anxious residents, but the night before she'd received an anxious phone call for help from the agitated white-haired gentleman who now waited, leaning on a cane, in front of her.

"You ready now?" he asked as Nancy looked up from her laptop. She nodded.

"I'm Bert Melstrom," he said, shaking Nancy's hand.

"Nice to meet you, Bert. Please pull up a chair." Nancy said. "What's the problem?"

Bert sat down in one of the comfortable lobby chairs. "Yesterday I got an email saying I'd ordered $5,000 worth of stuff from Amazon." The man was shivering in anger and distress. "I never did. I called the number they gave me, and they said if I paid it off with gift cards, then I could get a refund."

Nancy had heard this one before. "And did you buy the gift cards?"

He nodded.

"And you called the phone number they gave you and read

to them the gift card numbers, right?" Nancy hoped he had the money to lose.

"No, no," he said. "I came to my senses and decided to ask you about this. It seems strange to me."

"It's a scam. The crooks have no connection to Amazon and the phone number doesn't go to Amazon but to the crooks. They'll cash in those gift cards before you're off the phone, and you'll never see your money again."

He nodded. "That's what I was afraid of, but they threatened my credit rating and were scary on the phone."

"They're very bad people. Ignore them. Use the cards for yourself. Report the scam to the state consumer protection office. You can also report it to the Federal Trade Commission." Nancy had repeated this information so often she was on a roll. "Be wary of anyone who asks for money on the phone, internet or in the mail. Do not click on any links in their email or use any phone number they supply. Report a scam that happened with an online seller or a payment transfer system to the company's fraud department."

"Wait. I've got to write this down."

Nancy handed him a brochure. "You don't need to. All the information is in here." He took the brochure. "Thank you." He drew himself up, relief visible on his face. "I was really worried about this."

"Glad I could help. And for goodness sake, don't call the scammers back or click on any link in their message."

Bert rose, a different person. He smiled and winked at Nancy. "Thank you. I knew something was wrong. You relieved my mind and saved me a bundle."

Then he tottered down the hall to the elevator.

Nancy watched him leave, glad she was able to help and even gladder that he hadn't given the card numbers to the crooks. Then she noticed that Ashley had arrived at the lobby reception counter. No one else was around, so Nancy walked over to her.

After a brief greeting, she came to the point. "You see everyone who comes in here, don't you?"

Ashley was just taking the lid off her coffee. "Sure," she said, tossing her blonde hair out of her eyes.

"What kind of visitors came to see Bill Myers?"

"Visitors have to sign in, you know," Ashley said, sliding the login book to Nancy. "I'm not supposed to let people read through this log, but since it's you... Anyway, this only goes back about two months. You can look through it. It gives the visitor's name, date, time, and who they came to see."

"Perfect," said Nancy and began perusing the book. She found Mike Johnson's name several times. She'd seen him at Whisperwood arguing with Bill or searching for him, but she was surprised to see that he'd visited Bill four times in the last two months.

Don and Megan were frequent visitors, too. The other name on the list was Alice Tyson, the Pet Store owner. What would she want to see Bill about?" She tapped the counter. It was time for a visit. Anyway, Malone needed more cat food.

She went back to her laptop, read through her email, and found a new one from Emily.

HI, Nancy,

I've been job hunting in earnest, but brace yourself. I've got good news. After trudging through interviews at four P.I. offices, I was pretty depressed. I left them feeling like a naïve little girl swimming in waters too deep.

My mood was dark as I applied at the last P.I. Agency on my list for today. It was in an old office building with doors that had windows of etched glass. It reminded me of Sam Spade's office door in *The Maltese Falcon.* The name painted on the glass was "Jason S. Haines, Private Investigations." I figured this guy was new to the game and wasn't making much money.

Guess what? I worked a deal with him, and he's taking me on as his assistant. I'm only making a dollar in salary for the first month, and then we'll see if I prove my worth and we can work together. Win-win is the way I see it. With my lack of experience, none of the other agencies would even interview me. But he really, I mean really, needs me. He has no idea how much he needs me. I used to help Mike start up his business, so it's easy to see Jason has never run a business before.

Emily

Nancy smiled as she responded again with congratulations. Emily's excitement, enthusiasm, and imagination showed in every line. Mike Johnson had lost a treasure. She was going to turn Jason Haines's P.I. agency around.

Thoughts of Emily segued back to her husband. Nancy considered him a suspect in Bill's murder, but the connection was still tenuous and based on Mike's angry visits to Whisperwood. *We need more information about his activities with the commission.*

Louise was astute about governmental activities since she was an activist and kept track of what the local, state, and national government was doing on social and environmental issues. Nancy arranged to meet Louise in the Pub for lunch.

Nancy arrived first and found a table, and then spotted Louise as she walked in wearing a neon yellow T-shirt that couldn't be missed. Today, the button on her shirt said "Black Lives Matter." She swept off her sun hat as she walked to where Nancy sat. "I could use an iced tea," she said. "It's hot outside."

"Me, too." Nancy motioned to the server, and they both ordered BLT sandwiches and the iced teas.

"What's up?" asked Louise.

"You listen to the local scuttlebutt about the County Commission," Nancy said.

"That's right. Gotta watch those guys, or you'll find yourself out on the street."

"What do you know about Mike Johnson?"

Louise whistled. "Only what you know about the man."

"We know he was seen arguing with Bill Myers a few days before he was killed."

"And Bill was a muckraker," added Louise. "If Bill and Mike were arguing, it was probably about commission business. Bill had found suspicious activity in the county finances and was looking into the sneaky dealings to bring in a quarry."

"Embezzlement means jail time," said Nancy.

The server set their tea and sandwiches in front of them.

Nancy sighed as she picked up the sandwich. "The number

of suspects keeps growing, and that doesn't even include the people Bill was going to expose in this memoir he was supposedly writing."

"Which we haven't found yet," added Louise.

"True, but if any of those crooked government officials thought he would be exposed in such a memoir, he might have sneaked into Bill's apartment to murder him and then disappear, maybe taking a draft of the memoir or deleting it on his computer." Nancy paused to sip her tea thoughtfully.

Louise nodded. "Bill could have found evidence of embezzlement, bribery, fraud, womanizing, or conflicts of interest. Any of those could bring down a politician and affect his business."

"I could see Mike involved in all of that." Nancy shook her head. "We know he also has a hand in the selling of public lands behind Whisperwood to a company that plans to dig a quarry there. Bill was nosing into that deal. Gives Mike a bunch of motives." She finished her sandwich. "I'll spend the afternoon going through Bill's files. We need evidence, not speculation."

Nancy felt her phone vibrate. "Just a minute," she said, as she read the text message from Emily.

I had lunch with Jason today and asked if he would help me find my birth parents. He agreed! We went over the basic details I'd picked up from the census and I told him a DNA kit was ordered for me. Thank you for that! We decided to wait until we get the DNA results.

I'm spending the day putting cards announcing our

detective agency on community bulletin boards around town, and I suggested that Jason enroll in Toastmasters to improve his public speaking ability and join Kiwanis or Rotary or some other organization where he can make connections.

He calls me pushy and aggressive, but he says that's a good thing. At least I feel like I'm helping somebody and doing good work for a change.

Nancy grinned at Louise. "Emily's keeping me posted," she said. "She has a job in Savannah with a private investigator who is in over his head."

Louise gave Nancy a high five. "Good for her. You took a big risk in helping her."

As Nancy returned the phone to her purse, Louise added, "We've been looking for motives and opportunity, but we also need to check alibis. We have several strong suspects, but the one with the most immediate motive is…"

Nancy winced as she finished the sentence. "Tammy, the home health aide."

Louise nodded. "Tammy."

***

SIGN UP NOW!
Annual Hobby Fair: August 31

Looking for a hobby or have a hobby and want to find friends to join you? Whisperwood's popular Hobby Fair will be held Friday, August 31, from 2 p.m. to 5 p.m. Sign up now for space to exhibit your hobby or to staff a sign-up table.

The fair is open to everyone. No need to register to view the many exhibits. For more information, call Mary Ann Hopkins, Social Director, at 304-555-7223.

The Whisperwood Breeze,
Whisperwood Retirement Village Newsletter

Chapter 23

After leaving the Pub, Nancy stopped by Suzanne's office. Her door was open, so Nancy rapped on the wall and walked in. Suzanne looked up and waved at a chair.

"All going well," said Suzanne, sitting back in her chair, "despite current events. Any word on Bill's murderer?"

Nancy shook her head. "How is the detective doing?"

"I don't know. He won't tell me anything, but I think he's checking backgrounds of likely people around here to see what he can find." Suzanne tapped a pencil on the desk. "And alibis, of course."

"Good way to start," said Nancy.

"I guess." Suzanne shrugged and frowned. "Since the sheriff's office is involved, you and the 90s Club can stay out of it. You don't want to get hurt. This is a real murderer you're dealing with, not some fictional movie character."

Nancy didn't respond at first, but she felt a surge of anger. Suzanne was just doing her job, but she knew the capabilities of the 90s Club members. Her objection now was demeaning and uncalled for. It erected a barrier between the executive office and the residents. The ties of cooperation would be much more useful. Finally, Nancy responded with a bland statement. "We always contribute when we're needed."

"Let the cop do his job," Suzanne responded. "He's paid for it."

"Where is he?" asked Nancy. "Is he still using the temporary office space you gave him?"

"He hasn't needed it much since no one has come forward with information," said Suzanne. "I guess he is following whatever other leads he has somehow drummed up." She stood.

Nancy saw the signal and took her leave, but as she returned to her apartment, she thought of the grumbling among the residents about another rate hike in the monthly fees they paid to live at Whisperwood.

Fitz was napping on the living room sofa. He opened one eye. "You're back. Learn anything, Luv?" Malone was stretched out alongside Fitz, ignoring her.

"The plot thickens," said Nancy, but she didn't elaborate. Instead, she opened her laptop and began perusing the copies of Bill Myers' files sent from George's computer.

Nancy looked first at the file he'd kept on her. At first, it was benign and even a bit boring with an outline of her career, marriages, and addresses. Not impressive, not even interesting, thought Nancy with a grin. Then she came across police reports of the incident when she was wrongfully accused of shoplifting. Or the time she blundered into a barroom brawl, got socked in the jaw, and had to go to the hospital. How did Bill find out all this?

She scanned the files on Louise and George, but they were skimpy and offered no revelations. The file on Fitz bulged with news items in various languages, articles he'd written, and lists of work assignments around the world. Bill's scribbled notes about interview questions hinted that he was searching for dirt but not finding any. It was odd. Nancy wondered why Bill was digging deep into Fitz's past. Could he have been jealous of her relationship with Fitz? She rejected that thought as ridiculous.

Nancy quickly perused the files Bill had kept on several other residents, but there, too, she found nothing relating to anything questionable. Even Axel, it seemed, had nothing to worry about. Next to his name was a laughing emoji. Nancy wondered what that meant. Bill's quirky sense of humor, she supposed.

The file on Suzanne Craddock, on the other hand, contained extensive reports on the problems with the other nonprofits she had managed and included a list of her previous jobs and related phone numbers. Nancy printed that out, wondering how Suzanne could have been hired by Whisperwood with her dubious employment record. That bore looking into.

No matter who had embezzled much-needed funds from the other nonprofits Suzanne had managed, she was responsible for not providing adequate oversight. Perhaps the audit of Whisperwood's finances was a timely intervention. Still, she wondered how Suzanne could have been hired. Nancy had liked Suzanne, but her trust in the assistant administrator was rapidly eroding.

The file on Mike Johnson was also extensive and included a list of how he voted on various council concerns and a financial report on the garage he owned. Mike regularly voted against providing funds to nonprofit agencies, including the Humane

Society shelter, social services for children and women, and environmental protection activities. Fortunately, the other commissioners had more sense and overrode him to keep the funding for these important services in the county budget. Bill had taken many notes on Johnson's pontification on the need for more jobs and industry in the county, often citing the quarry for its economic and job creation potential. *He wanted the quarry.*

And nothing on Tammy Swann. *Maybe love was blind.*

Fitz rose off the sofa and walked over to stand behind her. "I looked through those files, too. I don't see anything but maybe embezzlement pointing to murder, do you?"

Nancy shook her head. "But Mike is the most obvious culprit," she said.

"I'd say maybe Suzanne, our esteemed assistant administrator," said Fitz.

"Mike, Tammy, Megan, Don. A lot of possibilities." Nancy sighed. "We have suspicions. What we need is proof."

***

Notice to Residents

Exhibit Honors Whisperwood's Contributions

Whisperwood residents contribute time and money to the many community service organizations in our county. They are thankful for our help. Next Monday at 2 p.m., these organizations are hosting an exhibit of their services that will honor Whisperwood's volunteers and contributions. All of us are invited to visit them in the high school auditorium. Refreshments will be served. Whisperwood will run a shuttle to and from the high school to make it easy for everyone to attend. If you have any questions, ask Mary Ann Hopkins, Social Director, at 304-555-7223. Come to the community exhibit! Enjoy the honor and find ways you can help our community.

Special Announcement
Mary Ann Hopkins, Social Director

Chapter 24

Hi, Nancy,

I'm all moved into my new apartment, and I love it. It's a made-over old garage, but it's cheap and livable. Just needs some paint and a bit of fixing, and it will be quite comfortable. The neighborhood is older with lots of trees and huge mansions (mostly apartments, now, I think.) Anyway, I like it.

Emily

Nancy read Emily's email with a smile, then logged out as Axel dropped by her table in the lobby. No one had shown up that morning with a scam story, so she was glad to see him.

"I've got it," Axel said, beaming. "The DNA results."

"Wonderful. Will they be useful?" Nancy hoped so.

Axel leaned over her table. "Come to my place now, okay? We can go over the results together."

"All right," Nancy said, checking her watch. Eleven-thirty. Time to pack up the table, and anyway, she was curious. What would the results reveal?

Nancy stood by as Axel sat at his desk and opened the email from the DNA company.

"You were right. They say I'm forty-six percent descended from Gypsies, the Roma people, originally from India, but I'm also English, German, Slovakian..." He laughed. "I'm a hodgepodge."

"We all are," said Nancy.

Axel pointed to the paragraph describing his lineage. "Roma is no surprise, thanks to you, but I still find it hard to believe."

Nancy smiled noncommittally. Hitler murdered not only Jews but the Roma, homosexuals, and other people he deemed unfit. Axel's parents were probably victims of the Holocaust. From what she'd read, the Roma kept to themselves and lived in tight-knit families and clans. How wrenching it must have been for Axel's parents to send their children away to a foreign land and a family much different from their own.

Also from what she'd read, few Roma had cameras. What if Axel's mother, who was presumably the photographer, came from outside the Roma culture? What if she had fallen in love with a Roma man and run away from her home? Nancy's imagination was in full gear. Perhaps Axel's mother was related to the family in England that adopted her children. That would explain how she knew them.

"But Nancy, look here." Axel interrupted her reverie, pointing to another paragraph. "I'm sending an email out to all the people who showed up in the DNA tests as relatives of mine. I hope someone will contact me who knows something about my family. Someone must have information, I'm sure of it."

Nancy was, too. "This is exciting news. I read that the Roma are often entertainers and include Charlie Chaplin, Elvis

Presley, Rita Hayworth, and others. Maybe that's where your aptitude for the violin comes from."

Axel became thoughtful. "Charley Chaplin? Elvis Presley? That isn't too shabby. I hadn't thought of that. I'll have to ask about music when I contact these people." His eyes glistened. "I am so happy. I thought only my sister and I and her kids were all that was left of my family. Now I find many other people related to me who are alive, and I have history behind me."

Nancy could see how profoundly affected Axel was by this revelation. "Let me know what you find out."

"I will, Nancy, I will." Axel walked her to the door. He seemed to stand taller.

Nancy wondered what he would learn. The Roma people were hated, feared, and discriminated against everywhere. Axel's parents would not willingly have let their children leave the clan to be raised by a family of *gandja* (non-Roma people) To do that, they must have been desperate indeed. Did they know that they were also giving Axel and his sister a better, healthier life where they would learn to read and write and embark on professional careers?

Nancy returned to her apartment but felt too restless to stay there. She picked up a deck of cards and strolled to the lobby. She sat at her usual table and laid the cards for a game of Solitaire. Out of the corner of her eye, she saw Tammy Swann, the home health aide, watching her from the receptionist's counter. Then Suzanne came out of her office, stopped to chat with Nancy, and when she left, Tammy was gone.

After lunch, Nancy returned to her apartment and played with Malone for a few minutes. She intended to check her email, but then she heard a soft knock on the door.

Tammy stood outside, hand raised for another knock. She looked nervous.

"Come in, Tammy," Nancy said, curious to see how the woman would approach the subject of Bill's will. That had to be the reason she was here.

"Thank you." Tammy walked in, saw Malone staring at her with eyes so malignant that she veered away from him nervously. Nancy gestured to a chair and took a seat herself.

"How can I help you?" Nancy asked as if she didn't know.

"I'm so worried I can hardly sleep," Tammy began. "I did not kill Mr. Myers. Just the same, I feel people are looking at me funny like they think I am a murderer."

"Has anyone said anything to you?" Nancy said, glancing at her desk, a few steps away from Tammy.

Tammy shook her head. "But they think it. I don't know why they assume Mr. Myers' left money for me in his will. I didn't even know he was my real grandfather until he told me."

"I'm sorry you have to go through this." Out of the corner of her eye, Nancy saw Malone planning some mischief and debated taking the cat into the back bedroom. She decided Tammy wouldn't stay long, but she kept an eye on Malone anyway. No telling what he might decide to do, and she didn't want blood on the carpet or an emergency room visit.

Tammy also watched Malone as she spoke. "Yes, I am worried and frightened."

"I'm sorry..." Nancy began.

"But don't you see? If you found the will, and I don't receive anything from Mr. Myers, then I have no reason to kill him, and the rumors will stop."

"What if he did leave you something in the will? Would you refuse it to show you had no reason to murder him?"

Tammy rose. "I don't think he left me any money in his will, and I didn't kill him. That's all I can say. I wish the will could be found. I just want to do my job."

Nancy refrained from reminding Tammy that even if she didn't inherit, she could think she did and that would be a strong motive.

"His daughter and her husband are looking for it." Nancy walked Tammy to the door. "My friends and I are also searching for it. We hope it will be found soon."

Tammy stared at Nancy a moment as if she were assessing Nancy's statement. Then she turned to go. "Thank you," she said. "That's all I ask."

Nancy watched Tammy step down the hall, head bowed as if in thought. Nancy didn't blame Tammy for being worried, but she had fraternized with an elderly man who was her patient, even if he might also be her grandfather. Nancy shook her head. She hoped Tammy was innocent, but she did have the air of protesting too much.

Nancy wondered about Tammy as she did about everyone she met. What was Tammy like as a person? How did she live? Nancy made a snap decision and called Louise. "Care for a drive?"

"Sure. I'll be right down."

Nancy stopped by Whisperwood's executive offices during the weekly staff meeting in Suzanne's office. No one was in the outer office to stop her as she searched the cabinets for the human resources files. She hoped they weren't located in some other room. She listened for signs of the meeting breaking up, but the low buzz of discussion in Suzanne's office continued. Nancy found Tammy Swann's personnel file in the bottom drawer, picked out Tammy's home address on her resume, and was back in the lobby before the staff returned to their desks.

She met Louise chatting with Ashley at the reception counter, and they walked out to the parking lot.

"Where to?" asked Louise.

"I want to see where Tammy lives. Might give me some insights." Nancy drove out of the lot and followed her GPS to a rutted country road that ended at a trailer on a scruffy piece of yard. The trailer was painted an aquamarine color and seemed to be in good shape. Three concrete blocks lay crookedly side by side to form the front steps.

Nancy turned the car around and parked on the roadside headed out. Two other trailers were parked close by. One had a rotted roof and was overgrown with vines. Broken toys and trash surrounded it. A dog barked from inside the other. Both trailers sat back from the road. Tammy wouldn't be home for at least three more hours, but whoever lived in the other one could be home anytime. Nancy viewed Tammy's trailer. She was already getting insights into Tammy the person rather than Tammy, the home health aide.

Her trailer looked neat and clean from the outside. Had Tammy been the one who chose its aquamarine color and painted it?

Louise folded her arms and surveyed the scene. "What are we doing here?" She glanced at Nancy. "I'm not getting out of the car. Not for anything."

"Don't," said Nancy, unlocking her safety belt. "I'm going to take a quick look around." She stepped carefully to avoid thorns and stickers and broken bottles tossed on the side of the road. No one was around. She stepped up a well-worn path and rose on her toes to peer into a trailer window. Again, like the outside, everything looked neat and clean, and the furnishings were a mix of old and new. On the wall were framed travel posters of New York, Chicago, London, and Paris. Tammy did indeed have dreams. Two shipping boxes lay open on the floor, but they were empty. Three dresses were laid out on the couch, tags hanging from their collars.

Tammy had been shopping. Was that because of an expected windfall or were those purchases bought from her earnings? Could Bill have given her money or gifts?

As Nancy returned to the car, the door to one of the other trailers opened. A man stood in the doorway, holding back a barking German shepherd. "What are ya doin' here," he yelled. "I seen ya sniffin' around that trailer. What do you want?"

Nancy was only a few steps from her car. In a flash, she analyzed the situation, decided the man could contribute nothing to their search, and she didn't want to test her skills with dog behavior. She leaped into the car, started the engine, and drove the car back down the rutted road and away from the trailers.

"Good. I didn't want to get friendly with that guy," said Louise.

"Nothing to be gained by talking to him." Nancy glanced into her rearview mirror. The man had released the dog. It chased her car a short way but was soon left behind.

"Find what you were looking for?" asked Louise.

"Maybe," said Nancy.

"All right. Now there's a place I want to go."

"Ready. Directions, please."

Louise routed her back to the road going to Whisperwood. About a mile from the retirement village, she pointed to a side road. "Take that," she said.

Nancy turned onto a road that circled behind the Whisperwood property. "Okay. Stop here," said Louise.

Nancy pulled to the side and parked. They both got out of the car and gazed at a scenic expanse of woods and fields. Beside the road, a narrow stream bubbled along, and birds sang in the trees. Behind them in the distance, rising over the trees, was the main building of Whisperwood.

"Beautiful, isn't it," said Louise.

Nancy took a deep breath, feeling the serenity relax her body. "It certainly is."

"You can see this from the back of Whisperwood," said Louise. "I love to look at it from my windows."

Nancy nodded.

"This beautiful scene in front of us," said Louise, "with its biodiversity, birds, animals, and unpolluted streams will be gone in a year if Mike Johnson, the commissioner, has his way. This is where his buddies want to dig a quarry. That means removing all natural vegetation, topsoil, and subsoil. It means noise, dust, pollution, and contaminated water."

"We can't let that happen," said Nancy.

"Wait a minute," added Louise. "I'm not finished. Pits and

quarries disrupt the movement of surface and groundwater and stop the recharge of natural water. That means less and poorer quality drinking water for residents and wildlife near or downstream from the quarry." Louise stood, arms akimbo, a sturdy defender of the environment.

"And when they've taken everything they can," she continued, "they probably won't rehabilitate the site the way they're supposed to by law. We're talking permanent negative impacts on the landscape."

"I'm glad you're organizing Whisperwood to fight this," said Nancy.

"A lot of money is riding on the quarry," Louise grumbled, "for some people."

***

Reuse and Recycle:
What You Can Do to Protect Our Environment

West Virginia is a beautiful state. Its parks, woodlands, forests, and streams are a joy to all of us. Whisperwood is designed with low-use faucets and showers, LED lighting, and recycling bins. The landscaping is planted with native plants and is pesticide free, thanks to our master gardeners. What can you do to help? Louise Owens will discuss these and other initiatives Whisperwood and its residents can take to protect West Virginia's environment and help prevent global warming. Come to the meeting in Classroom A, Lower Level, at 2 p.m. on Thursday.

The Whisperwood Breeze,
Whisperwood Retirement Village Newsletter

Chapter 25

Early the next morning, Nancy drove into town and parked in front of Alice's Pet Store on Main Street. Alice was just hanging out the "Open" sign as Nancy walked up. As she anticipated, Alice had no customers yet.

"What can I do you for," asked Alice cheerily, putting a broom away behind the counter and taking a place at the cash register.

"I want to talk with you for a few minutes," said Nancy walking up to the counter. "It's serious."

"Uh oh, Malone's all right, isn't he?"

"No problem with Malone—except his obnoxious personality," said Nancy with a smile. "I do need a bag of cat food."

"If nothing's wrong witih Malone, then what's on your mind?"

"You belong to the Chamber of Commerce and probably know a lot of what's going on in this town."

Alice shrugged. "It's a small town, like any other small town."

"Did you know Bill Myers?" Nancy asked.

"Myers?" Alice said. "Bill? Should I know him?"

"He lived at Whisperwood. Old newspaperman. He was murdered a few days ago. "

Alice nodded. "I see. You mean *that* Bill Myers, the former newspaperman."

Was Alice buying time? She must have known Bill better than she's pretending she did, Nancy thought, but she played along. "He fought with a county commissioner," Nancy said. "Since you're a business owner in town, I wondered if you knew anything about that." Nancy kept her eyes on Alice.

Alice nodded. "He was in here talking to me the week before he died, asking about Mike Johnson, but I'm not sure what he was looking for. I had problems with Mike. Most people did—especially if you were a woman. He was a pretentious, condescending ignoramus, and I wasn't on his 'favorites' list."

Nancy nodded. "What about how he served as a commissioner?"

"I own a business in this town. It behooves me to pay attention to what the county commissioners do. I questioned some of his decisions. I'm not sure I could say there was anything dishonest about them. I visited Bill at Whisperwood a couple of times. He wanted to know what I knew and vice versa."

"Did Bill focus on anything particular when he talked with you?" Nancy asked, trying to pull some insights from Alice's cagey answers. Alice probably knew a lot more than she was saying.

Alice stared at the ceiling for a moment. "There was one thing," she said. "A granite company wants to build a quarry outside of town on the other side of Whisperwood. They've been trying to be hush-hush about this, but the word is getting out, and some of our older citizens are enraged about this idea. The younger ones are in favor because it means jobs, but that company's record is to take everything and leave an ugly scar in the landscape. Haven't you heard about it at Whisperwood? It would be behind the buildings there."

"Not much," Nancy hedged.

"You should because if that company gets its way, you'll have one hideous eyesore out your windows."

Nancy summed it up. "Mike was in favor of this company's plans."

"That's right. It will mean jobs like I said," said Alice. "We need more jobs, but I think that's too high a price to pay."

Nancy agreed. "That must be what Bill was digging into and what the argument with Mike was all about."

Alice began arranging sales items on the counter. "I would bet so."

"Who owns that land?" asked Nancy.

"A couple in D.C. I've never met them. Doubt if they ever come out here. They will probably sell in a second. Maybe they've already sold that parcel."

"You said Mike and the company are trying to keep the lid on their plans?"

"That's what I've heard, and since you at Whisperwood hadn't heard about it, I would guess they're succeeding."

Nancy frowned. "Why didn't Bill tell us about it? He had plenty of opportunities. Louise formed a Citizens Action Committee. They could be organizing protests."

"You can't ask him," said Alice. "Someone shut him up, didn't they?"

One of many reasons to murder Bill. She returned home and found a new email from Emily.

> I've got my toe in the door, but I know more about running a business than my boss does. I arrived early for work today. Jason didn't get there until 9:30, and I didn't have a key. What if a client had shown up? I suggested that maybe if he wanted to succeed he had to come on time. I've got a key now, so if he's late I can let myself in.
>
> Just wanted to say the small garage apartment I'm renting is working out. It's quiet but near the downtown area and stores, and I can walk to work!
>
> Emily

Early that afternoon, as she passed by the Pub, Nancy spotted Bill's son-in-law, Don, eating a sandwich alone. He was wearing a gray suit and tie. Most men at Whisperwood dressed informally in polo shirts and often in jeans. "Where's Megan?" Nancy asked in a friendly way.

"Beauty salon," mumbled Don. "Do all you ladies spend fortunes getting your hair done?"

Nancy laughed, not sure if his remark was angry or an innocent off-the-cuff comment. It did make her wonder how hard up Don and Megan were and how desperately they needed her Dad's money.

"Mind if I join you?" she asked.

"Help yourself." He took another bite of his sandwich.

Nancy ignored the surly tone and signaled the waiter. "Iced tea," she said. She studied Don. "Is Megan doing okay? She must miss her dad."

"You'd think, but he was getting to be a problem," Don said. "Big problem."

"How's that?"

"Losing it," Don twirled a finger beside his head. "Coming up with bogus scandals and dribbling his money away. We had to take control of his bank account."

"He seemed okay to me," Nancy responded, sipping tea as she tested the waters.

"Yeah, well, you didn't see him when we did." Don munched on the sandwich. "Another month, he would have been broke. A few more months and he'd have been bonkers." He leaned forward and eyed Nancy. "And then there was that greedy little nurse."

"She was a home health aide," Nancy corrected.

"Whatever." Don shrugged. "Filthy old goat. He should have known better than to get involved with a…"

Nancy interrupted. "Those aides work hard."

Don raised an eyebrow. "Really? She was working hard, that's for sure…to get Bill's money. That's all she was interested in."

"She wasn't allowed to fraternize with the people she worked for, the residents," Nancy said.

"If she didn't fraternize, why was Bill putting her in his will?" Don finished his sandwich and glared at Nancy.

"Did he?" she asked.

"We can't find it," Don admitted, "but the lawyer insists there is one. He should have had a copy, but he says Bill wrote it himself and kept it. That aide's been sniffing around us, pretending to be sorry about Bill dying and all." He snorted. "She's only interested in his money. But if she thinks she's getting a penny, she's sadly mistaken. And you can bet on this. You'll find she did it. Greedy little …" He stood. "Got to go."

Nancy watched him stalk angrily out of the Pub and down the hall. Of course, he and Megan had Bill's keys. They could have gotten into any door from the outside with those keys and made their way secretly to Bill's apartment, then done away with him. But did they? If so, how could she prove it?

She left the Pub and dropped by Axel's apartment. "Anything new on your search?" she asked as he led her into the living room.

"I'm not sure how it works, Nancy. I used my name and gave the DNA company my email address. Anyone who wants to get in touch with me can do it through the company. I got a lot of names on my list of people I'm supposedly related to," said Axel with a wide grin, "according to the DNA results, that is. And I've already contacted a lot of them through the company. I'm very excited."

"Excellent," said Nancy. She was as curious as Axel to find out what happened to his family.

Then Axel's grin disappeared. "I've been reading more about the Roma people," he said. "Poverty struck, no education, illiterate..." He shook his head and sighed.

"Everyone takes that risk when they contact people they don't know," Nancy said, "but now that you have learned about your Roma family, you can support organizations fighting the discrimination against them. Don't forget these connections are the only way you're going to learn about your parents and what happened to them."

Axel was beginning a life-changing journey, but Nancy had another concern. "Why did you think Bill Myers had a folder on you?" she asked.

"That's what I say to myself. Why did he ask my friends questions about me? Did he ever talk to you about me?" asked Axel. "Maybe he was a Soviet spy, but me, I don't think so. Even if he was, why would he be interested in me?"

"He was a former newspaper reporter and interested in anyone here who might have a story. He probably has a folder on me and for sure on Louise with all her environmental causes. You've probably mentioned to people about your background, which is unusual. Bill would home in on that out of curiosity alone."

"I suppose so," said Axel, "but I'm an open book."

"What was your career?" Nancy asked.

"I was a chemist with a pharmaceutical company. Did he think I sold drugs on the black market?" He raised his shoulders and opened his palms to Nancy. "Like I said, I'm an open book except for before I was five years old. I am British except I became a U.S. citizen many years ago. I am not planning to overthrow the American government or concoct illegal drugs to sell on the street. I did not plant marijuana in my garden plot here." He paused for breath.

Nancy smiled. "I don't think you have to worry." She didn't add that they thought he was too weak and incapacitated to hurt anyone.

That evening, she relayed what she'd learned about the quarry and Mike Johnson to the other 90s Club members. "Bill must have been working up an exposé on Mike and the quarry company's plans. Whisperwood would be a powerful opponent," she concluded. "Most of its one thousand residents are voters and interested in what happens in the area."

"I'm organizing the opposition here at Whisperwood," said Louise, determination showing in the grim set of her jaw. Nancy had seen that look before, and it meant a battle ahead. Louise's "Buy Local" button shone on her khaki shirt. "A barrage of fluff has been coming out of the commission office," she said, "trying to smother us with petty stuff, so they can sneak the quarry through the system."

"They've got to hold public hearings on this," said Nancy. "We need to find out when and organize the local citizens to protest."

"I'm on it," answered Louise.

"Ahem," said George. "You do realize that this might be why Bill was murdered. Sounds like there's big money behind this. And when a lot of money is involved…" He crossed his throat with a finger. "Sayonara."

Louise glared at him. "I refuse to let murdering thieves stop us."

"Good for you," said Nancy. "They can't do away with everyone at Whisperwood."

"And an alternate plan is on the table," added Fitz. "Turning that land into a state park sounds like a great idea."

"Do you suppose Megan and Don have an interest in the quarry?" asked Nancy. "That would explain their opposition to Bill's activities."

"From what I've been hearing," added George, "they could

use his money."

"I'm writing a flyer to send to all the residents about the quarry," said Louise, "and I'll be talking to a reporter tomorrow."

Nancy sipped her wine thoughtfully. "You know," she finally said, "if Bill was murdered because he opposed the quarry, whoever killed him is going to be unhappily surprised when they find out it had the opposite effect."

***

Whisperwood Alert: STOP THE QUARRY!

What do you want to see as you gaze out the back windows of Whisperwood? A new state park with hiking trails and a clean stream for fishing and boating? Or a quarry with bulldozers and machines leaving behind a bare and ugly plot of land that pollutes the streams and destroys the beauty of our scenery. A state park will provide jobs our citizens can be proud of. STOP THE QUARRY! Join other Whisperwood Residents in the protest. Find out how you can help at the meeting in Classroom B tomorrow at 11 a.m. For more information, contact Louise Owens, Resident, Apt. 405.

Message from Whisperwood's
Community Action Committee

Chapter 26

Nancy was working on her laptop that evening. Fitz was reading a book while petting Malone who snuggled next to him and purred. Fitz laid the book aside, stood, and stretched. "I've got an idea," he said as he glanced at his watch.

Nancy looked up from her laptop. "I'm listening."

"It's after ten, Luv. Nobody is in the executive offices, and the front doors are locked."

"True. Except for the security guard sitting at the front desk."

Fitz folded his arms with his chin in one hand. "Forgot about that guard. He puts a wrinkle into a midnight foray in the executive suite."

"What are you thinking?"

"As residents of this cooperative enterprise, we get copies of the budget and treasurer's reports, but we have to trust the bookkeeper and treasurer that the reports are true and correct. Our esteemed assistant administrator, Suzanne, hired the book-keeper, who is new and inexperienced in the job. The Board treasurer takes what he's given without question, and our top administrator Harry Doyle, Suzanne's boss, is away on leave with his family for a month."

"I see where you're going with this," said Nancy, "but I don't believe Suzanne would try any funny stuff with the finances."

"It would be good to take a closer look," said Fitz.

"The books are audited every other year," said Nancy. "We're almost due for another audit."

"I'll talk to the bookkeeper tomorrow." Fitz rapped on the table as if to emphasize his resolve.

Nancy turned away from the computer with a nod. "This is a cooperative, owned by the residents. We have a right to look at the books."

***

The next day, Fitz returned from a visit with the Board president. "Over Suzanne's objections, the Board gave me access to the files," he said gleefully, "and permission as a resident to conduct a cursory examination of the bookkeeping procedures pre-audit. I played down what I plan to do, but I want to go through the files for the last two months."

"Congratulations," said Nancy.

"I don't want Suzanne to be nervous or anxious," Fitz said. "She has to give me access, but she insists that I cannot take them out of the office. She did give me a work table in the executive suite."

"Ask for a contact list for the vendors they use," Nancy suggested as she walked with him to the bookkeeper's office.

***

Two days later at dinner, Fitz folded his arms and said in a low voice, "Whisperwood has a big problem."

"Well, yeah," Louise snorted. "A man was murdered here."

"And I think I know why," said Fitz.

"Fitz has been studying Whisperwood's finances," said Nancy.

"That's right. I've been working on it for two days. I did a lot of tap dancing to assure the staff that all was well and that I was simply checking the procedures to pave the way for the auditors.

"What I found was embezzlement," Fitz continued. "Big time. I found falsified receipts and a fake office supply company charging big bills to Whisperwood for supplies never delivered."

"Didn't Suzanne catch that? Who's responsible?" asked George. "What about Harry, our esteemed administrator? He's her boss."

"He's on a well-earned vacation, remember?" said Nancy. "He took his wife and kids out west in a Winnebago for a month. He told me Suzanne is perfectly competent, but he or anyone on the board could call him on his cell phone if they needed help."

"Excuse me," said Louise, "but we all know Harry tends to be naïve. He didn't catch on to the shenanigans with the former owner and his assistant when we solved the mystery of the hidden staircase."

George nodded. "He tends to take people at face value, but he's a good administrator."

"Suzanne took advantage of Harry's absence. I think she's the culprit, and Bill was onto her." Fitz looked up as a server delivered water and rolls and took their orders. "The funny business I've found is recent."

Once the server left, Fitz sipped his water and continued. "That's why Bill had a file on Suzanne on his computer. I read through that file and found quite a few questionable actions on her part."

"Reason enough for her to get rid of Bill," said Nancy.

"There's still Tammy," said George. "And she is strong enough."

"I think it's down to Tammy, Mike Johnson, or Suzanne. Any ideas on how to zero in on the killer?" asked Fitz.

"Don and Megan are still in the picture, too," said Nancy.

They looked at each other as the dining room manager brought their wine and left.

"Could we set a trap?" asked Louise.

"I'd like to say," George began, "that I've rethought my position. Tammy is probably innocent. She could anticipate that Bill was on his last legs. If he left money for her in his will, she would no doubt be pleased, but that was only a rumor. If she inherited money from one of her patients, she'd stand to lose her job. The whole situation is too iffy for her to risk killing Bill, who didn't have long to live anyway." He cleared his throat. "What I'm saying is that Tammy could wait. We're looking for someone who had a more immediate need to get rid of Bill."

Nancy's mind flicked to the travel posters in Tammy's trailer, the glamour poses she affected when she thought no one was looking. Tammy had big dreams. How patient was she? Some residents lived for years after their anticipated death date, especially at a place like Whisperwood with all the health care services and social interactions they'd need.

"I don't want to rule Tammy out yet," said Louise, "but I still think Mike is a more likely suspect. He probably had finagled deals with the mining company and had a lot to gain from that quarry."

"As the assistant administrator, Suzanne was never considered the culprit by any of us until now," said Nancy. "I liked her very much, but I'm feeling betrayed. And she would have a lot to lose if the embezzlement was discovered. Whoever is responsible, Suzanne had oversight and should have caught the problem. I'm glad the audit is scheduled soon."

Fitz nodded. "If she hears that I've been going over the bookkeeping files, she may get worried. She knows about the audit, but that's several weeks away. She won't know for sure if I found anything."

"If she's innocent, she'll ask," said Nancy.

Fitz shrugged. "I haven't kept it a secret, but if the bookkeeper is guilty, she probably has the ego to think she was too clever for me."

"Suzanne and that bookkeeper think we're all over the hill, you know," said Louise. "Whenever I ask the bookkeeper a question about my bill, she patronizes me and acts as if I'm too gaga to understand. Probably hoping I'll kick the bucket and be out of her hair."

"If I talk to Suzanne about my suspicions, what is she likely to do?" asked Fitz.

"Skedaddle," said George.

"If Suzanne's not guilty," said Nancy, "she'll listen to you and launch an investigation to have the culprit arrested. If she is the culprit, she'll stonewall. And if she is guilty, this probably isn't the first place she's embezzled." Nancy paused to think. "I'll call the Residents Board of Directors tomorrow to get a copy of her references and call them."

"I'm sure they did that before they hired her," said George.

"They better have." Nancy shook her head. "But how thorough were they?"

Louise frowned. "Please remember a murderer is running around Whisperwood who has a lot to lose. It may not be Suzanne, but whoever it is probably has their eyes on us. We all need to be careful."

***

Sign Up Now for Investment Seminar

CPA and Investment Counselor Byron T. Vanderhoot, III, will lecture on "Protecting Your Investment" on Friday, August 26, at 2 p.m. in the Auditorium. Frauds, scams, and investment schemes are all likely to flaunt their glitter in front of the unwary investor. Learn how to tell the difference between a real opportunity and a fraud designed to leave you penniless. Sign up for this important lecture at the reception desk by Thursday at 5 p.m.

The Whisperwood Breeze,
Whisperwood Retirement Village Newsletter

Chapter 27

The next morning, Nancy called the president of the Residents' Board of Directors.

"Suzanne's resume?" he said impatiently as if he were busy. "Get it from Suzanne's assistant. It's on file in the office. Eleanor Baffin, Board secretary, called the references. Ask her any questions. I assure you, it was all aboveboard. Suzanne checked out."

Nancy hung up the phone. She knew Eleanor Baffin, an airhead if there ever was one. She tapped in Eleanor's number.

"Yes, I certainly did call Suzanne's references." She paused. "Two of them, anyway."

"What did they say?" Nancy asked.

"You know how those HR people are. Won't say anything they could get sued for." Eleanor sounded defensive. "They said she had worked for them, all right."

"Did they say why she left their company?"

"I think they said she moved on for better opportunities." Eleanor paused again.

"No red flags, then."

"She seemed perfectly all right," said Eleanor defensively.

"What's this all about?"

"Nothing. I wondered how it was done, that's all." Nancy hung up. Eleanor had maybe talked to two of the references but probably only one, got minimal information because most people were afraid of litigation these days. She and the Board decided they could hire Suzanne without further checking. Typical kind of thing Eleanor would do.

As nice a person as Suzanne seemed—and Nancy had liked her—her references were dubious, and her resume was not to be trusted. Nancy had worked on cases of serial killers who worked in hospitals and went from job to job because the current employer was glad to see a questionable employee move on, and the prospective employer conducted only a limited and careless check into the applicant's background.

Thinking of medical serial killers led Nancy to wonder about Tammy's background. She still had the fax she'd received from Tammy's last job, but it was noncommittal, only confirming that Tammy had worked there for seven months before she came to Whisperwood. She'd probably get the same type of information from other employers and schools.

She and Louise had visited Tammy's home, a trailer on a dead-end road. You couldn't blame her for hoping for help to something better, like a $100,000 bequest.

Unless she found stronger evidence against her, Nancy decided to accept the fact that Tammy performed well in her duties. George liked her and Louise said she was "all business," but others saw her as opportunistic. Bill had thought enough of her to designate $100,000 for her in his will. Whether Tammy was really his granddaughter was a moot question.

***

Announcement

Everyone Invited to the Board and Staff Tea

The Residents' Board of Directors at Whisperwood invites all residents to an informal tea reception to chat with the staff and board. The board will introduce new staff members and outline major new initiatives planned for the next year. Refreshments will be served. The reception will be in the dining room at 2:30 on Tuesday afternoon.

Board of Directors,
Whisperwood Retirement Village

Chapter 28

Nancy had walked the halls of Whisperwood as exercise for almost an hour. She felt thirsty. She glanced at her watch. Mid-afternoon. Way too early for dinner, but an iced tea would taste great. She wandered into the pub where she saw Don and Megan sipping margaritas and looking bored. "May I join you?" Nancy asked.

"Sure." Don motioned to the empty chair at their table.

Nancy glanced around the room. People were milling, drinking the pre-dinner cocktail, and chatting with the other residents, but the place didn't have the same lively atmosphere without Bill. "Your Dad used to be the life of the party here during cocktail hour," Nancy said.

"I'll bet," Megan's eyes flashed. "Dear old Dad couldn't live without a drink."

"Now, honey," Don began, reaching over to pat her arm. "Nothing wrong with a drink or two in the evening."

Megan shrugged off his hand. "Or three or four."

She's in quite a sour mood, thought Nancy. "Did you find the will?" They couldn't have because it reposed in Nancy's desk, but she wondered how they would answer the question.

Don shook his head while Megan took another sip of her drink. "We can't figure out where it is."

"Been through everything in his apartment," added Megan. "Have you figured out anywhere it could be? Bill said you and this Axel Wright would know."

Nancy shook her head. "You would inherit everything anyway, though, wouldn't you?" asked Nancy, using hand signals to the server for a margarita, pointing to Megan's.

"I suppose so," said Megan with a shrug. "Just a lot more hassles and fees."

"Were you here the night he died?" asked Nancy casually.

"Nah. We had a big do in Washington that night." Don fiddled with the drinking straw. "Charity fundraiser. We'd helped organize it, so we had to be there."

"Which charity?" asked Nancy. "I might like to contribute."

'They need all the bucks they can get," said Don.

"It's the National Fund Against Trafficking. NFAT for short." Megan pulled a card out of her purse. "Here's their contact information. They can use your contribution. It's tax deductible."

"Thank you." Nancy tucked the card into her pocket and stirred the pot. "I heard Bill left part of his estate to his home health aide."

Megan snorted. "What a bunch of baloney that is. Don't believe it for a minute, but if she thought he left her a pot of money, she'd have a good reason to kill him, wouldn't she?"

"That's where we place our bet," added Don. "We think she killed him."

"We couldn't watch him every hour of the day," Megan said. "That little tramp took advantage of a sick old man. She should have been fired immediately."

"He was killed late at night after most of the staff, including the home health aides, had gone home." As Nancy said this, she thought of Tammy's late night visits with Bill. He was killed on Saturday night. The aides didn't work on Saturdays, but somebody saw Tammy at Whisperwood on Saturday evening. Someone else said they saw Don and Megan. But Don said they were at a big charity fundraiser in D.C. that night. If their alibi checked out, then the witness was wrong. The witness who saw Tammy could be wrong also.

Don finished his drink. "We don't need his money," he said. "Bill was fine where he was, but he was losing his capacity to make sound decisions. We took over his accounts and got his power of attorney solely to protect him."

"We were worried about him, that's all," added Megan. "Now we're trying to clear things up and get my dad's things out of the apartment. We need to vacate the place as soon as possible. Whisperwood charges a hefty fee for every day we keep it. That's mounting up."

"Are the police through with it yet?" asked Nancy.

Don gloomily shook his head. "Who knows when that will be? Meanwhile, ka-ching."

"It's okay. It's my dad's money, after all," added Megan. "I would hate to see that greedy little aide get any of it. She knew how to twist my dad around her little finger all right."

"People around here seem to like her," Nancy said, stretching the truth to see their reaction.

Megan wrinkled her nose. "She's playing all the possibilities. A lot of people here have money."

Nancy glanced at her watch. Time to join her friends for dinner. She rose, "I wish you luck getting everything straightened out."

"Thanks," said Don. "Looks like we'll have to move forward without a will when we can."

"Don't forget my dad's memorial service is scheduled for ten a.m. tomorrow morning," Megan called after her.

"I'll be there." Nancy gave a thumb's up.

***

After dinner, as she and Fitz walked back to her apartment, she thought of the unlocked back door to Whisperwood, open twenty-four-seven for anyone to use. If the witnesses were right, what was Tammy doing at Whisperwood on that Saturday night?

For that matter, did Mike Johnson have an alibi? Before going to bed, Nancy checked her email and found a note from Emily:

Hi, Nancy,

Can you find out how Mike and the boys are? I'm sure they are all extremely angry at me, but I do worry about them. I received the email from you asking me what I know about the quarry project and telling me about how you're searching for Bill Myers' killer at Whisperwood. Terrible thing to happen.

When Mike bought the garage and set up his own business, I spent hours helping him with the bookkeeping and all the details that go into establishing a business. I had nothing to do with his campaign to become a county commissioner, but I didn't like some of the connections he was making. He sees himself as a high-rolling businessman and that's how he got involved in the quarry project. The sharks are manipulating an easy mark is my take on it.

Sounds like Mike didn't get along with Bill Myers, but I know on that particular Saturday night, Mike was driving the boys back from camp in Pennsylvania. As I remember the schedule, the boys would be picked up that Saturday afternoon, and they planned to spend the night outside Hancock, Maryland. Then they would drive the rest of the way home the next day, Sunday.

Check on that, Nancy. If they didn't change that schedule, Mike has a good alibi. I know he couldn't kill Bill Myers no matter how antagonistic their relationship.

By the way, thank you for the DNA kit. It has arrived, and I have followed the directions and sent it off. I can hardly wait for the results!

Love,

Emily

***

Mondays are 2 for 1 Nights

The Whisperwood Pub offers drinks 2 for 1 on Monday nights beginning next week. Plentiful hors d'oeuvres served, too. Meet your friends for a good time and pleasant conversation at Whisperwood's friendly Pub. Cheers!

The Whisperwood Breeze,
Whisperwood Retirement Village Newsletter

Chapter 29

Fitz was out somewhere, and the apartment felt too quiet. Nancy picked up the album and climbed the steps to the second floor. She knocked on Axel's door and listened as he dragged his walker forward step by step and finally opened the door.

"Nancy! I'm glad to see you." Axel beamed at his visitor. "Come on in." He turned his walker and led Nancy into his living room. "Have a seat. Want some coffee?"

"Is it made?" Every movement was such a struggle for Axel. "I can get it." She set the old album on the couch.

"Sure. In the kitchen." Axel crept to a chair and sat with a sigh of relief, pushing the walker to the side.

Nancy brought out two cups with cream and sugar and gave one to Axel. She took a sip and set the cup aside. "I brought back your album."

"Good. The DNA kit was more useful, though."

Nancy nodded. "Have you heard from anyone else?"

Axel grinned. "Two cousins are visiting me this weekend. They live in Washington."

"That's wonderful." Nancy picked up the album. "You and

your cousins can go through the album."

"That's what I thought." He stared down at his hands with a faint smile.

"Be sure to let me meet them." She worried about these long-lost relatives and what they might want from Axel.

"Of course."

Nancy smiled. "And I certainly hope you'll share what you learn with me," she said, handing him the album.

He couldn't hold onto it, and it slid to the floor. "I'm sorry." Nancy retrieved the album and set it on the coffee table between them.

"Not as strong as I think sometimes," Axel said apologetically. "Bad day."

"That's okay. The album wasn't damaged." Nancy finished her coffee and took her leave.

Back in her apartment, she called the National Fund Against Trafficking. The woman who answered the phone sounded brisk and efficient. "National Fund, Judith Sherer speaking."

Nancy gave her name. "I'm with the *Whisperwood Breeze* newspaper," she said, stretching the truth. "I met a couple visiting here yesterday who told me they were on your board. Don and Megan Thompson. Your organization sounds very worthwhile, and I'm sure Whisperwood's thousand residents would like to know more about it." She knew a nonprofit executive would quickly translate the numbers into possible donations.

"I know Don and Megan," Judith said.

"They mentioned a recent fundraising event your organization held on a Saturday night."

"Yes?" Judith said cautiously.

"They said it was in Washington, D.C." Pulling information out of this woman, Nancy thought, was hard work. She wasn't a talker.

"That's right. In our headquarters office."

"What was the date again?"

Judith supplied it, and it was on the night Bill was murdered.

"I don't know if they were there or not..." Nancy waited, hoping Judith would fill in. She sounded impatient and impatient people often gave out information just to keep things moving.

"They were there."

"I guess they had to be. They were on the program, weren't they?" Nancy made that up. People would see them, and they'd have to stay there if they were on the program. Otherwise, they could have faked attendance any number of ways.

Nancy's question opened the dam. "Of course, they were," Judith said, "That's the night they received the Volunteers of the Year Award. They've been outstanding contributors to NFAT's finances and programs this year. We are grateful they are involved."

That gave Don and Megan an alibi for Bill's murder. Driving from Washington would take five or more hours on dangerous mountain roads. Flying was possible but also hazardous at night in the mountains and highly improbable. The nearest small airstrip was miles away. They still could have driven to Whisperwood early that morning, done the deed, and left, but probably not unseen by some early risers. Why would they?

"Do you have a brochure you could send me about the organization? It sounds worthwhile, and I'd like to include that information in my article."

"I'll need your address." Judith became gracious. "Most of the information is also on our website."

"That's right. No need to send it. I'll just look it up on the web. Thank you very much."

Judith hung up first.

Nancy glanced down to see Malone staring at her ankle as if speculating on its taste. She distracted him with a pat and a treat. "Malone, I'm scratching three people off the suspect list. Axel Cooper and Don and Megan Thompson."

Malone licked his paws unconcernedly.

***

Build Your Muscles with Strength Training

Physical Trainer Mark Gillespie will begin a new series of strength-training classes on Monday at 10 a.m. in the Gym. Don't let those muscles turn to mush. Keep fit and ready to take part in the physical activities you used to enjoy. The cost is $50 for the eight-week series. Register at the reception desk in the lobby.

The Whisperwood Breeze,
Whisperwood Retirement Village Newsletter

Chapter 30

That evening, Nancy and Fitz came back from dinner and turned on the television. They surfed through Netflix and settled down to watch a mystery. Malone licked his paws as he curled up comfortably between them. Sometimes, he was quite lovable, Nancy thought.

Her mind was too wrapped up in the question of Bill's murder to follow the mystery. Finally, Fitz hit the pause button and looked at her. "What's going on, Nancy?" he asked.

He startled her out of her thoughts. "I didn't notice you had put the show on pause," she said, chagrined.

"What's on your mind?" Fitz repeated.

"I'm sorry." Nancy sighed. "I can't get my mind off the Bill Myers problem."

"What, in particular?" inquired Fitz.

She turned to face him. "I've found alibis for Don and Megan. Axel has no motive and isn't strong enough. Emily says Mike was in Pennsylvania, picking up his sons from camp."

Fitz whistled. "That's making good headway. What's the problem, Luv?"

"How do I check Mike's alibi?" asked Nancy.

"I guess you can't ask Mike or his sons," Fitz said. "Awkward."

"I've got to find out the name of the camp." She stroked Malone as she thought and was surprised to hear him purr, which he didn't do often. Maybe Malone was a regular kitty, after all.

"Easy. Ask Emily," said Fitz, smiling down at Malone.

"I didn't want to worry her, but she would know, of course." said Nancy. She walked to the laptop on the dining room table.

"Glad you've found a job and a nice place to live," she wrote in an email to Emily. "Good work! You are a superstar go-getter. Now I have a question for you. What camp do the boys go to in Pennsylvania? I'd like to rule Mike out on the Bill Myers' investigation and thought I could do that by checking to make sure he did pick the boys up on that Saturday. Of course, he did, but I better check on it. You'll feel better, and so will I."

She read the message to Fitz. "I don't want to alarm her."

Fitz nodded. "Or damage the bridge with Emily. You're her support system right now, Luv."

"I know." She reread the message. "It's the softest I can make it. She's smart. She'll read between the lines, but she'll understand what I need to find out."

"Probably. The message looks all right to me." It was the best Fitz could offer.

Nancy pressed "Send."

The first thing Nancy did the next morning was to check her emails. She crossed her fingers when she saw a response from Emily.

I got your email, and I understand what you're trying to do. If he didn't pick up the kids on Saturday, I'd like to know why. I don't think he was murdering Bill Myers. The camp is Camp Old Hickory, not named after the former president but the old oak-hickory forest around it. That's what I'm told anyway. It's outside the small town of Bear Lake in northwestern Pennsylvania and here's a phone number: 717-555-2737. Please let me know what you find out.

By the way, Jason got a case! From the way he acted, I think it was his first.

Love,

Emily

.

Nancy checked her watch. It was too early to call the camp. She fed the cat, changed his litter box, and sat down to eat her regular breakfast of cereal and tea. Fitz wandered into the kitchen, yawning, at eight-thirty. "Heard from Emily?" he asked.

Nancy nodded. "I got the camp name. Emily knows what it's about, and she wasn't upset."

"Good." Fitz yawned again as he rummaged in the refrigerator. He pulled out a bagel and some butter and jam.

Nancy finished her breakfast and left for a brisk walk. When she returned, it was after nine o'clock, and Nancy called the camp.

She introduced herself as Mrs. Johnson, gambling on no one at the camp recognizing Emily's voice. "May I speak to the person in charge?"

A moment later, a woman came on the line. "Madelyn Ryback, Head Counselor. How can I help you?"

"I'm Ms. Johnson. My husband Mike picked up our sons from the camp a couple of weeks ago."

"Oh yes, I remember that. He was a little late on Saturday afternoon. A lot of traffic, he said. We expect the kids to be picked up in the morning."

"I'm sorry about that. I've been looking over their things, and they seem to be missing several shorts and T-shirts they brought with them to camp."

"Really? They're supposed to have their names on every piece of clothing they bring. Easy to get their stuff mixed up with the other kids' things."

"I guess there's no way to reclaim them if some other kid took them by mistake."

"They might send them to you when they realize the mistake. I've been through all the cabins and tents. Everything was cleaned for the next camp session, so I don't think we have them here."

"You said my husband was late picking them up? I've been out of town and wasn't here to check on things. He did pick them up on that Saturday, didn't he?"

"That's right. They told me they were driving down to Hancock, Maryland, for the night. That's a long drive on winding back roads. I remember thinking they'd be really tired when they got there. Good thing they didn't try to go straight through to home."

"Thank you for your assistance," Nancy said. "I'll have to hope someone finds their clothes and sends them to us."

"Sorry I couldn't be more help."

Nancy hung up the landline phone. Mike had an alibi. Nan-

cy relayed the news to Emily and Fitz. Emily's reply came
quickly.

> I'm relieved. He was late picking up the boys, natu-
> rally, but he has an alibi. They seem to be managing
> themselves all right then. That's good, because I am,
> too.

Fitz merely nodded and said, "Another one to cross off the
list."

"We need to go to the chapel for Bill's memorial service. It
starts in ten minutes."

Fitz took her arm. "Off we go."

When they arrived, the Whisperwood chapel was already
crowded, but Fitz and Nancy found seats in the back row. Bill
was an avowed atheist, and when he was working in Baltimore,
often attended services of the historic Unitarian-Universalist
Church there.

According to the program, the minister had known Bill for
many years and was a good friend. He'd traveled to Whisperwood to conduct Bill's service.

Despite the rigid layout of pews, the service felt informal
and friendly, beginning with the minister's reminiscences in-
terspersed with biographical anecdotes. Then everyone was
invited to share their memories of Bill. The many stories were
told with humor and poignancy. Nancy came away realizing
Bill had touched many lives in positive ways, which angered
her even more that someone had killed him.

"I listened to all the memories," she said to Fitz as they
walked back to their apartment hand in hand, "but I didn't get

any new insights into his murderer. Did you?"

Fitz shook his head. "Afraid not. I'm off to talk with the bookkeeper this afternoon. The books are being fiddled with, that's for sure. I need to find out more about how that's happening and who's responsible. I would guess the embezzler and the murderer are one and the same."

***

Mystery Weekend Trip Planned

Sign up now for the Mystery Weekend at the Alderman Resort near Carlisle, Pa. The weekend begins Friday night, Sept. 9, with a cocktail reception followed by a five-course dinner featuring fine Pennsylvania wines. It concludes at a Sunday Brunch with the surprise ending and prizes given to the best detectives among the guests. Don't miss this exciting weekend, Sept 9-11. The cost is $495 including all meals and luxury accommodations in this renowned resort. Register now to make sure you get a place. Sign up at the lobby reception desk.

The Whisperwood Breeze,

Whisperwood Retirement Village Newsletter

Chapter 31

Fitz was gone all afternoon. Nancy didn't worry about him until she arrived at the dining room for dinner, and he still hadn't shown up. She joined Louise and George at their customary table. He wasn't there, either.

"Where's Fitz?" asked Louise.

"Not like him to be late for dinner," added George, pursing his lips. "I never am."

Louise snorted.

"I don't know where he could be,' Nancy said, glancing at her watch. "Excuse me a moment. I'll be right back." Maybe Fitz was caught up in the bookkeeping records and had lost track of time. She took out her cell phone and called him. Her message went to voice mail. She walked down the hall to the executive offices. The rooms were locked and dark. Even the office assistant had gone home. Ashley was still on the job and was watching Nancy.

"Who are you looking for?" she asked.

Nancy walked to the reception counter. "Have you seen Fitz Connelly?"

"I saw him go into the executive office before lunch." She

shrugged.

"What about Suzanne?"

"She left early today. Doctor's appointment. Mr. Connelly went out with her." Ashley looked at Nancy. "Anything wrong?"

Fitz went out with Suzanne. "Did Mr. Connelly come back?" Nancy asked, knowing the answer. She felt sick.

"Didn't see him," Ashley said. "He could have come in some other entrance."

Nancy bit her lip, thinking. Why would Fitz go home with her? What if she were a criminal embezzler? Or a murderer? A chill ran through Nancy's body. She had to find Fitz.

She looked at Ashley. "Do you know where Suzanne lives?"

Ashley shook her head and shrugged. "They don't give me that kind of information."

Nancy walked slowly back to the dining room. Fitz had never gone missing before. He was a thoughtful man. He'd call if he could. Why did he go somewhere with Suzanne? Why hadn't he come back? What if Suzanne were the killer?

George and Louise looked up expectantly as she returned to their table. She shook her head.

"He'll show up. Probably forgot about the time," said George, reaching for his water glass. "Anyway, it's just a little after five."

Louise agreed. "Give him till after dinner. If he hasn't shown up by then, we'll organize a search."

Neither one seemed worried, Nancy thought, but she couldn't manage a smile. Louise and George might be right, but he had never disappeared like this before. Nancy went through the motions of ordering dinner and picking at her food, waiting for this interminable meal to be over, imagining the worst, and considering how to find him. Jumbled thoughts filled her mind.

Something had happened to Fitz. She knew it. Suzanne had gone home early. Unusual for her. Fitz had been in the executive offices, going over the books. Suzanne knew what he was doing. If she were guilty of embezzlement and thought Fitz was onto her, what would she do?

The answer became glaringly obvious. She'd get him away from Whisperwood on some pretext, and then she'd get rid of him. Nancy shook herself. *My imagination is running away with itself.* Fitz probably went out to check some files Suzanne kept at home and forgot the time. He was probably eating dinner at a restaurant in town. He had to be all right. But what if he wasn't? Why hadn't he called?

They finished dinner quickly and turned down dessert. Louise and George hurried with Nancy back to her apartment.

"It's not like him to go somewhere," said Nancy, her stomach doing flip flops, "without letting me know."

"Yeah, he's pretty reliable," said Louise. "What can we do?"

Nancy checked her answering machine. No message. No text on her cell phone, either. She opened her laptop. No email from him.

"Wait a minute. I've got Susanne's resume in my files," Nancy flipped through the files in her desk drawer and pulled out a manila folder.

"Why would you have her resume?" asked Louise. "They don't hand them out like peanuts."

"Curiosity," said Nancy. "I'll try her phone." She tapped in the number and waited. "No response," she said finally.

"Wasn't he looking over the Whisperwood accounts?" asked George. "Where'd he do that?"

"In the executive offices," said Nancy. "Suzanne must have known what he was doing."

George turned around at Nancy's door. "Let's go down there and find out what's happening."

"Nobody's there." Nancy looked at him bleakly. "Ashley said he went out with Suzanne. A security guard must be on duty now in the lobby."

"All right." Louise nodded at the note in Nancy's hand. "You've got her address. Let's go see."

"I'm worried," Nancy said as she wrote a note to Fitz in case he returned before they got back. "I hope he's okay."

On their way out, they stopped to talk to the security guard who had replaced Ashley at the reception counter. "I came on at six," he said. "The executive staff was gone by then." He glanced from one to the other. "Anything wrong?"

Nancy made up her mind. "We don't know," she said. "My friend Fitz Connelly hasn't returned from town. The three of us are going for a little drive to look for him. We'll be back soon."

"Fitz Connelly, you said?" The guard made a note. "If he comes in, I'll tell him you're looking for him."

"Thank you." Nancy herded George and Louise through the front door. She walked swiftly to her car with the other two hobbling along behind her.

Suzanne lived a mile down the mountain on a side road. Her house was set back in the woods and closely surrounded by overgrown rhododendrons. It was made of redwood and had only one floor. A large, screened-in porch led to the front door. No welcoming lights shone in the windows, and her car was gone.

"Spooky place," George observed.

"She's not here," said Nancy in disappointment, gazing at the dark house. "Could they have gone out somewhere? Maybe to dinner?" Even though she was quivering in fear, a brief pang of jealousy surfaced, but she quelled it. *Really. At my age.*

"Get your flashlight, Nancy," said Louise. "Let's check this out."

"I'll stay here," George said, "so I can hire you gals a good lawyer."

"You do that," said Louise. She and Nancy stepped up to the porch. The screened door wasn't locked.

Nancy walked to the front door, knocked, and put her ear to the door to listen. After a moment, she said, "I don't hear anything moving inside." She peered through the window beside the door. "I don't see anyone. I'll go around the house." She pushed through the dense shrubbery surrounding the house to shine her flashlight through window after window. Louise followed closely behind. At the kitchen window, Nancy drew a deep breath as the flashlight shone on a figure slumped at the kitchen table. She recognized the blue shirt. It had to be Fitz.

"Here he is," she whispered to Louise.

He sat with his head on the kitchen table and his back to her. Nancy rapped on the window. No response. On the table were a teapot and two cups.

Something was wrong with Fitz. Was he asleep or...? Nancy couldn't bring herself to finish that thought. She looked again and thought she could see him breathing. He seemed to be asleep, but at the kitchen table?

Probably drugged, Nancy thought, but he was alive. She stepped to the kitchen door and tried it. "It's open."

"Wait," whispered Louise, holding Nancy back. "It might be a trap."

Nancy pushed off Louise's hand. "Fitz is hurt.' She rushed in. "Fitz, Fitz! Wake up." She shook his shoulder. His eyes fluttered.

Louise wet a dish towel and patted his forehead with it.

Fitz groaned. "Nancy," he moaned.

"I'm here," she said, her voice weak with relief. "I think you've been drugged, but you're okay."

He closed his eyes again. "Give me a few minutes."

Nancy glanced around the kitchen and saw a jar of instant coffee on the counter. "Louise, you make some coffee. Strong. I'll try to get Fitz up and walking." She found a knife in a kitchen drawer and cut the ropes that bound him to the chair. She tried to lift him, but Fitz was too heavy for Nancy to handle alone.

Louise put a cup of water in the microwave and then joined Nancy in getting Fitz out of the chair. Together they pulled Fitz onto his feet and helped him stay upright as he stumbled around the kitchen. Louise made the instant coffee and brought it to his lips as he walked. She refilled the cup and together, Louise and Nancy helped Fitz through the kitchen door and down the steps. Then they propelled him to the car.

"You found him," George said in surprise as Nancy and

Louise opened the back door and pushed Fitz onto the seat.

"To the hospital," Nancy said as they belted up. She drove them down the mountain into town and up to the emergency room at the hospital.

Dwayne, the sheriff's detective, arrived as Fitz was taken to his room, but none of Fitz's rescuers were allowed to enter. A nurse blocked the door. "Only relatives allowed," she said.

Nancy paced the hall outside the room, while Dwayne, Louise and George sat on a bench watching her. She managed a wobbly smile at Dwayne. "The baby okay?"

He smiled back. "Right as rain."

As Fitz gradually came out from under the influence of the drug, he called out for Nancy. She came to the doorway.

"Are you Nancy?" asked the nurse.

She nodded.

"Okay. He wants you to come in." The nurse left, and the detective followed Nancy in to stand by the bedside. Louise and George stayed at the door.

"You're okay," Nancy assured Fitz. "Suzanne gave you chloral hydrate, the well-known knockout drug. I'll stay here with you, but Louise and George will be going back to Whisperwood. Detective Yost is here now, too. Can you tell us what happened?"

"I'm still a bit fuzzy," Fitz said drowsily, "and I feel sick. I was talking to Suzanne in her office about my findings…and she said she had receipts and other documents at home…that would clarify the issues…I was finding with the books." Fitz stopped. Nancy held a glass of water to his lips. He took a few sips and continued. "She suggested we go out to her place…

and read through them. Naturally, I took my findings with me…
so we could discuss them." He grimaced and took another sip.
"She drove… the idea was we'd go over her accounts and then
return to Whisperwood."

He looked from Nancy to Louise and George and tried
shaking his head but shut his eyes and groaned. "I have a terrible headache, and I deserve it. I was a dope," Fitz said, chagrined. "She led me like a donkey. And she was one of our
suspects as the killer. How dumb can you get?" He shook his
head and groaned.

Louise interrupted. "Suzanne duped all of us at Whisperwood behind that charming Southern manner. Bill's files should
have tipped us off. You found out she's an embezzler. A career
embezzler. We're not her first victims, I'll bet."

Fitz became agitated and tried to sit up. Nancy pushed him
gently back. "She fooled all of us, me, too," Nancy said. "But
I don't think she's a killer. She could easily have gotten rid of
you if she was, and she wouldn't leave you in her house, but
she knew we had found out about her embezzlement. She was
buying time to get out of town and disappear."

"I suppose so, and I played into her little scheme." Fitz held
Nancy's hand. "At first she tried to snow me with bookkeeping
and financial jargon and doubletalk. When I didn't bite, that's
when she suggested we go over everything at her home."

"How long do you think you were out?" asked Louise.

'We got to her place around two, I think." Fitz closed his
eyes. "Not sure. She made tea … and that's all I remember."

"She's got at least five hours head start," put in George.

"She's long gone," Nancy agreed.

"She would be," Fitz said. "Did you find any papers there? Spread sheets?"

Nancy shook her head.

"She took all the evidence, too." He closed his eyes and slept.

Dwayne had quietly stood by and listened. "All right. Thank you. We'll put out an APB for her." He left immediately to obtain the personnel file and a photo of Suzanne and then to organize a search for her.

Before he left, Nancy asked him if Suzanne had an alibi for Bill's murder. He didn't respond.

Suzanne was an embezzler. Had Bill found out? If she killed Bill, why didn't she kill Fitz?" Fitz had imcriminating evidence against her and had been led like a lamb to slaughter away from Whisperwood. Rather than kill him, she chose to disappear, which confirmed Nancy's guess that Suzanne was not a murderer.

***

Keep Your Home Records Organized and Safe

Attorney David Orkney, new Whisperwood resident, offers his expertise on home record-keeping in a seminar on Wednesday, August 24, at 10 a.m. in Classroom A, Lower Level. What records should you keep? How do you keep them safe? What information must you have on hand for your family? These questions and more will be answered at the seminar. Please register by Tuesday, August 23.

The Whisperwood Breeze,
Whisperwood Retirement Village Newsletter

Chapter 32

Fitz came home the next day eager to talk to the Whisper-wood Board of Directors. Nancy and Louise joined Fitz in the meeting. It took over two hours and began with Fitz's report on his findings. Then the meeting descended into blame-pointing, denials, and fault-finding.

Tired of the circular nature of the discussion with no resolution, Nancy suggested that the Board immediately set up a meeting with the Human Resources and the Finance staff and plan how to cope with the disaster to minimize the damage, and then to set up preventive safeguards.

She left Fitz and Louise to sit through the rest of the meeting. On the way back to her apartment, she pondered the immediate question bothering her: Despite her strong belief that Suzanne was not the murderer, she couldn't overlook the fact that Suzanne had motive enough to kill Bill. Did she have the opportunity? She had told Nancy she was out of town that weekend. Was she? How could Nancy find out? .

Bill had been smothered in his bed late at night. That meant premeditation. If Bill had confronted Suzanne about the embezzlement, he would also have contacted the board and the police at the same time. He would not have given Suzanne the time to kill him. He'd hinted at the malfeasance to Nancy, but he was still collecting data. Nancy decided he had not talked to Suzanne, and she was not alerted to his investigation. If all that was true, Suzanne had no reason to kill Bill.

Nancy took a detour and stopped by the executive offices. She pushed her way past the office assistant and into Suzanne's office. Suzanne's appointment calendar was spread open on the desk. Nancy shuffled through the pages to find the date of Bill's death. The Saturday and Sunday pages for that weekend were blank.

Dwayne must have asked possible suspects for their alibis. Did Suzanne qualify as a suspect? Did she have an alibi? Suzanne might not have noted weekend social engagements on her business calendar.

She walked out of Suzanne's office and found the office assistant. "Was Suzanne in town the weekend of Bill's murder?" she asked.

"She doesn't tell me what she does on her time off," the assistant said with a smug grin. She didn't want to help.

"Okay," Nancy said. "Doesn't matter."

Suzanne hadn't killed Fitz, hidden his body somewhere and disclaimed all knowledge of his whereabouts. Instead, she had chosen to drug Fitz to give her enough time to leave town and disappear. If Bill had hinted to her that he had discovered her embezzlement, she could have set the fire in his apartment to destroy the evidence.

She crossed the lobby and saw Tammy heading her way as if she were lying in wait for Nancy to appear.

"Ms. Dickenson, I just heard the news," said Tammy, walking along beside her. "Ms. Craddock must be the killer. She stole money here, then Mr. Myers, he found out about it. They can't think I hurt Mr. Myers now, can they?"

Nancy felt uncomfortable. Tammy wanted her to agree with this assessment, which must be a relief for Tammy. If only she wouldn't bring up the subject of the will.

"Has anyone found his will yet?" Tammy asked, offhandedly, pretending she didn't care.

"They're still looking for it," said Nancy. She unlocked her apartment door and stepped inside. "Nice chatting with you."

Tammy stepped back. "You will let me know, won't you? I will still worry."

"I'm sure you'll be fine." Nancy closed the door and leaned against it. Tammy could get to be a pest. This wasn't the first or even the second time Tammy had waylaid Nancy in the halls.

Nancy glanced at her desk. On top, Malone lounged, licking his paws. Inside the top drawer was the sought-after will. She couldn't keep it much longer. Dwayne didn't seem any closer to solving the murder, but he could easily assume Suzanne's criminal activities would make her a suspect, too.

Fitz came in not long after, shaking his head. "How that board gets anything done is beyond me." He gave Nancy a hug and a kiss. "I should have left with you, Luv."

"I've got to turn over the will we found," Nancy said.

Fitz nodded. "The longer you keep it, the harder it'll be to explain."

"Tomorrow," Nancy said.

Dinner entrees that night were baked cod, teriyaki steak,

and cobb salad. The 90s Club sat around their favorite table fifty-six and again debated the question of who killed Bill.

Louise twirled the end of her long braid as she argued that Mike Johnson needed to be in jail for something even if he had an alibi for the murder.

Resplendent in a pastel blue suit, George wanted to throw the book at Suzanne.

Fitz was noncommittal but remorseful. "Suzanne's probably changed her hair color and bought contact lenses to change her eye color."

George shook his head. "Doesn't matter. Cops don't look at that. They look at the ears."

"Eye and ear placement on the head," added Louise, breaking a roll in two. "Too difficult if not impossible to change those."

This is getting us nowhere, Nancy thought, looking at them all while sipping her cabernet sauvignon. "Excuse me a moment," she said, "I'm going to get a notepad, so we can put down the pros and cons."

"We'll be here," said Louise with a wave.

Nancy hurried down the hall to her apartment. She found the door unlocked and standing open. Sometimes she did forget to lock the door. This wasn't much of a problem at Whisperwood with its remote location and security guards, but she always, always closed the door to make sure Malone didn't get out. Could Fitz have been careless? She'd have to talk with him, but right now she was in a hurry.

She rushed in and was shocked to find Tammy, herself surprised in reading a paper at Nancy's desk. She saw Nancy but wasn't embarrassed, ashamed, or apologetic. She glared at Nancy. "I found it," Tammy said accusingly. "You had it all along."

"You broke into my apartment," Nancy said, stating the obvious. Malone stalked out of the bedroom and jumped up on the couch. He eyed Tammy with a calculating gleam in his eyes.

"So what? You stole the will," said Tammy. She hadn't noticed Malone.

"I was protecting you." After the initial surprise, Nancy was regaining her wits.

"Sure you were," Tammy sniffed. "Protecting me from getting my money."

"And from being accused of Bill's murder. I had nothing to gain from that will." Nancy added.

Tammy stared at Nancy, obviously putting two and two together. "I played the old fool like a violin, but I made him happy. He owed me that money."

"So what happened? Did you lose your patience?" asked Nancy, edging backward toward the door.

"I knew he'd written a will, and I knew what was in it," said Tammy. "Then the old man went and hid it."

"A bunch of us found it," Nancy countered. "We decided to hide it for a while to protect you."

"Ha!" Tammy sneered. "You're just another one trying to make sure I can't get the money. You and his nasty daughter."

"That's not true." Nancy ran her eyes over Tammy's sweatshirt and jeans. Did Tammy have a weapon? She carried a large tote bag. *That's where a weapon would be.*

"It's my money. I didn't count on a nosey parker like you actually finding the will and then hiding it." Tammy slipped the will into the bag. She withdrew her hand slowly, and this time it held a tiny revolver. "It's small, but it works," she said.

Chapter 33

Nancy stared at the gun in Tammy's hand while her mind whipped through ways to handle the situation. Threatening with a gun didn't necessarily mean she was the murderer, although it seemed more and more likely.

"I was wrong to keep the will, but Bill listed you as a beneficiary of $100,000. That gives you a strong motive and makes you a prime suspect."

"And you thought you'd protect me by making sure his daughter got all the money," Tammy said in a voice dripping with sarcasm. "Do you think I'm dumb enough to believe you gave me a thought?" She raised the gun and pointed it directly at Nancy's head. "No one else has ever tried to help me. Why should you? Anyway, the cops don't have a shred of evidence against me."

"Do you have an alibi for the night Bill was killed?" Keep her talking, Nancy thought, but she had wondered about an alibi.

"I signed out at five p.m. and everyone in the office saw me leave. After five and on weekends you can only come in the entrances that have either a receptionist or a guard on duty. Then you have to sign the visitors' book. No way could I have come back in without someone seeing me." Tammy put her hand on her hip with a swagger. "But no one did, did they?"

"You came in the back way. The staff keeps that door open, so they can duck out for a cigarette."

Tammy's eyes narrowed. "You know about that?"

"Of course we do."

"In that case, we're going for a ride. I'll have to rethink my plan. And put the will back someplace where it will be found this time."

"So you murdered Bill," Nancy said, intent on nailing that fact down. She saw Malone creeping towards Tammy while Tammy kept her eyes on Nancy.

"He was about dead anyway. Time for him to go bye-bye." Tammy gestured for Nancy to turn around and head out the door. "Now we're going for a little drive. No reason why Suzanne can't get the credit."

Playing for time, Nancy asked the question that had bothered her. "Was Bill really your grandfather?"

"What do you think? I had to have some reason to keep people looking for the will and that damned daughter from destroying it." She waved the gun. "Get moving. Now!"

Then Malone sprang for Tammy's shoulder. It was possibly his idea of play or perhaps prey, but his claws dug into her back and shoulders.

"Ow! Ow! Get this thing offa me!" Tammy screamed, dropping the gun as she attempted to push Malone off her shoulder. This caused Malone to get serious. He bit her on the cheek.

Nancy ran forward and grabbed the gun. Then she pushed

the emergency button for the security guard as Malone dug his claws in deeper, relishing the fight. Tammy screamed in fear and pain. In a few minutes, two guards showed up.

Nancy gestured to Tammy, still wrestling with Malone who was enjoying the game. "She killed Bill Myers," Nancy said. "I'll call the sheriff's office." She handed over the gun and then stepped over to Tammy to pry Malone off the screaming woman.

Nancy shut Malone into the bedroom, while the guards handcuffed Tammy and took her, crying and cursing, down the hall to meet the sheriff's car on its way up the mountain.

Then Nancy released Malone and gave him a bowl of people-grade tuna fish as a thank you for saving her life.

"Now I need a drink," she muttered to herself as she returned, without a notebook, to the dining room.

***

Shooting Wildlife With Cameras

The classroom showcases on the Lower Level proudly present an exhibit of wildlife photos taken by residents in the Wildlife Photography class offered by retired photographer William Boyd. Enjoy the exhibit and see Whisperwood in a different way. The exhibit begins September 1 and runs through October 31.

The Whisperwood Breeze,
Whisperwood Retirement Village Newsletter

Chapter 34

Before entering the dining room, Nancy stopped at the Pub bar and ordered a Manhattan cocktail for herself. She took a sip of the Manhattan as soon as she received it, then carried it with her back to the 90s Club table in the dining room. On the way, she asked the dining room manager to deliver a bottle of champagne to their table.

She arrived, slightly fortified by the Manhattan, and took her place.

"Where's the notebook?" asked Louise. "We've been brainstorming motives and opportunities here."

"How come it took you so long?" asked George, waving his fork in the air.

Drink in hand, Nancy sat back and viewed all of them with a beneficent smile.

"Okay, Nancy," said Fitz. "What's up?"

"Yeah, Nancy, what happened?" Louise echoed.

"Don't tell me you've solved the murder," added George as he adjusted the napkin on his lap.

"Yes," said Nancy, "I have."

"What?" the other three shouted.

"Pipe down," said Nancy. She sipped again at her drink, feeling a mellow alcoholic glow. "Whisperwood, all of us, and especially me, owe Malone a huge fish dinner. It's because of him that I'm back with you now, and Tammy is on her way to jail."

"Tammy? Really?" said Fitz.

Nancy nodded with a smile. "Tammy, really. She broke into my apartment and found the will."

George whistled. "No kidding. Then what happened?"

"She pulled a gun on me, but Malone attacked her and saved my life. I called the guards and talked to Detective Yost—that's why it took me a while to get back here." She raised her glass. "And that's why I decided I needed a strong drink."

"I guess that's right," said Louise. "I'm flabbergasted."

"Me, too," said George.

"And," said Nancy, "I've ordered a bottle of champagne to toast Malone and the 90s Club for another case successfully concluded."

***

Charleston Post-Gazette Employment Ad
Home Health Aide is needed at this respected, luxury retirement village. Applicants must be certified graduates of an accredited training program. Hours: M-F, 9 a.m. – 5 p.m. Full package of benefits. Contact Whisperwood Human Resources, 304-555-9939.

Chapter 35

After dinner, Nancy and Fitz walked hand in hand back to Nancy's apartment. Both of them were silent and thoughtful, but they greeted Malone with affection and gave him an extra treat. Then they straightened up the mess left after Tammy's arrest and sat side by side on the couch.

"I've been thinking…" Nancy said.

"Me, too." Fitz glanced at her. She felt his hand tremble.

"When we were at the hospital," said Nancy, "they wouldn't let me into your room."

"Why was that?" Fitz asked. "I was out of it, I'm afraid."

"I wasn't related to you." Nancy looked at his kindly dark face. She'd known Fitz since college days. They'd always been friends, even when they didn't see each other for years. She thought of how pleased she'd been to meet him for the first time after many years in the elevator at Whisperwood. He had moved to the village because he knew she lived there. She hadn't known how much she cared for him until he went missing. She never wanted to relive those moments when she saw him in Suzanne's kitchen and thought he was dead.

"When I woke up in that hospital room, the only one I

wanted to see was you," Fitz said, squeezing her hand.

"I don't want anyone to keep me away from you," Nancy whispered, "especially a hospital nurse."

"Only one thing to do, then," Fitz said.

"What's that?" She knew the answer and looked at Fitz to see her joy mirrored in his eyes.

"We've got to get married, Luv," Fitz whispered in her ear, "Then you'll be my next of kin."

***

"I haven't wasted any time," Axel gloated as he confronted Nancy at her table in the lobby. "The latest person I've heard from lives in Maryland."

"Wonderful," said Nancy, pleased that he was following up on the DNA results but concerned about what he might find. "Are you going to visit him?"

"Better than that," Axel grinned. "We're planning a concert here. He plays the violin, too. He's coming down next weekend to stay with me, so we can rehearse."

Axel knew nothing about this man coming to visit. Should she worry about him? She kept her thoughts to herself and worked at being supportive. "You can show him your album," said Nancy. "He might recognize something about the people in it."

"Sure," Axel grinned. "First thing on the agenda."

"Let me know when he arrives. I'd like to meet him." And let the visitor know Axel wasn't alone.

"Don't worry. I'm not expecting much." Axel shrugged. "He knows about the family. The war broke up his clan—and mine, too, I guess." He held up his hands and shrugged. "Who knows? But from what I learn about the Roma life, I am glad I went to England." He laughed. "All I've got left as a Gypsy is my violin." He mimed playing the violin. "A Gypsy violin."

Nancy smiled at his enthusiasm. "So I guess your concert will be all Gypsy music. At least I hope so."

"It will be magnificent," assured Axel. He took Nancy's hand and kissed it. "I have you to thank for giving me a family."

Nancy watched him practically dance with his walker as he made his way down the hall to the elevators.

***

The morning after Tammy's arrest, Louise and George joined Nancy and Fitz for coffee and donuts in Nancy's apartment. Malone sat on the couch next to Nancy, preening himself under everyone's grateful attention. It hadn't changed his disposition much, but he seemed happy and hadn't bitten or clawed anyone since the Tammy incident.

"What do you suppose Bill Myers meant when he said his stash was in an old clock?" asked Louise, flicking her braid.

Nancy grinned. "I figured out what clock he means," she said. "He was a sneaky old guy, wasn't he? But first, let's decide what we're going to do about his will."

"I have a suggestion." Louise sat back with folded arms. "Tammy claimed to have no interest in the money. She says she wanted only to clear her reputation to keep from losing her job. We can speculate on her real agenda, but let's take her at her word."

"Tammy's out of it," said George, holding Louise's hand. The red-flowered Hawaiian shirt and red slacks he wore blinded the eye. "She has confessed to murdering Bill. That means she can't inherit no matter what the will says. Anyway, she's blabbed about how she found the will in your apartment, Nancy. You don't have any place to hide now."

"I know and I've thought about that. I'll have to say I found it yesterday in some old magazines I'd borrowed from Bill," said Nancy.

Louise snorted. "They'll be so grateful they won't think to ask questions."

Fitz nodded. "Anyway, Nancy had no reason to keep the will. We know she was trying to protect Tammy from being an easy victim for targeting by the police. They would probably consider that an obstruction of justice, so we need to follow Nancy's suggestion.

Nancy placed the stack of Bill's magazines next to the door. "I think Tammy was playing me for a patsy all the time. That bit about Bill being her grandfather was all made up."

"I guess you fooled her," Fitz said with a wink.

"I saw Don and Megan in the lobby a few minutes ago," George said.

Nancy took the will out of her desk and picked up the magazines. "Let's find them. I want to get all this out of my mind."

"We'll back you up," said Fitz. "If they start any trouble about your having the will, they'll have to fight the four of us."

Louise nodded. "I'm ready for a walk. First the will, then Nancy can lead us to Bill's real treasure, the one he hid in a clock."

They easily located Don and Megan talking with the office assistant. Dwayne had assembled the other staff at the conference table in the suite. From the shocked looks on their faces, the staff was learning about Suzanne's misdeeds for the first time. Nancy interrupted Don and Megan's conversation to hand Megan the will. "I found it in a magazine I'd borrowed from Bill. I know you've been hunting for it."

Megan was too stunned to speak. Don absentmindedly took the pile of magazines from Nancy as he tried to peer over Megan's shoulder. "Aha," he said. His tone was gleeful. "Bill did leave $100,000 for that…that woman in his will." He grinned at Nancy. "Fat chance she'll get a penny since she's been arrested for his murder."

Megan looked up. "Thank you, Nancy, and your kitty Malone. I've been hearing how he caught the killer."

Nancy smiled. "He is very protective of me." She still shivered at the thought of Tammy and the gun. Maybe she'd feed Malone salmon tonight. He loved salmon.

"She was after the will," Louise put in. "She thought Nancy was hiding it."

This was too close to the truth. Time to move on. "I'm glad I found the will for you," said Nancy. "Now we have some errands to run. Perhaps we'll see you later."

"Probably not," said Megan. "We're closing up his place today and going home. We'll be back for the trial, I guess."

"Glad to be out of here," Don muttered under his breath.

Louise was already moving down the hall, pulling George along with her. "Let's go find the clock, now," she said.

Nancy waved good-bye to Don and Megan and caught up with Louise.

"Follow me." Nancy led them through the labyrinthine halls of Whisperwood, then down an elevator to a lower-level classroom used for occasional staff meetings. "I found this place in walking the halls for exercise," she said. They filed through the door.

In the shadows at the back corner stood an ancient, tall grandfather clock. It did not tick, and the pendulum didn't swing. It stood there, frozen in time and forgotten.

"There's a metaphor for you," said George. "I'll bet Bill felt like that clock."

They gathered around it. The bottom compartment was locked, no key.

"I'm sure the key is behind the clock," said Nancy, running her hand up and down the back of the clock. "Yes, here it is. Taped." She brought out a tiny brass key and fitted it into the lock.

She turned the key and opened the door. Inside glittered Bill Myers' real treasure.

Two bottles of Jim Beam whiskey, one bottle of Smirnoff vodka, and a pint of Bacardi rum.

***

Dear Nancy,

Thank you so much for all your help. I'm glad Mike didn't have anything to do with Mr. Myers' murder. Everything is going well here. I've started classes, love my new place, and Jason's business is taking off.

Best news: I have received the DNA results and found my birth mother and people who are close relatives. I haven't connected with any of them yet because hearing from me might be a shock, so I'll have to be careful. We'll see what happens.

I am grateful to you. If you hadn't supported me and

provided the push I needed, I'd still be a pathetic and miserable drudge.

Much love to you,

Emily

*****

Note from the Residents' Board of Directors
Please welcome our new Assistant Administrator Carter Marlowe, who comes to us with excellent credentials and recommendations from Hillcrest Retirement Village in Lancaster, PA. He is especially pleased to move with his family to this area. "We love to hike and kayak, and we're thrilled to be living close to forests and rivers." Carter is also pleased to live near his mother, Whisperwood resident Hilda Marlowe.

THE END

If you enjoyed this mystery, please post
a quick review on Amazon. Just a sentence
or two would be fine.

I always enjoy hearing from readers and
can be reached by email at
eileenmcintire2017@gmail.com.
Website: www.secretpanels.net.
Facebook: @eileen.h.mcintire
Twitter: @EileenMcIntire

Acknowledgements

I am pleased to offer this book, the fifth in the 90s Club series, as another homage to the Nancy Drew books so many of us enjoyed when we were growing up. My character Nancy Dickenson may or may not be an elderly Nancy Drew, but like Nancy Drew, she is a lifelong learner, and it's a pleasure for me to follow her pursuits as she seeks a killer. The astute reader familiar with the Nancy Drew books may find buried references they'll recognize from the original Nancy Drew series.

Many thanks to beta readers Maureen Klovers, author of culinary mysteries; Flo McCahon, who writes cozy mysteries as Millie Mack; Janis Wilson, author of *Goulston Street*; Mark Willen, author of *The Question is Murder* and the Jonas Hawke series; Jean Burgess, author of *Collaborative Stage Directing: A Guide to Creating and Managing a Positive Theatre Environment;* Fran Altman, author of *Destiny's Daughter*; and Trey Cunninghove.

Many thanks also to Officer Casey Ciou of the Howard County (MD) Police Department who provided technical help, and to Tracy D. Rezvani, Administrator, Howard County (Maryland) Office of Consumer Protection, for permission to reprint their ten tips. Any mistakes are my own.

I am also indebted to the Maryland Writers' Association and Sisters in Crime for their many benefits and the companionship of fellow and sister writers.

Special thanks and much love to my husband, Roger McIntire, author and Professor Emeritus, Psychology, University of Maryland, for his constant support of my writing efforts.

Eileen Haavik McIntire

10 Tips to Avoid Fraud and Scams

SCAM ARTISTS in the U.S. and around the world STEAL millions of dollars from people each year. Use these tips to PROTECT YOURSELF. Reprinted with permission from the Howard County (Maryland) Office of Consumer Protection—www.howardcountymd.gov/consumer.

1 **Know who you're dealing with.** Try to find a seller's physical address (not a P.O. Box) and phone number so you know exactly who the company is and where it is located. Do an online search for the company name and website, so you can decide if the offer is worth the risk.

2 **Know that wiring money or sending pre-paid cards** is like sending cash. Con artists often insist that people wire money, especially overseas; it's nearly impossible to reverse the transaction or trace the money. If the seller will not accept payment any other way, find another seller.

3 **Read your monthly statements.** Scammers steal account information and then run up charges or commit crimes in your name. Dishonest merchants may bill you for monthly "membership fees" and other goods or services without your authorization. If you see charges you don't recognize or didn't

okay, contact your bank, card issuer, or other creditor immediately.

4 **After a disaster, give only to established charities.** Basically, don't trust any charity that has seemingly sprung up overnight. Give only to charities you are familiar with, and remember scam charities will often sound like established charities to fool potential donors.

5 **Talk to your doctor before you buy health products or treatments.** Ask about a product's possible risks or side effects, and clear any new remedy you try with your doctor. In addition, buy prescription drugs only from licensed U.S. pharmacies. Otherwise, you could end up with products that are fake, expired, or mislabeled.

6 **Remember there's no sure thing in investing.** If someone contacts you with low-risk, high-return investment opportunities, stay away. Be wary of pitches that insist you act now, guarantee big profits, promise little or no financial risk, or demand that you send cash immediately.

7 **Don't send money to someone you don't know**. Not to an online seller you've never heard of, nor to an online love interest who asks for money. It's best to do business with sites (and people) you know and trust.

8 **Don't agree to deposit a check and wire money back.** By law, banks have to make funds from deposited checks available within days, but uncovering a fake check can take weeks. You're responsible for the checks you deposit. If a check turns out to be a fake, you're responsible for paying back the bank. There is absolutely no legitimate reason anyone or any business would send you a check and ask you to wire money back to them.

9 **Don't reply to messages asking for personal or financial information.** It doesn't matter whether the message comes as an email, a phone call, a text message, or an ad. Don't

click on links or call phone numbers included in the message, either. It's called phishing. If you get a message like this and you are concerned about your account status, call the number on your credit/debit card (or your statement) and check on it.

10 **Don't play a foreign lottery.** It is illegal to play foreign lotteries. While lottery and sweepstakes claims can be tempting, you inevitably will be asked to pay "taxes," "fees," or "customs duties" to collect your prize. If you must send money to collect, you haven't won anything.

***

More Cautions and Where to Report a Scam

Everyone, but especially senior citizens, is a target in the many criminal activities to steal your money and your identity. Your best defense is to avoid responding in any way to phone calls, emails, and mail scams that in one way or another, ask for money. or personal information. This includes:
- A youthful voice claiming to be your grandson or daughter who needs money for any reason.
- A phone call or email from someone claiming to be from Social Security, the Sheriff, the IRS, or any other organization threatening you with prison, bad credit rating, or fines, if you don't pay up.

Do not use any contact information included in scam messages. These are usually spurious ones that connect you to the crooks. Use contact information in the federal agency directory to report government imposters.

The Federal Trade Commission (FTC) is the main agency that collects scam reports. Report a scam online with the FTC complaint assistant, or by phone at 1-877-382-4357 (9:00 AM - 8:00 PM, ET). The FTC accepts complaints about most scams, including these popular ones:
- Phone calls

- Emails
- Computer support scams
- Imposter scams
- Fake checks
- Demands for you to send money (check, wire transfers, gift cards)
  - Student loan or scholarship scams
  - Prize, grants, and sweepstakes offers

The FTC also collects reports of identity theft. Report identity theft online at IdentityTheft.gov or by phone at 1-877-438-4338 (9:00 AM - 8:00 PM, ET).

You can also report the scam to your state consumer protection office. If you lost money or other possessions in a scam, report it to your local police too.

Report fake websites, emails, malware, and other internet scams to the Internet Crime Complaint Center (IC3). Some online scams start outside the United States. If you have been affected by an international scam, report it through econsumer.gov. Your report helps international consumer protection offices spot trends and prevent scams.

Scammers often pretend to work for the Social Security Administration (SSA) or Internal Revenue Service (IRS). Common signs include:
- Robo calls
- Threats of arrest or lawsuits
- Demands for payments
- Suspension of your social security number
- Cancellation of your social security benefits

Report Social Security imposters online to SSA's Inspector General. Call 1-800-269-0271 (10:00 AM - 4:00 PM, ET) to report by phone.

Report IRS imposters to the Treasury Inspector General for Tax Administration (TIGTA). To report by phone, call TIGTA at 1-800-366-4484.

www.ingramcontent.com/pod-product-compliance
Lightning Source LLC
Chambersburg PA
CBHW051136190726
48290CB00006B/1874